Anna JACOBS

Persons *of* Rank

First published in the United Kingdom in 1993 by Century

This edition published in the United Kingdom in 2024 by

Canelo
Unit 9, 5th Floor
Cargo Works, 1–2 Hatfields
London SE1 9PG
United Kingdom

A CIP catalogue record for this book is available from the British Library.

Print ISBN 978 1 80436 723 0
Ebook ISBN 978 1 78863 428 1

Look for more great books at www.canelo.co

Printed and bound in Great Britain by Clays Ltd, Elcograf S.p.A.

Persons of Rank

Anna Jacobs is the author of over eighty novels and is a natural storyteller. She grew up in Lancashire and moved to Australia in the early seventies. She comes back to England every summer to visit her family. Married with two grown-up daughters and a grandson, she lives with her husband in Western Australia.

Also by Anna Jacobs

Chapter 1

"Persons of our rank," declared the Dowager, quivering with outrage at the mere idea, "do *not* fall in love! They may, if they are that way inclined, come to feel some affection for their spouses – I have known it to happen, even in the best of circles, though I myself consider it extremely vulgar – but – are you listening to me, Beatrice? Eleanor? – I repeat, *persons of rank do not, under any circumstances, fall in love!*"

The two young women standing in front of her exchanged speaking glances but knew better than to argue, so made noises to signify they were paying attention.

The old lady rapped her cane on the floor by her chair to emphasize this point and added with monumental scorn, "Nor do persons of our rank read sentimental tales about lowbred persons and their amours! They leave such absurdities for menials and governesses who know no better!" Her eyes flashed with scorn as she surveyed her niece, Beatrice, and her granddaughter, Eleanor, both in severe disgrace for being caught reading a novel together.

Beatrice suppressed a sigh and schooled her face into the calm expression she could summon up at will. Heaven knew she'd had enough years to practice that since her mother's death, when she was brought to live here with her father's much older sister. She shot a quick glance sideways, but saw with relief that Eleanor was staring past the Dowager out at the gardens and didn't seem about to argue.

As she looked back at her aunt, another worry surfaced. What would happen to her if the old lady died? The Dowager had appeared so frail lately. Beatrice shut off that thought resolutely and tried to pay attention to what her aunt was saying.

"And both you girls come from good stock, so…"

On the other side of the room, Eleanor dug her fingers into her palm to distract herself. She was still filled with anger at seeing her enthralling tale thrown on the fire by her grandmother. Now she and Beatrice would never know whether poor Melissa managed to escape from the toils of the evil Count and be reunited with Gervaise, her childhood sweetheart!

And what's more, Eleanor decided, simmering with rebellion as the lecture continued, she had every intention of falling in love one day, whatever her grandmother said, and had already begun to inspect the unattached men she met with extreme interest and care. Bea said that was not the way you did it, but Eleanor didn't suffer from her young aunt's shyness and had every intention of studying the field of candidates. Not that there were many young men here in the depths of Hampshire, and sadly, none of the ones she'd met so far had troubled her dreams in the slightest.

She caught a worried glance from across the room and winked at Bea, but didn't defy or contradict her grand-mother, in whose charge she had been for nine years. One didn't get one's own way by outright opposition to her ladyship. In fact, poor Bea rarely got her way at all, but Eleanor was never quite sure whether that was because she was submissive by nature or because she didn't care enough to dispute Lady Marguerite Graceover's authority.

She herself was cast in a more resolute mould, Eleanor felt complacently, stealing a quick glance sideways to admire her reflection in the mirror over the fireplace. The new way of arranging her hair looked very well, but this gown was far too plain. White muslin, for heaven's sake, as if she were still a child instead of a mature woman of nineteen!

Well, she had no intention of allowing her grand-mother to plan her whole life for her, let alone choose her husband. Why, Grandmamma had spoken approvingly only last week about second cousin Maria's engagement to a quite elderly nobleman, who was thirty-two if he was a day. Just because his family had come over with the Conqueror!

Eleanor knew her own future was presently under consideration, because she'd just happened to overhear her grandmother talking to the family lawyer recently about marriage settlements. Unfortunately, one of the maids had come along at that moment and she'd to move away from the door. But there was no doubt she would be a rich prize for someone and she meant to make the most of that, whatever Bea said. Only – that would mean leaving her beloved Satherby to live with a husband and she hated the thought of doing so.

The Dowager paused for breath, then continued the attack. "Pray tell me, Beatrice, since you are the older, why you were reading such – such vulgarities?"

3

Eleanor watched an agonized expression creep over Bea's face, so rushed to the rescue. "We only wanted to see what such books were like, Grandmamma. How is one to know about love and – and such things, if one cannot discuss them or read about them?"

"You have only to ask me. I can always tell you exactly what is or is not suitable for a Graceover of Satherby Abbey." She saw a stubborn expression on her grand-daughter's face and added sharply, "I forbid you, do you hear, absolutely forbid you to read such housemaids' trash again! Love! Pah! Love is only for the lower classes, who can afford to become quite ridiculous under its influence! Or for those fools who have forgotten their station in life. Fools like my younger brother Warwick."

This was one of the Dowager's favourite cautionary tales and was regularly trotted out and brandished before them as a warning. "Look what happened to him! Married for love, dead before forty, wife and child left living in poverty. It is I who have had to provide for my poor niece! My brother's fate is a lesson to us all."

Beatrice was alarmed at how white her aunt had gone, her lips a thin blue-tinged line in a face like wrinkled parchment. She exchanged worried glances with Eleanor and shook her head in warning to say nothing more.

After a few gasping breaths, the Dowager abandoned the rest of her customary diatribe and ended with the same old warning, "To marry without money is the height of improvidence, as I have told you many times before, have I not, Beatrice? And why are you both standing there like maidservants waiting for an order? Go and sit down on the sofa like gentlefolk. You know I cannot abide people looming over me."

Beatrice nodded and obeyed, tugging Eleanor across the room with her. She had some sympathy with the Dowager's views, since she and her mother had lived in extreme poverty for a while after her father's death and she had never forgotten what it felt like to go to bed hungry. Or to be without the means to pay the doctor's bills.

"Mind you," continued the Dowager, in the softer tones of one determined to be fair, "Beatrice could perfectly well have found herself some curate or gentleman farmer to marry who wouldn't care about her lack of dowry. She's a Dencey, after all. *My* family's pedigree goes back even further than the Graceovers' and we can hold our heads up in any circles." She squinted at her niece, as if seeing her for the first time. "She's pretty enough to attract some gentleman's attention, too, were she to set her mind to it."

Beatrice picked up her embroidery and made a determined stab at it with her needle. Over the years, she'd grown accustomed to her role as the Dowager Lady Graceover's unpaid companion and had developed a genuine affection for her aunt; but once in a while she could not help thinking wistfully how pleasant it would be to marry and have a home of one's very own – and even, perhaps, to have a family. She'd always loved children, which was why she'd welcomed the chance to help raise Eleanor, who had been orphaned at the age of nine. But that wasn't the same as having a child of one's own. Or a husband.

"In future, kindly do not forget what you owe to the Family!" the Dowager said, in what was, for her, quite a mild tone. "I have better things planned for you, Eleanor, than falling in love! You'll be the last of the Graceovers, more's the pity, but you're rich enough to seek a husband among the True Nobility."

Eleanor perked up and leaned forward, eagerness in every line of her body. "What exactly have you got planned for me, Grandmamma? May I not know?"

But this was going too far for the Dowager. "No, you may not know, miss! I'll tell you what you need to know when the time comes. And what are you doing lolling about on the sofa like that? If you have nothing better to occupy yourself with, you may go and practice your music. I wish to have a word with Beatrice in private."

Eleanor breathed deeply and rose to her feet. It was no use arguing with her grandmother when the old lady was in this mood. As she turned to leave, she rolled her eyes at Bea, then composed her expression and left.

Still feeling thoughtful, she made her way to the Blue Salon downstairs, where her favourite piano had been placed out of her ladyship's hearing, since only inconsiderate persons inflicted the sound of their practice upon the ears of their families. There she sat down and began to play, for she loved music and could lose herself in it for hours.

But she kept wondering what was happening upstairs. Clearly her grandmother was seriously considering the question of her marriage. But to whom? She wouldn't marry someone she did not like, however well-connected his family; on that point she was quite determined.

–

In London a gentleman of high enough rank to satisfy even the Dowager and handsome enough to delight the most romantically-minded young lady as well, got ready to go to a small, pre-season ball designed to introduce some of this year's crop of young ladies to the ways of the ton. In the middle of tying his neckcloth, he paused, scowled at himself in the mirror and swore softly, tossing aside the piece of mangled cloth. "No, definitely not."

Turning round, he stared at his valet as if he had never seen him before, then said harshly, "I've changed my mind. I shall not be going out tonight, after all, Beamish."

"But sir—"

"That will be all, thank you."

Beamish breathed deeply, but said nothing. He picked up the pile of mangled neckcloths and walked out with his usual measured tread.

When the valet had left, the gentleman flung himself down in the comfortable armchair in front of the fire and stared blindly into the flames. If he set one foot in that ballroom tonight, everyone in the ton would know that he was seriously looking for a wife this season. And did he really want that? No, he did not! He loathed being a focus of gossip, absolutely loathed it.

The trouble was, his mother was growing very insistent that he marry. She had driven up from Bath to Hertfordshire to visit him twice in the past year, and the last time she had made him promise to spend at least part of the coming season in London.

He stretched his tall body with a sigh, feeling a sudden longing sweep through him for his home in the country, for a canter through the woods and a fresh breeze on his face. Then he sighed and scowled down at his feet, forcing himself to face facts. It was his duty to marry. His absolute and inescapable duty. His mother was right about that.

But somehow, he'd never met a lady who didn't bore him to death after a few encounters. They were all so obliging, so breathlessly eager to please him that it made him feel angry. If he'd said the moon was purple, they'd have agreed. And they'd be just as eager to please any other gentleman of fortune, anything to get themselves a wealthy husband. He gave a snort of bitter laughter. Oh, he was a fool, expecting the impossible. Persons of his rank did not marry for love, but for sound social and financial reasons. Why should he be any different?

He jerked to his feet and went to pour himself a brandy, then slumped down in the chair again with a growl of annoyance and stared down into the rich amber liquid. He was three and thirty, and his mother was right, damn her. He had to marry. He raised the glass in a mocking toast, "To my future Lady Wife!"

He wouldn't go to tonight's ball, though, but would wait for the season proper to start and proceed with caution, drawing as little attention to himself as possible.

He raised the glass in another toast to his reflection in a mirror. "Here's to the last of the Serles!" He would suit himself as well in choosing a wife, he decided. He didn't want just a woman of breeding and fortune, but one of a pleasant nature and with a reasonable intelligence. Surely there must be some women around who didn't use their beauty as a weapon, live for gossip and fashion, and regard men merely as providers of heirs and money?

"Ha!" he said a little later, as he refilled his glass, spilling some brandy on the polished surface. "Maybe I should look at the ugly ones this time. At least they'd be *grateful*!" He drank to that as well.

Beamish peeped in a little later, worried that his master had not come down for dinner. He gaped in amazement at the sight of the overturned glass and the figure sprawled in the chair, sleeping soundly. It wasn't at all like Mr Serle to dip into the brandy. Shaking his head in surprise and disapproval both, he woke his master and persuaded him, not without difficulty, to go to bed.

"She's pushing him too hard," he muttered as he closed the bedchamber door. "There's going to be trouble."

–

When Eleanor had left the room, the Dowager fidgeted and cleared her throat a couple of times, then snapped, "Put that sewing down and pay attention to me, Beatrice! This is important!" There was a pause, then, "It's time we were thinking of the chit's future, but I'm out of touch with the younger set." She scowled across the room. "Don't know who's who in the ton any more."

Beatrice was thoroughly mystified. "Why should you need to keep in touch with the younger set, Aunt Marguerite?"

The Dowager ignored this, as she ignored all questions she didn't wish to answer. "And I'm too old to do another Season, more's the pity." She glared at her twisted hands, then folded them in her lap and fixed a hawk-like gaze upon her niece. "So *you* will just have to go up to London for me."

"*Me? Go to London!*"

"Yes, you, ninny! Who else is there? No men left in the family now, are there? So we've only got ourselves to rely on. Ah, we women are weak vessels!" She attempted to look frail and ill-used, but only succeeded in looking even more ferocious than usual.

"But Johanna lives in London. Surely your daughter would be the best person to deal with any business you wish conducted there?" Beatrice protested. They'd occasionally visited Johanna in town until the last couple of years, though they'd never gone about in society during those visits, because the Dowager said the ton was full of nobodies these days and she had better things to do than say how-de-do to farmers and shopkeepers.

The Dowager's scowl deepened. "I shan't trust *her* judgment when it comes to finding a husband for Eleanor."

"F-finding a husband for Eleanor?"

"Stop repeatin' what I say! Makes you sound like a sheep." Marguerite Graceover looked down at her lap for a moment, sighed and said more temperately, "I shan't ask Johanna to attend to this for me! Look at the sort of men she allowed her own daughters to marry! Johnny-come-latelies, both of them. A mere baronet! And the grandson of a nabob! What's the world coming to when a descendant of the Graceovers marries a tea merchant?"

This connection had rankled with her for several years, Beatrice knew, though in the eyes of the world, Johanna's daughters had done well for themselves and the gentlemen in question were not only rich, but pleasant-natured and had made their wives very happy. "Though you'll stay with Johanna when you're in London, of course," the Dowager added. "You'll need her as a chaperone, and she knows everyone, whether they're worth knowing or not."

"But I—"

"Stop interrupting! How am I to get my tale told if you keep stopping me? I'll write and tell Johanna what I want and to whom you're to be introduced. Then you can do the Season and look 'em all over for me."

By now, Beatrice was feeling quite bewildered. "Look who over, Aunt?"

"I've just been tellin' you! Young people don't know how to listen to their elders any more! Why am I always surrounded by ditherers and half-wits? I'm talking about the younger set! The ton. Or what passes for the ton nowadays. Persons of rank, mind, not nobodies and tea merchants! You'll have to go and look 'em over for me! How else are we to find a husband for Eleanor?"

"But I can't—"

"Of course you can! I'll give you a list of acceptable families, then you'll only have to sort out one or two possible husbands and invite them down here to meet Eleanor. I'll do the rest. We should be able to get the knot tied before the end of the year – if *you* will only bustle around a bit, that is!"

"But Aunt, really, I couldn't possibly—"

The old face grew grim. "I'm not lettin' the chit loose on the town without me to keep an eye on her. She's not only pretty, she's far too rich for her own good. And too impetuous. But innocent, of course. I've seen to that. Brought her up properly, at least."

Beatrice wondered what her ladyship would say if she knew about some of the exploits which the innocent chit had been up to lately, the little excursions into the village unescorted, the flirting at social gatherings *just for practice*. "But surely, Aunt Marguerite, Johanna could – she could—"

The cane thumped down again. "Johanna could *not*! She encourages the attentions of upstarts and mushrooms! I want better breeding than that for my granddaughter."

She bowed her head for a moment, then looked at Beatrice and for once there was no hauteur in those knowing old eyes. "Thing is, the doctor don't think I'll last much longer, Bea. Get a pain in my chest if I do much nowadays. There's nothin' he can do about it. A year at most, he thinks. M'heart's failing."

"Oh, Aunt, I'm so sorry!" Beatrice moved quickly across the room to kneel by her aunt's chair and clasp her hand.

The hand squeezed hers once, patted it and was withdrawn. "I believe you mean that, for which I thank you, Bea, but I'm five and seventy, and I've had a good long life, so I'm not complaining." She looked across the room into some distance only she could see. "The pity of it is that with two healthy sons I didn't get even one grandson to carry on the name. That idiot, William Herforth, will inherit. No, he died, didn't he? I keep forgetting. All the fault of that stupid will! How my husband came to write it, I'll never know!" Her eyes closed for a moment, then she jerked upright. "What was I saying?"

These slight lapses of concentration were another thing which was beginning to worry Beatrice.

"You were talking about the Herforths, Aunt."

"Yes, so I was. It's Herforth's son who'll be inheriting, isn't it? What's the fellow's name again?"

"Crispin."

"Yes. Crispin! Did you ever hear such a ridiculous name? *Crispin!*" she repeated with awful scorn. "It's a name for actors or dancing masters."

"It's only a word," Beatrice said softly.

The Dowager's mouth worked, as if she were swallowing something distasteful. "I swore no Herforth would set foot across the threshold till I was gone, but I've changed my mind, *had to* change my mind. I've invited that Crispin fellow to come and stay here for a while, because he needs to learn how to manage the estate. Got to make sure he's up to snuff socially, as well." Her voice trailed away again and for a moment or two she dozed, as old people will, for the anger had exhausted her.

Beatrice went back to the sofa and sat on in silence, her thoughts in too much turmoil to go and face Eleanor yet. Once or twice she looked across at her aunt and felt tears come into her eyes. If her ladyship's heart were indeed failing, she had good reason to be worried about Eleanor's future. Her husband, who had died twenty years before, had left his wife lifelong use of and control over the estate, which was then to pass to the next male heir.

With two sons living when he wrote the will, he could perhaps be forgiven for expecting that one of them or their descendants would inherit, but although both had survived him, neither had lived beyond the age of thirty and neither had sired a living son, so now the estate would pass to Crispin Herforth, not Eleanor.

And there was another problem to be considered – what would happen to Beatrice herself when her aunt died? It was something she had worried about occasionally, but now it had suddenly become of immediate concern. She had no other relatives and not a penny to call her own. What was to become of her? Surely her aunt would make some sort of provision for her?

In Hertfordshire, Crispin Herforth read the letter which had just been delivered by a groom from Satherby in growing indignation.

> *Sir*
>
> *Since you are heir to Satherby and in view of my increasing years, I have decided that it is necessary for you to become acquainted with your future inheritance. I shall therefore expect you to make time during the next few weeks for an extended visit here.*
>
> *Please advise me of the date of your arrival and do not delay in setting matters in train.*
>
> *Marguerite Graceover*

"I shan't go," he told the spaniel snoozing in front of the fire. "She refused even to receive my father when he asked to visit Satherby, so why should I go to her now?"

But as the day passed and he rode round his own much smaller estate, the Dowager's words kept coming back to him "in view of my increasing years," she had said. Did that mean she was ill? Dying even?

"So what?" he told his favourite mare. "I've never even met the woman and I don't want to, either."

But what if she were dying? How would he reconcile a refusal to visit her with his conscience?

Not until he was getting ready for bed did he admit the other reason for going. Satherby Abbey itself. To inherit such a place was a sacred trust. So many people depended on you for their livelihood, so many generations of the family before you had given their lives to it. You simply could not turn your back on that.

It was two weeks, however, before he bowed to the inevitable and his reply was equally terse and to the point.

> *Dear Lady Graceover*
> *I thank you for your kind invitation. I am not*
> *at present at liberty to visit you, but shall hope to*
> *be free later in the year.*
> *Crispin Herforth*

He smiled as he signed it and remained in a good mood all day as he made certain arrangements. He would do this his own way. You did not walk blindly into a lion's den. Or a lioness's, either.

–

The Dowager woke up with a start, coughed and spluttered for a moment, blinked at her niece, then reverted to her topic. "Have to settle you both, but Eleanor's more of a worry, d'you see? She's a considerable heiress, even if she can't have this estate. Don't want fortune hunters buzzin' around. Can't rely on a gal of her age makin' a wise decision."

"Yes, Aunt."

"And it's only fair to leave you properly provided for as well, Bea." She saw that her niece was looking embarrassed. "Don't think I've forgotten you. I couldn't look for a husband for you before, because I needed you to help me bring up the chit. Too old to do it all myself. Never had much patience with children, anyway. And you did a good job, as well, young as you were."

Beatrice smiled. "That was a pleasure for me, as you know."

"Yes. You're a born mother. Y'should have had your own family by now. It's my fault you haven't. But it's not too late to amend that."

Beatrice flushed. "I'm nearly thirty, Aunt. Past thinking of such things."

"Twenty-eight last month. Don't exaggerate!" Rap! went the silver-headed cane that always stood ready by the chair. "Now! Hold your tongue and listen! I've fixed it all up with the lawyers and settled enough money on you to get yourself a husband of whose breeding we needn't be ashamed."

"I don't care to have you buy me a husband, Aunt! I should be grateful for a small annuity, certainly, but—"

"Hoity-toity!" The Dowager's face softened. "You'll do as you're told because it's my dying wish to see you settled and because I know you'd like to have a family of your own."

Beatrice shook her head, not wishing anyone to buy her a husband.

"*Please*, Beatrice! I beg of you! Please do this last thing for me!"

Never once had Beatrice heard this autocratic old termagant plead with anyone for anything. "But Aunt, I..." Her voice tailed away and she could only look beseechingly at her relative.

The sunken eyes stared at her unwinkingly. The body might be failing, but the mind inside it was still as sharp as ever. "Didn't think to hear me plead, did you? And I didn't think I'd have to do it, either. Just goes to show. Death is a great leveller." She paused, then asked sharply,

"What's got into you, girl? What have I asked you to do that sticks in your gullet?"

"I don't – I cannot like the idea of – of having a husband bought for me – someone who will only be interested in my money."

Her ladyship cackled loudly, sounding more like an ancient parrot than a respected member of the upper classes. "Is that all?"

"Isn't it enough?"

"No! It ain't enough! What other way is there for persons like us to make a proper match? Whether you admit it or not, marriage is a business transaction. And besides," she glared at Beatrice, angry for being made to continue pleading, "I can't die with you on my conscience, girl! I should have found you a husband years ago."

Beatrice shook her head. "Aunt, I just can't like the idea!"

The old eyes narrowed in cunning and the voice grew softly persuasive. "Eleanor will need you even more once I'm gone! And you'll be able to look after her much better if you're a married woman, not to mention looking after yourself, too!" She clicked her tongue in exasperation. "For heaven's sake, child, a woman's business in life is to marry, and marry as well as she can."

"I shall need to think about it, Aunt. I can't just – just snap up your offer straight away. *I can't!*"

Her ladyship nodded. "Yes, you *ought* to take the time to think about something so important. It's what I'd do myself in your place. Come here!"

When Beatrice approached her chair again, she pulled her niece's head down toward her own and planted on the soft cheek the first and last kiss she would ever give her. "You're a good girl, in spite of your mother. It's the Dencey blood coming out in you, I dare say. Quality will always tell." She patted her niece's cheek, then pushed her away again. "Go and do your thinking, then! But send my maid in to me first. And not a word about this to Eleanor, mind! Promise."

Beatrice's thoughts were in a turmoil as she took refuge in her own bedchamber. When Eleanor knocked on the door and demanded admittance, she made no move to open it, simply calling out that she needed a rest.

"But Bea—"

"Go away, Eleanor. I'll talk to you later."

She had locked the door, so she ignored a renewed tattoo on its venerable panels and plumped down in front of the fire. One of the few indulgences she allowed herself was to sit on the rug and toast her stockinged toes. The Dowager would have been horrified at such undignified behaviour, but Beatrice had long ago found that staring into dancing flames was a good way to sort out one's thoughts. She had needed to do that many times when she had first arrived at Satherby, a grieving and inexperienced girl of seventeen, with no understanding of her father's world and only a lawyer's assurance that she would find a home there.

Well, she had come to terms with many things since coming to live at Satherby, so she supposed she could come to terms with this as well. But, she decided, frowning into the embers, although she might not be able to find a husband whom she could love, as her parents had loved, she would insist on having some say as to whom she married. She couldn't marry someone whom she didn't both respect and like. That would be her one condition in agreeing to her ladyship's wishes.

A little later, Eleanor banged on the door again. "Are you ready for dinner, Bea?"

"Oh, sorry! I'm not changed yet. You go down without me."

With a shock Bea realized that she had allowed the fire to burn down low and was feeling thoroughly chilled. She put on more wood, then lit the candles with a taper, before changing her clothes and tidying her hair in time for the dinner gong. She didn't bother to summon the housemaid whose duty it was to wait on her if required. She'd never grown used to servants hovering over her while she performed her intimate tasks.

"I'll have to do it," she told her reflection in the mirror, "but the choice of husband will be mine, not my aunt's!" If anyone wanted her. Two clear hazel eyes stared back at her in a face anyone else would have considered remarkably pretty, but which Beatrice rather despised, for the full redness of her lips and the brilliance of her eyes were, to a mind schooled by long years with the Dowager, rather theatrical in appearance.

She smoothed the creamy skin of her cheek with one fingertip and turned to study herself from the side, then shrugged her shoulders. She supposed she'd have no trouble in finding some sort of husband if she had a generous dowry, but oh dear, she didn't want things to change. She had come to terms with her role in life and was quietly happy at Satherby, enjoying the beauties of the changing seasons in the country and the power she had to improve the lot of the poorer tenants on the estate. That meant a lot to her.

But when the Dowager died, everything would change. Her aunt was right. Beatrice needed to face that fact and prepare for it. She smoothed her full silken skirts, shaking the pale blue frills around her feet into place, then picking up a warm shawl to counter the draughts that abounded in this ancient house. No use worrying about the future now, when she hadn't even sealed her bargain with the Dowager. Taking a deep breath, she opened the door.

I can do it, she told herself firmly, as she walked down the stairs. Of course I can. My aunt would never expect me to marry someone I despised.

Chapter 2

It was dark and threatening rain when the old-fashioned Graceover carriage reached London, but the house before which the carriage stopped was glittering with lights and had attracted a small crowd of onlookers. The Satherby coachman had to wait for two ladies and a gentleman, all very lightly clad considering the inclement weather, to descend from another carriage before he could even pull up to the door.

Beatrice drew in a slow, painful breath at the sight of the other visitors' elegant appearance and confident demeanour, and pulled her travelling cloak more closely around her, feeling dowdy and countrified.

As the elderly footman, who had journeyed with them and who had served the Graceovers all his life, handed her down, he said quietly, as if he understood how she felt, "She always did like company, Miss Johanna did. Her ladyship, I should say."

It was an ordeal for Beatrice to climb the steps to the front door and face a house full of strangers, but the butler greeted her with a bow and a friendly smile, and that heartened her a little. As he took her cloak, she murmured that she wasn't dressed to meet company, and he nodded instant understanding, showing her straight into a small parlour away from the noise.

"I'll inform her ladyship of your arrival."

Servants were always so kind, Beatrice thought. With a sigh of relief, she sank into a chair. Then she realized that a gentleman was already occupying the high-backed armchair on the other side of the fireplace and started up again with a gasp of shock.

He rose and bowed with a flourish, elegance personified. Boredom personified, too, from his weary expression. His black pantaloons displayed shapely but muscular legs, and his coat, black also, was stretched across shoulders that needed no padding to give them a fashionable broadness. The coat's raised collar and reverse framed shirt collars were gleaming white, but only moderately high, and were embellished with a cravat tied in a neat Irish knot and fastened by one small gold pin.

Even the Dowager, Beatrice decided, could not have objected to his appearance, as she did to that of most of the younger gentlemen she met. They appeared, she was wont to declare and often to their faces, to have bandaged their throats or to be wearing horse blinkers, so high were their collars and so bulky their cravats.

"I must apologize for startling you, Ma'am. Permit me to introduce myself. Justin Serle at your service. Are you also seeking refuge from the merrymaking?"

Beatrice was quite tall, for a woman, but he was much taller, which made her feel at an unusual disadvantage. She had to look up at a face framed by dark hair and neat side-whiskers, and dominated by a long aristocratic nose. He had strong features, not exactly handsome, but forming an attractive whole, or would have done, she decided, if the expression in his grey-blue eyes had not been so chill and aloof.

She realized she'd been staring at him like an idiot at a fair and first blushed, then took an involuntary step backwards as the name sank in. Oh, good heavens! Serle! He was at the very top of the Dowager's list and was one of the few individuals specified by first name as well as by family. "I – I beg your pardon? What did you say, Sir?" she stammered, feeling stupid.

"I merely wondered whether you too were seeking refuge from the merrymaking, Ma'am."

He didn't really sound interested in her answer and that made her feel worse. She sought desperately for a suitable response, but could think of nothing to say.

Justin stared back at her openly, somewhat annoyed at the way she had been scrutinizing him. Who was she to stare so? Quite pretty, if you liked rosy-cheeked brunettes, which he did not particularly, but she had country manners and a wardrobe to match. She wasn't at all like one of Lady Johanna Ostdene's usual guests, in fact. Who was she? Some poor relative?

Beatrice found her voice and tried to answer his question. "Er – no. I'm not escaping anything. I've only just arrived. From – from the country." She could hear how flustered she sounded and saw a look of impatience flicker across his face. That made her feel worse, but it also made her feel angry. How dared he behave so arrogantly toward a complete stranger? Who did he think he was? Lord of all he surveyed?

Before either of them could say anything more, a voice interrupted them unceremoniously. "Serle! Are you in hiding already? I vow I'll not invite you to one of my parties again. Go back at once and talk to Mary."

He gave an exaggerated sigh and flourished a bow. "Must I, Lady Ostdene? She has the most foolish laugh it's ever been my misfortune to hear!"

Beatrice couldn't help staring. What an ill-mannered way to speak about a fellow guest! She did not, she decided, like the looks of this man, even if he did come from an ancient and respected line! She listened to the rest of her companions' banter with growing disgust.

"No, no! You're quite wrong there, Serle," Johanna retorted with a smile. "It's Isabella Mardsley who has the silliest laugh of anyone in town."

They both chuckled at that, then Johanna smiled at Beatrice and nodded to the gentleman, "I don't think you've met my cousin before, have you, Serle?"

"No, indeed. We were just about to introduce ourselves."

"Let me do it for you. Beatrice Dencey – Justin Serle."

They nodded to each other, neither making the effort to shake hands. Beatrice could only hope that her dislike for this type of supercilious gentleman did not show.

Johanna turned back and shook one finger playfully at him. "Well, Serle, we had an agreement about tonight, did we not?"

He threw up his hands in a gesture of mock defeat and gave an exaggerated sigh. "To my great dismay, yes! I shall keep my word, at whatever cost to myself. Miss Dencey, delighted to have met you."

He bowed languidly to them both and turned to leave.

Johanna chuckled as she watched him saunter out. "What a wretch he is! I knew poor Mary – she's my goddaughter, you know – wouldn't take his fancy, but he absolutely promised to give her a little attention tonight, for my sake, and I'll hold him to that. Where Justin Serle shows an interest, other men do not disdain to follow, especially when a girl is well-dowered."

Beatrice flushed scarlet. She, too, was well-dowered, now. Would her cousin have to bribe people to speak to her?

Johanna came to present a perfumed cheek for a kiss, then held her guest at arm's length to study her face. "So you're here to find yourself a husband at last, are you? Not to mention one for Eleanor as well! Mama wrote me a long letter explaining all her plans." She grimaced. "Typical of Mama! Full of contradictory orders. But I couldn't be more delighted to give you a Season, Bea! Truly, I couldn't! I've been offering to do it for years. It was such fun getting my girls married off that I wished I had a few more daughters to bring out. And now I have my wish granted."

Beatrice dredged up a smile. "It's very kind of you to say that, Johanna." She wished she could share her cousin's enthusiasm. Or her confident elegance. Plump as she was, Johanna always made her much younger cousin feel ill-groomed. Her curls might be greying now, but they were dressed in an elaborate style which flattered her still-pretty face. Her smooth white throat and soft hands sparkled with jewels and her gowns were miracles of the modiste's art. But most attractive of all was her lively personality, which made her such fun to be with. As Beatrice knew she herself was not. She was far too serious and had little small talk.

"She's a happy soul, my Johanna," the Dowager had once said. "Married well, lives in comfort, has two perfectly satisfactory daughters – birthed them without the slightest trouble, of course – and didn't long mourn that nonentity of a husband when he died young and left her a fortune. Can't ask for much more in life, can you?"

Beatrice would have asked for far more. Love such as her parents had known might not come to many people, but to hope for affection between oneself and one's spouse didn't seem to her to be unreasonable.

Johanna hugged her again. "You poor lamb, you look exhausted!" She linked arms with Beatrice. "Let me show you to your room. You'd be welcome to join the party – it'll go on for hours yet – but I can see that you're nearly asleep on your feet. This way! I've given you Penelope's old room. It's got a fine view of the square and the most comfortable bed in the house. People always sleep well there, I don't know why." Almost as an afterthought, she added, "And how's Mama?"

"Oh – er – much as usual." The Dowager had strictly forbidden her to divulge anything to Johanna about her declining state of health.

"And Eleanor? Is she still as pretty? It must be a year or more since I've seen her. I really must make the effort to visit Mama more often."

"Oh, yes. Eleanor is very pretty. At least, I think so. And – and with very lively taking ways." Though a little rash at times, she added mentally, already starting to worry about what Eleanor would be getting up to, now that she was left to her own devices.

"Then we should have no difficulty finding her a husband, should we?" Johanna escorted Beatrice up the stairs, waving to several people en route and promising to introduce her cousin to them another time.

Anyone less like her formidable mother would be hard to find, thought Beatrice. Johanna was always so affectionate and comfortable to be with!

Left alone at last, she sighed and sat down on the edge of the bed. Noise and laughter floated up from below and she wondered how anyone could possibly expect her to sleep with a party going on. Within half an hour, however, she had allowed a young maid to unpack her travelling case, drunk a glass of hot milk sweetened with honey, eaten a piece of cake and settled down for the night.

She expected to have difficulty falling asleep, but instead, she proved her hostess's point that it was, indeed, the most comfortable bed in the house.

–

When she awoke the following morning, it took Beatrice a minute or two to remember where she was, then she sat bolt upright in the bed. She was in London already and rushing toward a fate she definitely did not relish. What sort of man would want to marry a woman as old as she was, and one, moreover, whose family connections were not all they should be? An older man, of course! A widower, probably.

Her imagination ran riot for a few minutes, picturing a series of elderly gentlemen creaking down onto their knees to propose to her, then she gave a shaky laugh and banished the images from her mind. She would take one step at a time. First, she must grow accustomed to London ways, for her Aunt Marguerite had never gone about much in society on their occasional brief visits to town, confining herself to receiving, in much state, the few people of her generation still alive whose ancestry she did not despise.

Beatrice stared across at her trunks, remembering the elegance of the people she had seen the previous evening. She must purchase some more stylish clothes. She smiled at the thought. That prospect, at least, was a pleasant one. Who would not enjoy buying a completely new wardrobe? She took a deep breath and told herself that not until all that was accomplished need she think of the other thing. Not for another week, anyway. This decision made her feel much better.

Her determined expression faded slowly, however, as she remembered the arrogant gentleman she'd met the previous evening. Oh dear! It had started already, without her wishing it to, for she'd met one of the Names within minutes of entering the house. Justin Serle, of Melbury Park, Hertfordshire, the list said, with a tick beside the name to indicate that he was a highly preferred candidate. She could still see his handsome, disdainful face looking down at her with controlled politeness, and she blushed again as she remembered how she'd stammered and stuttered in reply to his questions. How stupid she must have appeared to him!

And how arrogant he had appeared to her!

She gasped aloud and giggled suddenly, as it occurred to her that he exactly fitted the description of the villain in the novel her grandmother had burned. The Conte di Maggione! Oh, she definitely had to purchase another copy and find out how the tale ended, ridiculous as it was.

A knock on the door heralded the entrance of the same small maid who had helped her unpack the night before, this time come to light the fire. "Shall I fetch your hot water up yet, miss? And would you like a tea tray? And if you please, her ladyship says to tell you that I'm to help you get ready and look after your things until you find a lady's maid of your own."

"I don't need any help, thank you."

The girl's face fell so dramatically that Beatrice was moved to ask her what was wrong. The Dowager frequently grew angry with her for paying so much attention to servants, but it was one thing she refused to change. Servants were people with the same feelings as anyone else and one of the few powers she had was to make their lives a little more pleasant by showing her appreciation for their services.

"Please miss, I know I'm not a real lady's maid, but Sarah, what maids for her ladyship, she's been giving me lessons and she says I have a knack with hair, and I'm good with the ironing and mending, too. I won't let you down, honest I won't!"

Beatrice realized from this that she would be blighting the young maid's big chance in life if she denied needing any help. She couldn't possibly refuse such a plea. "Very well, then."

The thin face was instantly radiant. "Oh, miss, you won't be sorry! I'll be ever so careful, you'll see. Now, I'll just go and fetch you a tea tray, then I'll get your hot water, and afterwards, I'll get your things ready. Sarah's shown me 'zactly what to do." The words poured out in an enthusiastic stream.

"Just a moment!"

"Yes, miss?"

"You haven't told me your name."

"Ooh, so I haven't! Sorry, miss! I'm Tilly. Short for Matilda."

So Beatrice submitted to the first of her London ordeals and allowed herself to be attended by the eager Tilly, who wouldn't let her do a thing for herself, but who really did have a deft touch with hair and who absolutely radiated happiness as she reverently performed her duties.

Breakfast was not until nine and Beatrice, an inveterate early riser, felt the day was half gone by the time she made her way down to the small dining-room. She was already at table when Johanna floated in, still dressed in a chamber gown.

"Ah, there you are, Bea! Did you sleep well?"

"Very well."

"Of course you did go to bed much earlier than I did. But then, I've never been much good in the mornings. How dreadfully energetic you look!" She yawned again and languidly helped herself to a piece of toast. "Did Tilly look after you all right? Sarah thought we might give her a tryout, but if she's not suitable you must tell me. In any case, we'll soon find you a proper lady's maid."

"Oh, no!" Beatrice exclaimed involuntarily.

"Why, whatever do you mean?"

"I – I prefer to look after myself."

"Well, you can't do that in London, silly, whatever you do at Satherby. Why, I dare say I change my clothes four or five times a day, and you'll be doing the same. You're going to *need* someone to look after your things. Mama said I was to find you the best lady's maid to be had, and never mind the expense. In fact, we're not to consider the expense of anything. What delicious fun we're going to have!"

"Oh, dear!"

Johanna grinned at her. "Has she been laying down the law to you about what you're to do and not do?"

"Well, she has, rather. And I've no ambitions to look like a fashion plate. I prefer to feel comfortable. A real lady's maid would be sure to despise me! Your Sarah does already!"

Johanna burst out laughing. "No, she doesn't! She wouldn't dare! That's just her way of maintaining her dignity." She studied Beatrice carefully. "You know, if you don't mind my saying so, I think you're shyer than either of my girls were, Bea, and they were years younger than you when they came out. You shouldn't be so modest! I prophesy you'll take very well. Any maid would be pleased to look after you. They have their pride, you know, and you're prettier than I remember, or you will be, once we've got you properly gowned and your hair dressed to better advantage. Besides which, you have a very substantial dowry, and that's sure to—"

Beatrice dropped her knife. "I have *what*?"

"Surely Mama told you how much she's decided to settle on you?"

Beatrice's cheeks were burning. "No!"

"Didn't you even ask?"

"No!"

"Well, isn't that just like her? She adores making mysteries. And how like you to be embarrassed by it. Don't colour up, you silly goose! In my opinion, a woman should know her own worth to the penny. Why, my girls knew exactly what they would bring to their husbands before they were even twelve years old!"

Beatrice was speechless. Aunt Marguerite always said that marriage was a business, but to calculate the exchange rates so openly filled her with embarrassment. A very substantial dowry might buy her a husband whose birth didn't displease the Dowager, but would it bring her a man to whom she herself could warm?

"Anyway," Johanna went on, not noticing her guest's utter demoralization, "Mama's decided to settle twenty thousand pounds on you. That should give you a good range of choice, once the word gets about. Beatrice! Beatrice, where are you going?" She stared open-mouthed at the half-open door. The sound of her cousin running up the stairs floated back to her.

"Well, Mama said you were nervous about all this, but she didn't tell me you were so very touchy!" she said aloud. "No wonder she left it to me to tell you about the dowry!"

After a minute, she smiled to herself and murmured, "Still, such modesty might set a new style, if I play it well." She reached for another piece of toast and smeared it liberally with butter and blackberry conserve, her thoughts busy with plans for launching her cousin. An evening party first, with a full-scale ball later. A few dinners and visits to the theatre, and who knew what else would be on offer from other hostesses? What fun it would all be!

Upstairs, Beatrice was staring unhappily out of her bedroom window, breakfast forgotten. "What am I to do?" she whispered, pressing her palms to her burning cheeks. "How am I to face it all? *Twenty thousand pounds!* It's far too much! No one will care what I'm like – they'll just be interested in my money! And Aunt Marguerite knew, she knew perfectly well, that I'd have to accept it after my promise to her!"

It was over an hour before she could calm down enough to face Johanna again. The only thing which kept her to her promise of finding a husband was the thought that as a married woman she would be better placed to protect Eleanor. And her niece's happiness mattered very much indeed to her.

Tilly came up to find her eventually, to let her know that her ladyship was nearly ready to go out shopping. Beatrice asked automatically for her cloak, but Tilly shook her head. "Cloaks isn't worn for shopping in London, miss. I'll unpack the rest of your things for you while you're out, but perhaps you can tell me if you've got a pelisse or spencer you like to wear with that dress? If it needs ironing, I can easily run down to the maids' room and smooth it over. We always keep the flat irons near the fire on a special stand."

She was obviously bursting to help and was as good as her word, returning within minutes carrying Beatrice's perfectly-ironed pelisse reverently across her arms. "Here you are, miss."

As she smoothed the pelisse with tender hands, Beatrice watched her thoughtfully. She hated the idea of having her life invaded by a starchy lady's maid, like the one who served Johanna. The majestic Sarah ruled her mistress with a rod of iron where her appearance was concerned. That would not at all suit Beatrice. Perhaps, though, if she could persuade her cousin that Tilly was able to cope, things might not turn out too badly. She already felt comfortable with the girl, who was cheerful and willing.

"Is it your ambition to become a lady's maid, then?" she asked casually as she prepared to go downstairs.

33

"Ooh, yes, miss! And Sarah says I may just do and she's been giving me lessons for ages now. I'm to be available to help guests, you see, now Mary's left, and I'm to get an extra guinea a year if you're satisfied with me this time."

She looked so anxious about it all that Beatrice smiled and said in her gentle way, "Well, you've been doing an excellent job so far, Tilly."

She was rewarded by another beaming smile.

Beatrice nodded as she studied her reflection, for Tilly had managed to tame the heavy hair that gave its owner so much trouble and it now lay in sleek waves on her brow, with the back hair looped neatly up. If I really do have to have a maid, she thought, watching Tilly's still-smiling face behind her in the mirror, I think I'd much prefer a cheerful young girl like her. Did Johanna say we'd have to change our clothes four or five times a day? Oh dear! How tedious! However many clothes will I need for that?

Johanna looked her cousin over critically when she came downstairs again, then nodded. "Not the height of fashion, but a neat enough turnout. Trust Mama to find you a good country dressmaker. Anyway, we'll soon improve on that and have you cutting a dash in town." She hesitated before adding, "Are you over the shock of finding yourself a rich woman, yet, love?"

Beatrice shook her head ruefully. "I'm sorry if I seemed rude, but Johanna, I still can't believe it! How can I accept so much money from your mother? I have no right to it!"

"Just say thank you and be grateful. Mama's extremely rich, you know, and she never does anything she doesn't want to. And look how you've put up with her for all these years. We all know what an autocrat she is."

"She's been very kind to me – in the circumstances."

Johanna screwed up her nose. "Well, I think it was quite gothic of her family to cut your father off without a penny like that and leave everything to Mama!"

Beatrice shrugged. "That was all over and done with long ago. It still doesn't entitle me to such a – a fortune!"

"You've earned every penny, I promise you. Now, let's forget about all that nonsense and go and see Odette. She's been my modiste for years. She charges prodigiously high, but she's a genius, my dear, an absolute genius. You'll soon be setting the fashion if you put yourself in her hands. And Mama did say we were to spare no expense."

Beatrice sighed audibly.

"Don't you like clothes?" Johanna's tone was incredulous.

"Well, I do normally, of course I do, but at the moment I feel like an offering being prepared for sacrifice. I – I dare say I'll grow used to the idea." She smiled bravely.

Johanna roared with laughter. "Oh, Bea, you'll be the death of me yet! Grow used to it, indeed! You should *revel* in the idea of being worth twenty thousand pounds. Mama's kept you too quiet, but don't worry, I'll soon teach you how to enjoy yourself."

Wisely Beatrice did not try to contradict her, but she rather doubted that she would enjoy city life among so many strangers. She allowed Johanna to gossip about fashions all the way to the modiste's, but her own thoughts were still in turmoil. *Twenty thousand pounds!* she kept thinking. Too much. Far too much.

It'd attract fortune hunters.

She couldn't help remembering the hardships she and her mother had suffered and it occurred to her that only a fraction of that dowry disbursed earlier would have made them both comfortable and perhaps kept her mother alive for longer. Fate could be so capricious! She took a deep breath and reminded herself, as she had many times before, that the Dowager hadn't known of their circumstances and thus could not be held to blame for their difficulties.

The two ladies were granted the honour of an immediate interview with Mademoiselle Odette herself, and Johanna explained her cousin's needs and aspirations so frankly that Beatrice was soon blushing again.

Odette nodded briskly and turned to study her new customer. Even Johanna's tongue was stilled as she watched the modiste.

"Will you please stand up and walk about, Miss Dencey? Yes, now sit down. Stand up again. Turn round. Hmm! Let me think. Do please sit down again!"

Beatrice sank gratefully onto a spindly gilt chair and stared at the carpet, feeling more than ever like a sacrificial victim.

After a few minutes, during which Odette moved to survey Beatrice from several angles, her impersonal fingers turning her new client's head first one way, then the other, the modiste nodded. "We shall set a new fashion with Miss Dencey, I think, your ladyship. Restrained, ladylike elegance. Simple, but exquisite. The shyness will enhance this. Good colours, wonderful fabrics, no fuss. You'll see." She began to take Beatrice's measurements, nodding in approval as she called them off to an assistant.

When that was over, Johanna nodded in a friendly way. "I'll leave it all to you, then, Odette. How soon can you have something ready?"

"Within a day or two. Which garments would you like made up first, Lady Ostdene?"

"Something for paying morning calls, something for walking in the park – oh, and an evening gown, of course."

"I'll send them round as soon as they're ready, your ladyship. A fitting of a toile tomorrow, if you please, Miss Dencey, to give us the exact sizing, then we'll make up a padded figure for everything but the final fittings. Price?" She cocked her head on one side like a bright-eyed bird.

Beatrice had no idea and looked to Johanna for help.

"The price is irrelevant, Odette. As long as you live up to your usual standards. I wish my cousin to be *noticed*."

Odette's eyes gleamed. "Have you ever known me to fail, your ladyship?"

Johanna was admiring herself in a mirror. "No, you don't normally fail. This is quite one of my favourites, Odette."

"It does look well on your ladyship."

Johanna turned her attention to Beatrice. "My cousin is a little different from the usual young lady making her debut in society."

"Yes, indeed. Colours will make a nice change from whites and pastels, your ladyship. And, if I may say so, Miss Dencey may be older than the usual young lady making her debut, but she has character and resolution in her face. With her height and figure, we cannot fail to make a good impression."

By this time, Beatrice was again scarlet with embarrassment. She felt as if she'd done nothing but blush and stutter since she arrived in London. She hated to be a focus of attention, absolutely hated it.

"Please let us have samples of the materials you've chosen as soon as possible, so that we can purchase accessories."

"Certainly, your ladyship."

As they settled back in the carriage, Johanna sighed happily. "Now, accessories. Stockings, gloves, shawls, bonnets. We'll go and inspect a few things today, but we won't buy much until we have our sample swatches. Oh, what fun it will all be!"

"Don't we have any choice – about the colours and materials, I mean?" ventured Beatrice.

"*Choice? With Odette?*" Johanna hooted with laughter. "I wouldn't *dare* tell her what to use! She's a genius, my dear, a pure genius! Just leave it all to her!"

They spent a busy morning shopping, first at the premises of Harding, Howell and Company, who had a most amazing emporium, situated in Schomberg House in Pall Mall. It actually consisted of several shops all under the one roof, each separated from the others by glazed mahogany partitions, and to Beatrice's dazed eyes it seemed enormous. The shop even contained a refreshment room upstairs where customers could be served with wines, tea, coffee and sweetmeats. Johanna confessed to a weakness for the pastries sold there and proved it by consuming three of them before they continued on to Grafton House in New Bond Street. This was so crowded that they had to wait for quite fifteen minutes before they could even be attended to.

At both shops, Johanna introduced Bea to a bewildering number of ladies whose names she was sure she would not remember. By the time they left, her head was spinning with not only names but also the huge numbers of items for sale.

As the two ladies were walking out toward their carriage, a haggard-looking man with one arm missing, who had been begging near the corner, collapsed suddenly in the street. Before Johanna could prevent her, Beatrice had rushed across to his aid and was actually kneeling down to help him sit up, ignoring the dirt on both the ground and his person.

Johanna, horrified, remembered her mother complaining that if Beatrice saw an injured bird, it had to be brought home and tended. Well, she wouldn't be able to tend all the beggars in London! And this one appeared to be as dirty as the rest of them.

"Bea!" she called. "Bea, come back!"

She was ignored.

"I'm sorry for causing trouble, miss." The man let the lady help him to his feet then leaned against the wall, looking white and ill.

Even then Beatrice couldn't leave well alone. While her cousin watched in horror, she commanded a small boy loitering nearby to fetch something hot to eat and drink, held out a sixpence and promised double that amount as a reward for himself if he carried out the errand swiftly.

"Give that man some money and come away!" hissed Johanna, stepping closer to twitch at Bea's sleeve. She glanced round, terrified that someone she knew would see them and gossip about the strange behaviour of her visitor.

She was again ignored. Within minutes, Beatrice had found out that the man was an ex-soldier and was currently without means of support, also that he had been ill for the past week and had nothing to eat for two days. Not content with giving him money, she quickly discovered that his ambition was to become a pie-man, but that he lacked the capital to launch this business venture.

Tipping the change out of her purse, she provided him with enough money to do that, together with some sound advice and her name and address. He was to come and let her know how things went.

Only after this was all arranged, the boy had brought back some food and the man had promised to keep in touch would Beatrice consent to return to the carriage.

"You really shouldn't hand out money to such people, you know!" Johanna protested, once they were safely inside the carriage. "And just look at the dirt on your dress!"

Beatrice looked down in surprise, then shrugged. "That man lost his arm defending his country and no one seems to care. What does a bit of dirt matter if I am able to help him?"

"You'll never hear from him again."

"I think I will." She stared at her cousin. "I can remember myself what it's like to go hungry, you know."

Johanna could only gape at her. A few seconds later she asked in hushed tones, "Did you really go hungry, Bea? Actually," she gulped, "not have enough to eat?"

"Many times. My mother and I had very little money to live on and you know how food prices rose during the war. We weren't the only ones to suffer, either."

"Goodness, why have you never said anything about it before?"

"What was the point? What's past is done with and can't be changed. Even my aunt didn't know till afterwards how bad things had been for us. My mother had her pride, too, you see. It was only when she realized she was dying that she wrote to the Graceovers' man of business. And by the time he replied, she was dead."

Johanna could only pat her hand. It was beginning to occur to her that Bea might not be quite as meek and amenable as she'd expected. Then, putting such an unwelcome idea from her mind, she quickly recovered her good humour, leaned back in the carriage and changed the subject, smiling once more. "Spending someone else's money is such fun, Bea, even better than spending one's own. I'll ask the housekeeper to send a message to a Domestic Employment Agency when we get home and tomorrow we can start interviewing lady's maids."

Beatrice screwed up her courage and shook her head firmly. "I don't wish for a strange lady's maid, Johanna. Couldn't I – couldn't we, I mean – just see how Tilly goes on?"

"Tilly? She's a nice child, but you'll need more help than she can give you."

"Johanna, please believe that I really dislike the idea of having a fashionable lady's maid!" Beatrice took a deep breath and said in a voice that was a little unsteady, "It's Tilly or no one!"

"Nonsense! You can't mean that!"

"I do mean it! I'm not used to all this." Tears gathered in her eyes. "Please, Johanna, let's just try Tilly for a few days. That can't do any harm, surely. I like her cheerful nature and she's better with my hair than I am."

Johanna eyed her shrewdly, realized that her cousin was genuinely upset and capitulated. "Oh, very well!" After all, Sarah would be there to help out and Sarah was obviously enjoying training Tilly. It had put her in a good mood for weeks now. "But the girl is only on trial, mind," she added. "Don't say anything to her about a permanent place till we see how she goes!"

"Whatever you wish, Johanna." Beatrice sank back in relief.

—

When they got home, it was to find the house in an uproar. A carriage stood at the door and there were trunks and parcels all over the floor.

A head peered over the banisters. "It's me, Mama!"

"Jennice! What are *you* doing in town?"

Johanna's younger daughter chuckled naughtily. "Fleeing, Mama."

"What on earth do you mean by that? And come down, will you? I'm getting a crick in my neck talking to you like this."

A very pretty young woman descended the stairs. Beatrice stared at her. How Jennice had changed since her marriage! She was plumper than she had been, but Beatrice wished she looked even half as assured and elegant as the newcomer. In that, Jennice took after her mother. The pair of them made Beatrice feel very dowdy today.

Jennice planted a hearty kiss on her mother's cheek and a fleeting one in the air above Beatrice's ear. "So nice to be here safely!"

"*Safely?*" Johanna quizzed. "It's only a two-hour drive from Lymsby."

Jennice scowled. "Well, to hear Boris talk, you'd think we had to drive through forests full of highwaymen to get here."

Johanna swept them both into her own small sitting room, calling out to the butler to send them in some refreshments before she perished of hunger. "Now, young woman, kindly explain yourself!" she said with mock sternness as she sat down. "What exactly are you fleeing from?"

Another chuckle. "From my husband, Mama!"

"Oh, that's all right, then. What's Boris done this time?"

"Threatened to keep me at Lymsby for the rest of the year."

"Goodness, what a dreadful fate! Why should he want to do that?"

Jennice's expression became positively smug. "Because I'm about to make you into a grandmama!"

"*What!*"

When the shower of hugs from Johanna was over, Jennice explained how excited Boris had been at the mere possibility of a child and then how unbearably despotic he had become once its existence was confirmed. "As if I were ill or something! I told him childbearing is a perfectly natural thing and that common women continue working until the very last minute."

"And what did he say to that?"

"He turned up his nose and said that *his* wife was neither common nor required to work for her living, and would be looked after as befitted her station. So there was nothing for it but to show him how silly he's being."

"Oh, I do agree! It's fatal to allow a husband to dictate to one."

"I waited till he went over to a friend's to look at some horses – I'm sick and tired of him going out and leaving me alone! – and then I left straight away. I just hope nothing sends him home early. He shouldn't get back to Lymsby till after dark, so he won't set out for London

43

tonight, but I dare say he'll be here tomorrow, breathing fire and brimstone."

Johanna beamed at her. "Dear me, I'm terrified at the mere thought."

Beatrice, watching, could only wonder at the way they made the relationship between husband and wife seem a mere game. She couldn't help feeling some sympathy for Boris, whom she had not yet met.

Jennice smiled. "I'll soon bring him round, you'll see – at least I will if you'll only help me by telling him how dangerous it is to thwart the wishes of a woman carrying a child."

Johanna threw back her head and laughed. "You never change, Jennice! Very well, I'll help you. But when you get bigger, I do think you should retire to Lymsby and set poor Boris's mind at rest. Husbands are always so much more fussy with the first child. He'll probably leave you in peace with the others – at least, he will if this one's a boy. And you *will* have to cosset yourself a little more than usual, you know."

"Well, of course I'll retire when I grow bigger! You don't think I wish to be seen in public looking like a – a cow in milk! You know how gigantic Penelope got and I dare say I'll be the same. But I have a million things to do first: buy all the latest novels to keep myself entertained during my incarceration, arrange for some new clothes to be made – oh, all sorts of other things that one can only do in town!"

She turned to Beatrice. "And I must apologize, Bea, for ignoring you like this. What are you doing in London? Have you fled from Grandmamma?"

Chapter 3

Two days after the visit to Odette, the first of Beatrice's new clothes arrived, thanks to the efforts of three seamstresses who had stayed up until late each night sewing. Odette herself came to supervise the final trying-on, a rare attention, but the modiste was rather pleased with what she had created and wished to see that her efforts were properly appreciated.

Tilly stood in awed attendance as Odette's assistant helped her mistress don a soft apricot-coloured street dress with a high waist.

Beatrice studied herself in the full-length mirror, her eyes shining with wonderment at how flattering the dress was. Two lines of simple tucking gave body to the fabric just above the scalloped hem, and the long full sleeves ended in tucking, too, with narrow cream lace ruffles. These were matched by a soft lace frill rather like a ruff around the high neckline. To wear with the dress, there was a pelisse in a deeper colour of apricot velvet. She had never possessed anything which suited her half so well.

She turned to Odette first and reached out to clasp the modiste's hands, "Thank you!" she said, with a catch in her voice. "I never dreamed I could look so elegant!"

Johanna noted in amusement that the modiste was completely won over by this egalitarian treatment and

45

watched her press Beatrice's hands in return, before releasing them and stepping backwards.

"You will set a fashion, Mademoiselle," Odette prophesied. "I shall make sure of that. And, if I may suggest, to go with this dress a simple poke bonnet would be best with a full brim and very little trimming. Perhaps *un tout petit peu de dentelles*, not too much lace, mind! And one spray of flowers in a colour to match the pelisse?"

"Whatever you say." Beatrice turned next to her cousin. "I – I don't know what to say, Johanna."

Her cousin's eyes softened. "You don't need to say anything, Bea. I'm thoroughly enjoying all this. And you look lovely. Now, try on the ball dress! I think Odette has excelled herself with that."

Beatrice retired behind the screen with Tilly and the assistant in attendance and Odette stood there, a small smile curving her mouth. When her newest customer emerged like a butterfly from its chrysalis, she made no attempt to moderate her delight.

The dress was in a soft creamy silk which glistened slightly. It was trimmed above the one frill which graced the hem with three rows of narrow satin ribbon just a shade or two darker. At one point the frill rose to a higher point and the ribbon also curved upwards a few inches to meet a near-flat spray of delicate silk roses in a lighter cream. These were echoed by a matching spray on a satin fillet for the hair.

Beatrice's delight in the dress lent a sparkle to her eyes and soft colour to her cheeks. She had been dreadfully afraid that the dictates of fashion would force her to dress in multiple flounces and gaudy trimmings, or fussy strands of artificial flowers like the pictures in *La Belle Assemblée* and *The Ladies Monthly Museum* – Johanna's favourite reading material. Odette had captured Beatrice's wishes exactly in this elegant simplicity.

"I have just the thing to wear with that!" Johanna left the room abruptly, to return with a huge shawl, two and a half square yards of fine satin-striped Lyon silk, with a scalloped edging. "There! You'd think we'd matched the colour of the ribbon purposely, wouldn't you? Drape it round your shoulders, Bea!"

She stood back to gauge the effect and was rewarded by another nod of approval and complicity from Odette, who was becoming more French by the minute in her excitement. "*C'est parfait*, Your Ladyship. *Absolument parfait!* Everything should be of the purest lines for mademoiselle, but of the very finest quality. *Très simple, mais très chic.* I've found some materials which are rather special. I think, *non, j'en suis sûre*, that you will be pleased with them."

Johanna nodded. She wouldn't have dared disobey Odette's commands, even if her own fashion sense hadn't told her the same thing. "That's exactly my opinion," she agreed, "but it won't do for the court dress."

"Certainly not!" Odette's eyes gleamed. "For that, we shall need more elaboration, or it will be taken as a lack of respect for Her Majesty."

"Do I *have* to be presented?" pleaded Beatrice, though she knew she had little hope of escaping this ordeal.

Two shocked faces were her only answer.

She sighed. "I shall feel so ridiculous! Hoops! And feathers on my head! I shall seem six feet tall! I can't bear to think of it."

Johanna shook her head. "My dear, we all go through it and we all survive. And hoops are not nearly as much

47

trouble as you might expect, since you won't be sitting down in them, even on the carriage ride. Sitting down really is difficult to manage elegantly." She saw Beatrice's mouth open for another protest and held up one hand. "No! Not another word!" She turned to the modiste. "Odette, we shall leave the design of the court dress entirely up to you. White, of course."

"*Bien sûr.*"

Beatrice sighed again. She had forgotten about being presented in her anxiety about her aunt's list of eligibles. Now it loomed before her as yet another ordeal to be faced, perhaps one of the worst. She was quite sure she'd make a fool of herself, as she had in her encounter with Mr Serle. And why she kept thinking of him, she couldn't imagine.

–

The next day she wore the new apricot dress as she sat with Johanna in the salon, it being her ladyship's day to receive visitors. Her natural serenity lent her the gentle dignity which best suited both her looks and nature, but she was completely unaware of how well she looked, for she was concentrating on trying to remember people's names and on learning what sorts of topics ladies discussed when they went out and about in society.

Justin Serle arrived just as the last visitors were leaving. He was apparently a frequent caller, being a friend of Johanna's son-in-law. An expression of obvious surprise crossed his face as he gazed at the transformation of the foolish woman in crumpled travelling clothes whom he'd met a few evenings previously and whom he had dismissed out of hand as a nonentity.

Beatrice could easily guess what he was thinking and felt her indignation rise. How dared that man judge her by appearances? What a frivolous creature he must be! She gave him only the tips of her fingers to shake and removed her hand from his as quickly as politeness allowed, turning away and giving him no encouragement to linger by her side.

When he crossed the room to sit next to Jennice, who was in high fettle today, Beatrice retreated to sit in the bay window and stare down at the street. She had found the last hour or so rather tedious. Did no one talk about anything but parties and fashions and the latest gossip here in London?

The sun was shining outside, but no one seemed to wish to go out and enjoy it. Poor men from Manchester were so hungry that a group of them had tried to march on London to demand help, but no one cared. The news-papers seemed glad to see the Blanketeers dispersed by troops, but the sufferers had all her sympathy.

The doings of Princess Charlotte had been the main topic of conversation for several of the ladies that day. Beatrice had already seen Her Highness in the distance, driving past in a carriage: a plump young lady with yellow hair and undistinguished features. She had been extremely disappointed by the appearance of the much-fêted Heiress of England.

Across the room, Justin stared at her. He hadn't missed the look of disapproval on Miss Dencey's face as she took his hand, or the way she turned away from him as soon as she could, and he decided that even if his first impression of her as a country dowd had been wrong, he had not been mistaken in her character, which was serious to a fault. She would definitely not take in town, with that prim expression, and she was certainly not to his taste, however well she looked now.

Putting her firmly out of his mind, he began to flirt outrageously with Jennice whom he had known all his life and who therefore knew better than to take him seriously. When he glanced sideways again, he saw Beatrice's look of disapproval deepen and felt a sense of triumph.

"So, Justin, how do you find this year's crop of young ladies?" Jennice demanded, lounging back on the sofa in a manner which the Dowager would have condemned instantly as hoydenish.

He pulled a face. "Much the same as last year's. Sweet, innocent and deadly dull."

"I vow you're too demanding. The poor girls haven't got a chance with you! It's time you took a wife, for you're past thirty now. 'Tis your duty, sir, your solemn duty!" She wagged one finger at him in mock reproof, but her laughing eyes belied her words.

He bent his head for a moment as if in shamed acceptance of her reproof. "I admit it and I have tried, believe me! But if a girl possesses one good quality, she inevitably possesses two bad ones. And surely it's not too much to ask that a wife should be pleasant in appearance? You will note I do not stipulate beautiful. That would be to ask too much of Providence."

"Well, there are any number of pleasant-looking girls for you to choose from!"

"Yes, but I require one or two other qualities. Absolutely insist on them, in fact."

"Such as, sir?"

"A soft voice, a modicum of intelligence and the capacity to act as my hostess and châtelaine without tittering like a laundry maid."

As Beatrice listened, she watched them enviously, admiring the dexterity with which Jennice handled the light-hearted repartee and wishing she were similarly skilled. She could maintain a conversation, for that had been part of the Dowager's training, but not with such verve and lightness. Indeed, she felt herself to be extremely dull and prosaic by the standards of her Cousin Johanna's set.

In the middle of Mr Serle's visit, Lord Boris Newthorpe arrived at last to confront his errant wife, and since he was boiling with rage and was acquainted with or related to all the persons present, he did not scruple to start a quarrel in front of them.

He struck a pose in the doorway, one hand on the door frame, the other on his hip, and waited until all eyes were on him. "So, Madam, I find you here at last, do I?"

Beatrice could only gape, for she was not aware that Lord Newthorpe was given to a melodramatic turn of phrase when his ire was roused.

Jennice tilted her nose upwards and allowed a few moments to pass before saying sarcastically, "Since I left a note to tell you I was coming to visit Mama and since I was with you only two days ago, I cannot understand either your difficulty in finding me or your tone now, Sir!"

The aggrieved husband ground his teeth quite audibly. "You know what I mean, Madam."

"I'm sure I don't! I never do when you get on your high horse, Boris! *And* – if you've been so very worried about me – why has it taken you two days to get here?" She tossed her head at him.

"Majesty had sprained his fetlock! I had to see that it was properly tended. You know how ill-tempered he is with anyone except me."

"I'm well aware that *that horse* is more important to you than I am!" Jennice stood up, turned her back to him and pretended to study her reflection in a mirror, patting a curl into place while watching him from beneath her eyelashes.

He glared at her and turned to bow coldly to his mother-in-law, who took the opportunity to reintroduce Beatrice to him. But his thoughts were clearly not on the introductions. As soon as he had bowed over the visitor's hand, stared blankly at her and said through gritted teeth how delighted he was to see her, he turned back to his wife. "Kindly instruct your maid to pack your things, Madam!"

Jennice spun round, mouth open in shock. "Certainly not!"

"If you don't," Boris was growing redder in the face by the minute and rapidly losing his dignified tone, "then I shall give Susan the order myself."

Jennice's dignity also began to slip. "Well, she won't obey you, so there! She's *my* maid and she answers only to me!"

"In that case I shall be compelled to turn her off and find a maid who *does* recognise her master, shan't I?"

Jennice lost the rest of her elaborate poise abruptly and took a step toward him. "You wouldn't *dare*!"

He put one hand on his heart and struck a noble pose. "I dare do anything to protect my unborn child!"

"My dears, pray calm down!" murmured Johanna, who was finding it hard to conceal her amusement. Neither of the combatants paid her the slightest attention.

"I never heard of anything so mean in all my life!" declared Jennice, both hands clasped at her bosom and tears sparkling on her eyelashes. "Threatening to turn away Susan, who has been with me for years just because you're miffed! You're a beast, Boris Newthorpe, an absolute beast! What sort of a father will *you* make? Oh, my poor baby!" She pressed her hands protectively over her stomach.

"You have only to obey your husband's lawful commands, Madam, and the woman may stay on as your maid!"

"Obey your commands! *Obey your commands!* I never heard anything half so gothic! And that from a man whose horse is more important to him than his wife!"

Boris scowled at her and abandoned his pose. "Dash it all, I explained about that, Jen. If it had been any other horse than Majesty…"

She sniffed scornfully. "Anyway, you deserved that I should leave. Ordering me about like that and then going off to look at horses and leaving me on my own! What sort of husbandly care is that, pray? And who do you think I am anyway – your slave?"

"You're my wife and have promised to obey me."

She brushed that away with a careless gesture of one hand. "Oh pooh, whoever means that? It's just words."

He drew himself up again and tried to regain lost ground. "Madam, I insist that you do as you're told!"

"Well, I won't! And I think you're a beast to call me 'Madam' like that. And if you *dare* to even *begin* to carry out your threat about Susan…" Jennice was unable to think of anything dire enough to threaten him with in return, so she hid her dilemma by bursting into tears, which usually brought him to heel.

This time, however, all the tears elicited from her husband was a scornful, "Hah!" and another dramatic pose, this time with arms folded.

Beatrice, by this time scarlet with embarrassment and distress at the public nature of their altercation, felt a gentle touch on her arm. Mr Serle was standing beside her.

"May I suggest that we leave them to complete their quarrel in private and go out for a stroll round the square, Miss Dencey?"

His eyes were brimming with laughter as he kept an eye on the tragicomedy being played in front of them, but he had noticed that his hostess's cousin was genuinely upset by the quarrel and for some strange reason that had touched him. She must have a very tender heart and be very naïve about the games husbands and wives played. Well, that was better than some of the brass-faced harpies you met in town, who cared for nothing but themselves. In fact, for some strange reason Miss Dencey reminded him of his grandmother, whom he had loved dearly and who had also been very tender-hearted. "We're certainly in the way here," he added quietly, offering her his arm.

She stood up quickly. "Oh yes! They must wish to be alone!"

He rather doubted that, since both the Newthorpes loved playing to an audience, but he didn't voice his disagreement.

Jennice sobbed twice as loudly when Boris didn't rush to her side, then, after looking at him covertly, sank gracefully onto the sofa and demanded that someone bring her a vinaigrette before she fainted quite away. "Oh, how did I come to marry a monster like you?" she declaimed, one arm covering her eyes. "What a father you will make for my children! You will care more for your horses than for my poor babies!"

Beatrice took Mr Serle's arm and let him guide her toward the door.

Johanna turned her head away for a moment, shoulders shaking with suppressed laughter, but her guest didn't notice that.

Justin left Beatrice waiting in the hall and went back to whisper in his hostess's ear.

Johanna nodded permission. She knew it would be a while before Boris could be brought to heel and Jennice calmed down, and although she thoroughly enjoyed watching the minx's antics, she could see that her young cousin was suffering from acute embarrassment. Poor Bea had always been oversensitive about quarrels, while Jennice and Boris enjoyed theirs thoroughly – not to mention the tender reconciliations that always followed them!

Beatrice stood in the hall with Mr Serle, waiting for her new velvet spencer to be brought down.

When Tilly had assisted her mistress to don it and a simple straw bonnet, the butler stepped forward to open the door for them.

"I think," Justin told him quietly, "your mistress will not wish to receive any other callers this morning."

Jennice's sobbing was quite audible even from the front door. A shriek of rage punctuated it suddenly, making Beatrice gasp, but the butler didn't flinch. "Quite so, sir," he said. "Miss Jennice does get a trifle upset at times. Lady Newthorpe, I should say."

"We'll just take a walk round the gardens here in the square. You can send someone out to fetch us when the fireworks are over."

"Certainly, Mr Serle. Fine clement weather we are enjoying, are we not, Miss? The spring flowers are just coming out nicely in the gardens. I fancy you'll enjoy the displays."

Not until they were outside in the weak spring sunlight did Beatrice realize that Jennice's quarrel with her husband had thrown her into close proximity with someone who was almost a complete stranger and to whom she had taken a strong dislike. She stopped abruptly. "I – er – should we be…?" and couldn't think how to phrase her question without sounding impolite.

"If you mean is it proper for us to be out walking together without a chaperone, yes, it is, that is as long as we keep to the public gardens here. I'm sure you'd prefer to be out of the house while those two continue their quarrel. My friend Boris can be a trifle arrogant at times, but I think he's more than met his match in Jennice. Do you know why he's so eager to take her away from town? I had thought they were planning to come up here for the whole season. They usually do."

"She's expecting a baby," Beatrice replied without thinking, then flushed and stopped dead just as she was about to take his arm. "Oh dear! I'm not sure whether I should have told you that! Pray don't tell them. I mean…" Her voice faded and she could only study the flower bed to her left in an attempt to hide her blushes. Why did this man make her act so foolishly? She had only to be in his presence to feel flustered and breathless.

He began to feel bored at this missish behaviour, but offered her his arm. He studied her as they began to walk. A woman of her age should have more social confidence, though the flushed face and over-bright eyes became her very well. In fact, she was far more attractive than he had thought at first. He preferred taller women like her. It was annoying to have to bend down to talk to someone. "You needn't worry about telling me the news, Miss Dencey. Boris is a childhood friend of mine – we more or less grew up together – and I'm bound to be one of the first to know about the baby. No wonder he wants her to return home!"

Beatrice nodded and looked down at his arm, feeling a little bemused by how conscious she was of touching him. And how strong his arm felt! She glanced sideways at him and caught her breath at how handsome he was looking today. For a moment the world seemed to fade around them and she was conscious only of him, then she realized he was speaking again and tried to pay better attention. She must learn to behave more sensibly in his presence.

"The two of them have been married for four years without a sign of the precious heir," Justin said, his voice rather scornful.

As they strolled on, Beatrice protested, "It's only to be expected that he would wish for children. It's one of the main purposes of marriage, isn't it?" Apart from the money aspects, a voice said inside her head. People of her class seemed to marry more often for money than for love.

"Besides," her voice grew softer, "what woman does not wish for children?"

Her longing for a child echoed clearly in her voice, which made him slow down to stare at her in surprise. Not many of the young ladies he'd met in town were so honest about their feelings. In fact, it wasn't fashionable even to speak of one's children, except perhaps to very close friends and relatives.

"Jennice was delighted about the child, I think," Beatrice said thoughtfully, "though not about Boris wishing her to stay in the country."

"I'm not an expert on children. Most of the women I know complain loudly of the tedium of the breeding process and then leave their offspring to the care of nurse-maids. Jennice won't enjoy being cloistered at Lymsby, nor can I see her devoting herself to her children – well, not once the novelty has worn off."

He and his younger brother had rarely seen their own mother and had been raised by their nurse. Fortunately, that redoubtable woman had furnished them with the permanent affection which all children need and as well, they had each other's company. There being only eighteen months difference in age, they had been as close as many twins.

The same nurse was now in charge of the house-keeping at Melbury and had lately taken to reinforcing what his mother said by scolding Justin roundly whenever he visited his country estates. She made no secret of the fact that she considered it shameful and selfish for him to remain single for so long and thus omit to provide an heir for the Serle line.

"If you are not careful," Mrs. Powis had told him bluntly only a week previously, "your unmarried state will become a habit and you'll end up a crab-tempered old bachelor, with no one to love you in your declining years."

Mrs. Powis had been far more successful in persuading him to consider his duty than his mother had, for she hadn't hesitated to remind him that the lack of an heir would also mean that his cousin would inherit the estate. "And what will become of all the tenants then?" she had added ominously? "Have you thought about that, eh, Master Justin? If not, then you had better start doing so at once! Your Cousin Luke has already gambled away most of his own inheritance and will be happy to waste the Serle fortunes as well, for a more reckless, spendthrift creature I have yet to meet. He should have been spanked more often as a child."

"You never spanked us at all, Powey!" Justin had teased, in an attempt to divert her from this tedious topic – but he had failed.

"You two never needed spanking. Master Luke did. I mind him visiting here and breaking your toys – *on purpose*." She drew herself up to her full height of five feet and one inch, and finished, "I had thought better of you, Master Justin, than to see you neglect what you owe to the family like this. I had indeed."

Justin turned the corner of the square automatically, still lost in his thoughts. The matter of an heir had not seemed important while his elder brother was alive, but Peter had been killed at Waterloo nearly two years previously. Justin still missed him desperately and was quite aware that he had grown cooler with the world since his brother's death, for he had no one to make him laugh now, or to tease him out of his dignity.

This time Mrs. Powis's words had been reinforced, unknown to her, by the fact that his cousin Luke had recently asked for a loan to cover his gambling losses, to prevent the heavily mortgaged Mendleton estates being seized by creditors and sold. Justin had refused to supply that loan. Even as a boy Luke had never returned the things he was lent; as a grown man he had turned into a dashed loose fish. Why, the fellow had even tried to pledge his cousin's name to certain debts, though the family lawyer had soon put a stop to that.

So as a result of all the pressure, Justin was trying very hard indeed to steel himself to the idea of marriage. The trouble was, apart from the lack of a suitable lady, he had a private worry, which he was unable to discuss with anyone, about whether he could actually bring himself to make love to a silly young chit who did not attract him purely for the sake of begetting children. The mere thought of failure to do so made his blood run cold.

Beatrice glanced sideways at Mr Serle, saw he was lost in thought and didn't try to make conversation. He was looking sad and she couldn't help wondering what he had to be sad about. Perhaps Johanna would know. It was none of her business, of course, but if he were such a close friend of the family, she ought to know which subjects to avoid introducing with him. She noticed that one lock of hair had fallen across his brow and couldn't help smiling a little to see how boyish that made him appear, for all his elegant clothing. She definitely preferred men with dark hair. They looked so much more distinguished than fair-haired men.

'"I couldn't leave *my* children to be brought up by servants," she said after a while, voicing her thoughts aloud. Was that the sort of behaviour a gentleman of rank would expect of his wife?

Justin made a noncommittal noise, not at all interested in what she, or any other unmarried lady, intended to do with their as-yet-unborn children. At least her soft voice didn't grate upon his ears and she didn't constantly demand his attention, so it was no great trial to walk with her, though it was a pity she had that tendency to grow flustered for no reason.

"I think children need as much love as you can give them," she added, sighing as she thought of dear Eleanor, whom she was missing dreadfully.

"And are you – er – an expert on child-rearing, Miss Dencey?" he asked, resigning himself to a discussion of this topic. It was amusing, really, for he knew she was a spinster well past the usual age of marrying. What could she possibly know about raising children?

She flushed at the mockery in his voice. "I've had the pleasure of bringing up a young relative from the time she was nine until now, and since Eleanor is nineteen, I know a little about such things, Sir."

Her gentle dignity made him feel suddenly ashamed. "I cry pardon, Miss Dencey. I didn't mean to mock you. I was unaware of your exact circumstances."

She bowed her head in acknowledgment of his apology, but her expression told him plainly that she didn't really care what he thought and he was rather surprised at that.

"Do you mean to make a long stay in London?" he asked idly, it being a standard question to put to a newcomer.

"I suppose I shall have to stay for the whole Season." Her tone was despondent.

The unexpectedness of this answer made him look at her in surprise. "You don't sound very enthusiastic about that. Most young ladies can't wait to have their London Seasons."

She spoke impatiently, her mind still on Eleanor. "Well, as you've no doubt noticed, Mr Serle, I'm not exactly young. And to tell the truth, I'm not at all thrilled about doing the Season!" Nor was she thrilled to be thrown into the company of an arrogant person like this man, who spent his time either making trite meaningless comments or else being odiously sarcastic! Why, he would make Eleanor's life an absolute misery! she decided indignantly. I shall cross his name off my aunt's list the minute I get back to my room!

He smothered another sigh and wondered if the Newthorpes' quarrel was over yet.

"I'm here at my aunt's behest, not by my own choosing," she went on, thinking aloud. "And I'm not at all sure that I shall enjoy spending so long in the city. I much prefer life in the country."

He didn't really believe her. So many people said such things for effect, especially those trying to sound blasé. What woman would not relish the opportunity to buy a wardrobe full of new clothes and sample all the pleasures of the London Season?

After another awkward pause, he began to speak of the parties planned by his friends, assuming Miss Dencey would be attending them all with her cousin and she dutifully followed his lead, thinking how tedious these festivities would become, crammed one upon the other as they seemed to be. As she murmured responses, she wondered which wildflowers were out in the woods at Satherby and whether in London she might sometimes be allowed to go out for proper walks, not like this boring dawdle round and round the square. A few spring flowers were certainly out in the gardens here, which consisted of four narrow flower beds containing stiff rows of plants. Poor little things! She had a fellow feeling for them. Already she was feeling restless and penned in.

On their next circuit Beatrice paused to stretch out a hand and caress a frond of soft spring foliage on one of the bushes. "The young leaves are so beautiful. But everything's all caged up here in London, isn't it?"

As she resumed her walk and her silence, Justin realized with surprise that she was just as happy to study the beauties of the garden as to indulge in polite conversation. In fact, he thought, smiling wryly, he rather got the impression that she preferred the flowers to his conversation. Which was most unusual for a lady favoured with his attentions. He walked in silence for a while, determined to make her furnish the next topic of conversation, and was amazed when she suddenly stopped dead.

"Oh, there's Tom! Would you mind, Mr Serle, if I just had a word with him?"

She left his side without waiting for his permission and he turned to see who this Tom was. To his utter astonishment, the man turned out to be a poor haggard creature, lacking an arm and with a rather grimy and tattered sleeve pinned across his chest. He was an old soldier, from the

63

looks of him. The streets of the capital were still full of men like him, though the war had been over for nearly two years. Intrigued, Justin followed Beatrice across the square.

"Oh, Tom, I'm so glad to see you looking better!" she exclaimed.

The man touched his cap, as if saluting an officer. "Came to show you me tray, Miss."

"Yes, it's exactly right! Now, you must be sure to keep it clean. That makes *such* a difference, you know."

Justin watched in amazement as his erstwhile tongue-tied companion, who seemed to have completely forgotten his presence, laughed with Tom over some escapade or other and then questioned him closely about the details of his business plans. When her face was animated, as it was for this shabby creature, Miss Dencey was quite startlingly lovely. As he listened, he found that Tom's business appeared to consist of selling hot pies from a tray slung around his neck to people he met in the streets, and the whole contraption seemed to have been recently funded by Miss Dencey.

It was Tom who, after a while, ahemmed and begged the gentleman's pardon for taking up the lady's time.

Beatrice's animation vanished abruptly. "Oh yes, I had quite forgotten. I do beg your pardon, Mr Serle! I was just so glad to see Tom looking better. He's been very ill, you see. You be sure to keep your chest warm, Tom! I shall keep an eye open for you when I'm out shopping tomorrow." She watched as he touched his cap and walked away, then turned back to Justin, her expression schooled to that of a dutiful listener once more.

He was irritated enough to say unguardedly, "That's a strange kind of acquaintance for a lady!"

Knowing how annoyed Johanna would be at this further encounter with Tom, Beatrice could feel herself colouring. "I saw him collapse in the street a few days ago from hunger and was able to help him. All he needed was a little assistance and he was quite capable of earning himself a living. It's shameful the way these old soldiers are abandoned by their regiments. The government ought to do something about them, if no one else will! Tom lost his arm at Waterloo, poor fellow."

She sighed and dropped her eyes. "I'm sorry. *You* cannot be interested in him. You were saying…?" Her eyes became glazed as she waited for him to take up their conversation again.

Justin felt indignation surge up within him so strongly that he almost allowed himself the pleasure of giving her a set-down. Here he was, honouring her with his company for over half an hour and she could hardly be bothered to listen to him! Then she left him in mid-sentence and became animated at the sight of a shabby old ex-soldier, a mere ranker!

His expression was for a moment so savage that Beatrice stared at him in astonishment.

"I can be very interested in anyone who was at Waterloo," he snapped, "since my own brother was killed there! And I applaud your generosity in helping that man, Miss Dencey. I do, indeed." He would keep a better look out himself for old soldiers fallen on hard times from now on, he added mentally. Peter would not have liked to see his men in trouble. He'd thought the world of them, and they of him. Some of them had even written to the family after Peter was killed to say that. Justin had found their ill-spelled letter signed by six names very touching and still had it in his possession.

Beatrice flushed. "Oh. Well – I thank you for the compliment, but it's a pleasure to help people like him."

"Not all ladies feel that way. You are to be commended."

An embarrassed silence fell and they were both relieved to see a footman coming across the square to tell them that her ladyship was waiting for them with a light luncheon as soon as they were ready to return.

Justin was certainly happy to join the others, for Miss Dencey was not at all a comfortable companion. And the memory of her laughing face as she spoke to Tom still rather piqued him, if truth be told. Few ladies were so transparently impervious to his charms and none had ever before shown herself to be actually bored by his conversation.

Beatrice stifled a sigh as they turned back toward the house. "It seems a pity to stay indoors on such a lovely day." Forgetting her London manners, she walked back with what could only be described as a stride.

Justin noticed that she turned at the door to look back longingly at the sunny sky. She clearly meant what she said about wishing to be outdoors. She was, he decided as he watched her, the most puzzling lady he had ever met.

–

Indoors, they found Johanna waiting for them alone, her eyes still crinkled in amusement.

"Has the battle been won?" asked Justin lightly.

Beatrice frowned to hear him talk so flippantly about something as serious as a quarrel between husband and wife.

"It has indeed. The combatants are indulging in a touching reconciliation at this very moment."

"And who won the engagement?"

"Who do you think?" she countered.

"Jennice, of course. I'd back her any day." There was a tinge of scorn to his voice. That was what you got for marrying. A wife who wheedled and wept, doing anything to get her own way. He had seen it happen all too many times.

Johanna inclined her head. "Correct! Jennice is to stay in town with me for a month or two before returning to Lymsby. Boris will join us here from time to time."

Beatrice occupied herself with her food as the other two joked about the Newthorpes. Would she ever grow used to the way members of the ton poked fun at serious things? If she were expecting a baby, the last place she'd want to come to would be London and the last thing she'd wish would be to run away from her husband. She indulged herself briefly in a little fantasy of a home and family of her own – and why Mr Serle's face should figure in that fantasy, she couldn't understand. As if she'd want to marry a man as fashionable and uncaring as him – however attractive he was – and you couldn't deny that he was attractive! Even Jennice responded to his charm.

"And did you two enjoy your walk?" Johanna asked, intrigued to find out how Justin, who usually bestowed his attentions only upon spirited ladies of dashing habits, had coped with a quiet, serious-minded companion.

"Very much!" he said automatically, inclining his head toward Miss Dencey.

"Beatrice?" Johanna asked, for her cousin was avoiding her eyes.

"Oh, the gardens are very pleasant, Johanna, and it was very – um, kind of Mr Serle to escort me. Though I have to admit that I prefer real walks in the countryside. One is so restricted in the town."

Johanna raised her eyebrows in surprise at this luke-warm statement. "You'll have to grow used to taking the air in such a way, I'm afraid, my dear," she said. "I'm not one for long walks myself, and certainly not brisk ones. I much prefer shopping." Her grin at Justin showed him just how amused she was by his failure to charm the lady.

He responded with the tiniest of shrugs.

Beatrice, who hadn't noticed the interchange, kept her mouth resolutely closed on the truthful comment she would have liked to make. "Shopping can be very pleasant, too," she muttered, unable to think of a better response without telling an outright lie.

Once Justin had taken his leave, Johanna asked curi-ously, "Did you not enjoy his company?"

"Whose?"

"Whose do you think? Serle's, of course!"

"It was kind of him to take me away from the quarrel. I'm not – not used to such things."

"Serle is accounted very good company by most young ladies, not to mention being thought handsome. Why, he's one of the most sought-after bachelors in town! Now, he would make a very proper match for you or Eleanor."

Beatrice didn't like to see everyone fawning over a man who cared so little about the people around him.

She abandoned caution and politeness to say roundly, "Well, I'm not a young lady and if you really want to know, Johanna, I prefer people whose conversation is less frivolous and who don't spend their time mocking other people."

Her tone was severe and dismissive. She had definitely decided now that Justin Serle would make the worst possible husband for Eleanor. Dear Eleanor needed someone more serious-minded, someone who would counter her impulsiveness. But not someone stuffy. That would be just as bad! Oh dear, this was all going to be so difficult!

Beatrice wished, and not for the first time, that her Aunt Marguerite had entrusted this task to someone else.

Chapter 4

Within a few days, Beatrice had grown more used to her cousin's indolent habits and to the patterned behaviour of the upper classes in town. On their brief visits to London, before her aunt grew too frail to travel, she had suspected that such a life would not suit her; now, as the slow days passed and she struggled to stay awake until late at night, she grew more and more certain of it.

Back at Satherby she had been able to keep more rational hours and had a myriad occupations to keep her busy, what with visiting the tenants, helping the sick, managing a large household for her aunt, practising her singing, talking to Eleanor or simply walking in the home park. Here in London Johanna's house ran smoothly without the need for much attention from its languid mistress. And no one Beatrice met here ever seemed to say what they meant or to discuss anything interesting.

In order to avoid upsetting anyone, she developed the habit of walking out with her maid early in the morning, when Johanna and her daughter were still in bed. She loved to watch the street life that teemed in London once you got away from the calm oases inhabited by the rich.

Johanna expostulated with her in vain. "But such creatures are *dirty*!"

"So would you be if you had to share a water pump with a dozen other streets!"

Johanna couldn't even begin to imagine that situation, so ignored it. "Well, don't let anyone see you on these expeditions – and for heavens' sake, take a footman with you for protection!"

Beatrice didn't actually refuse to do this, but simply ignored this instruction. A starchy footman would drive away the very people she wanted to talk to. Tilly was quite enough company, thank you.

Unfortunately, this innocent desire to help her fellow creatures led her into trouble the week after Jennice's arrival in town. Early one morning she was watching with amusement an old woman buying a pie from Tom and making a big fuss about which one to choose from his tray. The two of them had already had sharp words because he had refused to let the customer feel all his stock to see which pie was the warmest, and they were now vigorously debating which was the plumpest pie on offer.

Smiling, Beatrice wished she had her sketch book, for she would have loved to try to capture the old woman's expression and the way her whole body was absorbed in the choosing of that one pie.

Then Tilly screamed and shouted, "Stop thief!" and Beatrice realized with a shock that a small boy had cut the strings of her reticule and was even now darting along the street with his booty. If it hadn't been for Tilly's quick eye, he'd have got away unnoticed, for Beatrice had felt nothing.

Angry at being caught like that, she started to run after him, following him round a corner and off the main street. She saw him turn another corner and increased her pace.

Tilly, puffing and gasping, was soon left behind.

Beatrice had spent most of her youth roaming the countryside, as she grew older, fending for herself and her mother. She reverted instinctively to the same mode of behaviour in this crisis, forgetting that it was shocking behaviour for a lady to run like that.

Suddenly, as she turned yet another corner, she felt herself falling and was unable to prevent it. She thudded to the ground and lay there, half stunned. A figure loomed over her and a filthy hand reached out toward the gold chain around her neck.

"Tut! Tut!" said a hoarse voice. "Very careless of me to trip you up like that! What a pretty necklace, my dear!"

Beatrice slapped his hand aside and covered the chain with her own hand. When she tried to roll away from him, however, it only brought her into contact with another pair of legs clad in ragged fustian trousers. Another man was barring her way on the other side and another set of black-nailed fingers was reaching down toward her.

A voice screamed, "There she is! *Help!*"

Beatrice's new assailant cursed and tried to grab the gold chain. She fought him off, but then something struck her head and pain exploded around her. As she felt the chain snap, the world receded into a red mist.

It was some time before she came to her senses. Through a blur of noise and pulsating colour, she gradually became aware that she was leaning against a man's chest, with Tilly crouched beside her fanning her face.

"What – happened?"

Tilly stopped fanning for a moment to clasp her hand. "Oh, Miss! Are you all right? You gave us such a fright!"

"What on earth were you doing chasing someone down these unsavoury lanes?" demanded a furious voice above her head. "Had you taken complete leave of your senses, Miss Dencey?"

"I was… they'd stolen my reticule." She had to force the words out, for her head was still swimming. She fumbled at her neck. "And they took my chain."

"That's when one of them kicked her, sir," Tilly put in.

"You should have let them take it, Miss Dencey. They wouldn't have hesitated to kill you for it! These are the back streets of London, not some country village! Such men would cut your throat as soon as look at you!"

"It's Justin Serle," Beatrice said, who was still feeling very strange. "How did he get here, Tilly? And why is he so angry with me?"

"I don't think she's come to herself proper yet, sir," the maid whispered. "An' she's that pale! I've never seen her so white."

"She'll probably be sick in a minute," he said, still sounding angry. "People often are when they've been hit on the head. Can you run and find us a hackney cab?"

"I don't think I ought to leave her," said Tilly dubiously. "If she's sick, she'll need me. And what if they come back again?"

"I can defend her if those villains return, believe me." His expression was steely, though his arms were still gentle as he supported Miss Dencey. To his surprise, he was again feeling protective toward her. What was there about her that elicited this response in him?

Tilly stood up, hesitating, seeming uncertain where her duty lay.

"Mr Serle has a very strong heartbeat," announced Beatrice. "I can hear it quite clearly." She nestled against his chest with a happy murmur.

Justin jerked his head in the direction of the main streets. "On your way, girl! I want to get Miss Dencey home as soon as possible. The best way you can help your mistress at the moment is to find us a cab!"

Footsteps clumped up to a point behind Beatrice's head, but she couldn't summon up the energy to turn round and see who it was.

Tom's voice announced gruffly, "They got clear away, sir, I'm sorry to say. I couldn't keep up with them. Look, I can go an' get you a hackney, if you need this young woman's help."

"I'd prefer you to stay here with me, Tom, in case we're attacked again. *Move yourself, girl!* Tom, go and stand on the street corner and keep an eye on Miss Dencey's maid. We don't want her getting attacked as well."

Tilly bowed to the voice of authority and moved off.

Beatrice, lying there dreamily, heard the conversation continue.

"I doubt I'd be much help to you in a scrap, sir." Tom's voice sounded tight and angry.

"You've still got one hand and two feet, haven't you? Of course you'd be some use."

The other voice became more cheerful. "Well, I'd certainly do my best, sir. Nicest lady I ever met, Miss Dencey is. Lucky day for me when I collapsed in front of 'er, I can tell you."

Justin stared down at the pale face so close to his. He hadn't realized before how long Miss Dencey's eyelashes were, or what a pretty colour her hair was when the sun was shining on it.

She looked up at him for a moment with unfocused eyes, then grimaced. "I feel s-sick." She was finding it hard to form the words. "But I can't – can't sit up properly."

Deftly, Justin moved her into a sitting position and held her until she had finished vomiting, then lifted her in his arms, carrying her a short distance along the street before stopping again. He fumbled in his pocket for his handkerchief and wiped her mouth.

She allowed his ministrations, leaning against him again when he had finished, for he felt so warm and comforting. The world was beginning to make a little more sense now. "I'm sorry to be so much trouble."

"You were quite feather-brained to take such a risk!" He glanced around, alert to the possibility that the thieves might come back with reinforcements. Then he looked down and saw tears come into her eyes at his sharp words and his voice became gentle again. "I'm sorry. I shouldn't be scolding you now. You must be feeling dreadful."

The world was still hazy around her, but she felt a need to explain. "Didn't like to – to be robbed."

"He dropped your gold chain when I hit him with me tray, Miss," volunteered Tom. "I've got it here safe for you."

"Oh, Tom! Thank you so much!" She tried to turn her head toward him, but winced as pain shot through her.

Justin's voice sounded in her ear. "You should be resting, Miss Dencey, not trying to talk. Or move."

"Oh. Yes." She closed her eyes and tried to do that, but could still hear what they were saying, as if it were at the far end of a long tunnel.

"Remind me to reimburse you for the pies you lost," said Justin. "Miss Dencey is very obliged to you. As am I. You bore into that villain like a good 'un."

"Ah, you should 'ave seen me when I 'ad both me arms," said Tom regretfully. "I'd ha' caught one of 'em for sure in them days. Nor I don't need payin' to 'elp a regular trojan of a lady like Miss Dencey."

"You've more than earned a reward."

"Well, all right, then. No, not that much. I wouldn't take nothin' at all, sir, only I need money for more stock, you see. Mine got spilled – full tray, it was, too – an' all the pies will 'ave been picked up and et. I ain't got nothin' saved yet, with you see, me only just starting in the trade."

Beatrice felt Mr Serle fumble in his pocket and one of his hands momentarily left her. As the hand returned to hold her more tightly, she gave in to the temptation to snuggle more closely into the crook of her rescuer's arm. "You're stronger than you look," she murmured. "Not just a dandy."

Justin, who prided himself on his sporting prowess, stiffened and exclaimed in astonishment, "*A dandy!* Is that what you think of me?"

"Always talking about fashions and parties," she explained, still feeling light-headed and more than half convinced that this was just a dream and a bad one at that. It didn't really matter what she said in a dream. She'd never dare say such things to anyone in real life, of course, though she had often longed to.

Justin's lips tightened and Tom hid a grin.

"Always immaculately dressed," she continued. "In the height of fashion. That's a dandy, isn't it?"

The rattle of wheels and the sound of Tilly's voice interrupted Beatrice's ramblings, and she felt herself being lifted up and settled in a vehicle which smelled of stale sweat and mouldy straw. She couldn't help moaning, for being moved made her head stab with pain, but a gentle voice promised she would soon be safe in her bed, so she subsided against Serle once more, clinging to him with her free hand. "I feel safe with you," she confided. "Don't let them hit me again!"

"No, I won't."

As the cab began to move, Beatrice could feel herself drifting away into a warm darkness. The dream must be coming to an end. She would be glad to wake up. Her head was hurting so much she couldn't think properly.

Justin stared down at her beautiful hair, tumbled on her shoulders now and brushing against his chin. He had a sudden urge to stroke it, so lustrous was it, and he barely prevented himself from doing so. Fortunately the maid didn't seem to have noticed anything. But the strange impulses continued to bombard him. He could feel Miss Dencey's breasts rising and falling against his chest. She had a woman's figure, warm and soft, not a slight girlish frame, like so many young ladies, some of whom had barely turned seventeen. It surprised him that he hadn't fully appreciated before what an attractive woman she was. Perhaps that was because she wasn't showy, didn't set out to attract. She was just – herself.

His expression became grim as he remembered what she thought of him. *A dandy, indeed!*

Another period of jolting was followed by a chorus of voices and by more movement and light, which hurt her head again. Beatrice sighed in relief when a man's deep voice told the others sharply to be quiet and then ordered someone to show him where Miss Dencey's bedchamber lay.

"You're breathing very deeply," Beatrice told the person who was carrying her. "Where are you taking me? Oh!" For as he started to climb some stairs, the increased jolting made her head begin to throb again. She clutched his shoulder tightly.

"Is it hurting you?"

"Yes." Her voice was a mere thread of sound.

"I'm sorry. But see, we're here at your bedroom now."

As he laid her on the bed, she opened her eyes, only to find the room spinning about her. With a sigh, she let herself spiral down into the darkness, glad to leave the pain behind.

–

When Beatrice awoke, it was dark and Johanna was sitting by her bed. There was a rustle of silk, then a whisper of, "Bea?"

"Johanna," she managed. "What – what happened?"

"At least she seems to be in her right senses," Johanna commented to someone invisible beyond the pool of light thrown by a single candle.

Beatrice frowned. "Of course I'm in my senses? But why am I lying here with... Oh!" Memories came flooding back.

"You were attacked in the street."

"It wasn't a dream."

"No. And fancy running after a thief like that. Don't you know how dangerous those alleys are?"

A cool cloth was laid on her forehead and Beatrice sighed. "Nice," she managed, closing her eyes.

"Does it help?"

"Yes. Head's aching!"

"I'm not surprised! Those villains *kicked* you! Such people should be hanged!"

"They were probably hungry." Beatrice tried to see who else was in the room, but gasped as her head throbbed in protest against even a slight movement.

Johanna patted her hand. "Never mind that! Just try to rest, Bea! The doctor said nothing is broken and you'll be all right in a day or two."

"Yes. I'd like to – rest." There was a fire flickering in the grate and its cheerful flames were tugging at the corners of her eyes. She couldn't keep them open. She could not…

–

It was light when she woke again and this time her maid was sitting beside her.

"How do you feel, Miss? You look a bit better now, I must say. Got a bit of pink in your cheeks again. You slept for most of the night, though you was a bit restless just before dawn."

Beatrice's head was still aching, but she could think more clearly, at least. She gasped as she started to remember what had happened and tried to persuade herself that it was just a dream that she had accused her rescuer of being a dandy – but somehow, her memories of that conversation seemed only too real. "Tilly!" she said, after a minute or two.

"Yes, Miss?"

She simply had to find out whether she had really spoken her thoughts aloud and been so rude to poor Mr Serle. "Did I – um, say anything – um, anything impolite to Mr Serle yesterday?"

Tilly giggled. "Well…"

"Tell me!"

"Well, Miss, Tom says you told Mr Serle he was a dandy an' said that he only talked nonsense, an' Tom says he wasn't best pleased with that."

"Oh dear!"

"Don't you worry, Miss! He'll soon forget it, Mr Serle will. He's a kind gentleman and he knows you wasn't yourself."

Beatrice groaned. Out of her senses or not, she'd been extremely rude! How would she ever face Justin Serle again? What must he think of her? Especially as, dandy or not, he'd come to her rescue and driven away her attackers. She lay there for a minute or two, then tried to turn her head to look at Tilly, but the effort made her head throb again.

"Just you lie still, Miss. I'll go an' tell them you're awake."

Beatrice dozed off after that, until she became suddenly aware of a debate between Johanna and Tilly as to whether the doctor should be summoned again. "I'm all right," she managed and opened her eyes. "I don't need a doctor. Johanna!"

Her cousin leaned over her. "Is there anything you do need, love?"

"I'm thirsty."

"Tilly, get your mistress a drink of that barley water the doctor ordered. Afterwards, we'll sponge you down, Bea, so that you feel fresher."

"Yes. Yes, I'd like that."

She drank a whole glass of liquid, then allowed them to do as they would with her. Almost before they'd finished their ministrations, she could feel herself drifting into sleep again. "So tired," she sighed.

–

By the following day, apart from a slight residual headache, Beatrice felt well enough to be helped to a couch by the fire in her room.

Jennice came to visit her, but Beatrice couldn't seem to concentrate for long on what her visitor said, for the loud, cheerful voice and lively conversation made her head throb. Johanna came in later and was a more comfortable companion, because she talked quietly and softly, not demanding answers.

Tilly was best of all, because she said very little and that in hushed tones, seeming to notice what her mistress needed without being told.

Justin Serle had sent a huge bunch of hothouse flowers, which gazed accusingly down at Beatrice from a wooden plant stand in the bay window. In the end, after trying in vain to ignore it, she told Tilly to take them away, pretending their perfume made her headache worse.

It was several days before she felt strong enough to resume her normal life again, days in which she worried about the fact that she had insulted Mr Serle and must definitely apologize to him as soon as she possibly could.

During that period of convalescence she was fussed over by every servant with a claim to attend her. From the start of this visit, Johanna had watched with wry amusement as Beatrice gradually won over *her* servants and had them eating out of her hand, even Moreton, who was famous for being one of the most supercilious butlers in town. But he was not haughty with Miss Dencey. With her, he was fatherly and helpful, especially since her accident. For her, he would unbend amazingly and the two of them held long conversations about the manners of the ton nowadays and those in his youth, or the difficulties of maintaining standards during the recent war, with prices so high and food and goods so scarce.

While Miss Dencey was ill, there was distinct rivalry between the various servants as to who could do most for her, and it was noticeable that Moreton found several excuses to visit her upstairs, even carrying up the notes from well-wishers himself, a signal honour.

Tilly had now become very possessive of her temporary mistress and Johanna could see that there would be no chance of hiring a more experienced lady's maid after this.

Even that man Tom had appeared at the kitchen door every day, begging for news of Miss Dencey.

-

Once she had recovered, Beatrice resumed her social engagements, somewhat embarrassed by the notoriety she had acquired because of her adventure. Justin Serle, she found, was cast in the role of hero rescuing a poor foolish lady. People spoke of his bravery in the most extravagant terms, as if expecting her to swoon away at the mere thought of it.

No one seemed to give her any credit for trying to fight off her attackers, but rather, they hinted at how foolish she had been to try to follow the thief. She had to dig her fingers into her palms several times to prevent herself from answering sharply, but thanks to her years of training with the Dowager, no one suspected how angry she sometimes felt. Well, she hoped they didn't.

Mr Serle came to call upon her as soon as he heard she was out and about again, and though she had been dreading this meeting, she couldn't refuse to see him. When he sat down, Johanna, forewarned of her need to apologize, tactfully went into the next room, leaving them alone.

Beatrice took a deep breath and began the speech she had prepared. "I wish to tell you that I – I'm grateful, no, I mean *extremely grateful* to you, Mr Serle, for – for rescuing me from those men." She knew the words had come out woodenly, so that she sounded insincere, but she couldn't help that.

"I'm happy to have been of service to you, Miss Dencey."

His voice was as stiff as hers, his expression cold and accusing. He must still be angry at what she had said. "I believe," she said, head bent, fiddling with the fringe of her shawl, "that I owe you an apology as well."

"What on earth for, Miss Dencey?"

She couldn't now imagine this man holding her so carefully in his arms. The memory of the way she had nestled against him had made her blush several times, not to mention haunting her dreams. "I'm sorry for – for saying things. About you. Things I had no – no right to – to…"

"There is no need to…"

But she couldn't leave it at that. She knew she had to make him understand. "I didn't realize, you see, that it was real. I felt so distant. I thought I was dreaming."

If that was how she dreamed, she must have a very low opinion of him. He tried to contain his anger. He couldn't understand why he was still so annoyed with her. What did Miss Dencey's opinion matter to him, after all? "Pray give it no more thought. Your wits were wandering after the blow. I do assure you that no one could possibly take offense at what you said while you were in that condition."

"You still sound angry, though." She looked at him uncertainly, her expression vulnerable.

He felt his eyes soften as he looked at her. "I meant what I said. Pray give the matter no more thought. We shall blame it on the blow to your head. And you said nothing to which I could take offence."

She knew this for a lie, but she couldn't think what else to say, how to mend matters between them. In the end, she was relieved when Johanna rejoined them.

The conversation at once turned to the social inanities Beatrice so despised and thereafter she made little attempt to join in.

Justin responded automatically to his hostess's remarks, but kept wishing he could say something to take the anxious expression from Miss Dencey's face. But he couldn't think of anything conciliatory to say to her. When he glanced sideways, he saw that Lady Ostdene was observing him closely, which made him feel even worse, for she knew him only too well, being like the aunt he had never had.

He made a greater effort to maintain a light tone and hoped he had succeeded, for if he behaved differently toward Miss Dencey from the way he behaved toward other young ladies, his hostess would notice at once and wonder why.

Just before he left, he remembered something which would please Beatrice – and why ever did he keep thinking of her by her first name when she was no connection of his, not even a friend? "I've seen Tom once or twice, Miss Dencey, and have kept an eye on him for you. He's doing well with his pies, has found a better supplier and is becoming quite popular in certain streets."

She beamed at him. "Oh, I'm so glad! Thank you for that information, Mr Serle!" Her voice was warm again, as if she had completely forgotten their differences.

He smiled back at her, delighted to have pleased her. "I was glad to help. He's a decent sort of fellow and came to your aid without a thought of himself."

They parted on a more friendly note.

Afterwards, Johanna, who had been eavesdropping unashamedly in the next room while they spoke privately, insisted on knowing what her cousin had said to Justin that required an apology and nearly choked with laughter when Beatrice confessed. "Well, that's probably the biggest set-down Serle has ever received in his life," she said, wiping tears from her eyes. "Calling him a dandy! Justin Serle, of all people! Oh dear, I wish I could tell our friends, but of course that would be unpardonable when he so kindly rescued you. Besides, I have some fondness for him myself."

"Well, I've apologized to him about it," muttered Beatrice defensively, "so I don't see what more I can do!"

Johanna, still chuckling, informed her cousin that Serle was a noted Corinthian, a famous sportsman and rider, and in no way a dandy. "A dandy, my dear, is likely to lisp at you, to wave his hands when he speaks and to waft flowery perfume all over you."

"Oh dear! Why did I not know that?" Serle's movements were all decisive – though graceful, too, and he had smelled of some crisp cologne, whose scent she found very attractive.

"Why did you think it in the first place?" Johanna could not stop chuckling. She wished she had been there to see Serle's face.

"Well, he puts other men quite in the shade by the way he dresses. He always looks so – so elegant."

"That's because he's *not* a dandy! Simply a gentleman of exquisite taste."

"Oh, dear. Ought I to apologize again. I didn't do it very well." Beatrice frowned and added, "But that still doesn't explain it all. Johanna, why does he behave so languidly? And talk only of frivolous things? It's as if – as if he didn't really care about anything." Yet he was so strong and masculine. He had rescued her, held her in his arms and carried her up to her room. And she was no fragile flower. She remembered the way his chest had moved, as he breathed deeply, labouring under her weight. And – she flushed – he had held her when she was sick and been very gentle with her afterwards. She remembered it all quite clearly now.

"By no means must you apologize again! I told you: it'll do him good to know how others see him sometimes. I'm very fond of Justin, but he has lived behind a barrier since his brother's death, concealing his feelings from the world. He does have a serious side to him, you know, but he doesn't care to broadcast it. He takes a keen interest in improving his estates and in agriculture generally. His tenants and employees are very well looked after, I can assure you."

"I'm glad of that."

Johanna saw that Beatrice was still looking thoughtful and suddenly began to wonder about the two of them. It was not like Justin to show that he cared about someone's opinion and it was not like Bea to worry so much about something so unimportant. She would, she decided, keep an eye on them the next time they met and see how they behaved with each other. Was it possible…? No, Serle would surely marry a more dashing lady than quiet Beatrice. But still…

During the following few days, Johanna couldn't help noticing that for someone who affected complete indifference to Mr Serle, Bea mentioned his name rather frequently. And for someone who had been so greatly insulted, Justin paid an amazing number of visits to check on Miss Dencey's recovery and to report to her on Tom's progress.

Was it really possible, Johanna wondered, that her quiet young cousin was proving attractive to Justin Serle, the man of whom matchmaking mamas had despaired for years? How very amusing it all was! And what a feather in her cap it would be if she could promote a match between Bea and Justin.

Even her fussy mother would approve of that connection.

Chapter 5

The Dowager was upset. "Look at this!" she said, brandishing a piece of paper at Eleanor. "How dare he?"

"What's wrong, Grandmamma?" Now that Bea was away, Eleanor found herself expected to listen to her grandmother more attentively over their midday meal – which made her realize how skilfully Bea had smoothed things over before and kept the old lady tranquil. She tried to do the same, but had to admit that she was not as good at this as her young aunt was.

"You can never trust a Herforth to do what's right!" the Dowager said bitterly. "Although he is the heir to Satherby – an honour he does not deserve, I might add – he has written to say he will not be available to visit until later in the year."

"I didn't know you were expecting him, Grandmamma."

"I invited him expressly to come here so that I could make sure he's up to snuff. But," awful scorn filled her voice, "he cannot even make the effort." She scowled down at the letter. "Ignorant clodpate! Placing farming and such menial occupations before the well-being of estates which have belonged to The Family for two centuries and which it is now his bounden duty to preserve and protect."

Eleanor was surprised at the depth of anger in her grandmother's voice. "But he cannot just leave his other responsibilities, surely?" she ventured. "And he *is* going to come here later in the year, so that will be all right."

"Satherby is by far the most important of his responsibilities. And I had planned to have him here *now*. He must learn to behave in a way consonant with his new and totally undeserved status in life." She breathed deeply, crumpled the letter in her hand, then let it drop beside her plate.

Eleanor returned to her breakfast, but when she glanced sideways she was worried at how white and frail her grandmother looked.

Indeed, after this expenditure of nervous energy, the Dowager admitted to her maid that she felt quite washed out, and agreed to rest and recruit her strength for a few days while she decided on what tack to take next with the elusive heir.

Her fretting and fuming at mealtimes would have made Eleanor's life quite intolerable had that young lady not had several other things to divert her. She had lately found another supplier of romantic novels in the nearby town and had her head stuffed full of the adventures of a series of dashing heroines so reckless they regularly landed themselves in the direst straits just as the dinner bell rang. Then poor Eleanor had to endure an evening's suspense before she could find out how their problems were resolved.

In addition, there was Snowy. The fluffy white puppy, which Beatrice had given her before she left, needed training and exercising, and that occupied a considerable amount of Eleanor's time. A dog which was to be allowed inside the Dowager's residence when he grew older needed impeccable manners and must be perfectly groomed at all times.

Best of all, however, Eleanor had made a new acquaintance, quite unknown to her grandmother, and this added considerable interest to her days.

Only Eleanor's groom, Anders, was aware of her new friend, and although he objected strongly at first, she managed to persuade him to suspend judgment.

Anders had been her father's head groom and had brought Eleanor to the Abbey himself after the carriage accident which had killed her parents and younger brother. Her governess, who had broken her ankle a week previous to that, had declined absolutely to subject herself to the jolting of a journey across country, and the rest of the staff, who lived in dire terror of the Dowager's rare visits, were glad to abnegate responsibility.

Once at Satherby, Anders had been offered the job of becoming Miss Eleanor's personal groom, for the Dowager, grim-faced in flowing black, did not neglect her duty to look after her favourite son's faithful servants, however much she might be grieving over his death.

From that day onwards, Anders had supervised Miss Eleanor and her riding with the utmost care and now boasted that she was the best lady rider in the county.

As the sole link with her past, he was the only other person apart from Beatrice who was able to cheer up the solitary child mourning the loss of her parents and brother. He had chosen Miss Eleanor's horses for her, guided her through the mysteries of learning to jump and accompanied her to her first hunt. He was generally reckoned by the other servants to be willing to kill for her, if necessary.

Left to her own devices and feeling more than usually restless that day, Eleanor went for a walk in the woods, disobeying the Dowager by doing so unescorted by either maid or groom – and disobeying Anders too, for he agreed absolutely with the Dowager on this point.

Eleanor felt she desperately time to herself. It had been a trying week since the letter from Crispin Herforth, with her grandmother's temper fluctuating between rage and scorn, and Eleanor was finding it hard to remain cheerful.

The puppy strayed from the narrow path to follow a quite irresistible scent and refused to obey a command from his mistress to return to heel. Terrified of losing her pet, she ran after him and caught up just in time to see him disappear down a rabbit hole. Some of the soft earth fell in on him, so although he managed to turn round, he was unable to get out again and cowered in the narrow tunnel, whimpering with fear.

With no thought for her own appearance, Eleanor fell to her knees and at once began trying to dig the puppy out, scolding him all the time in a tender voice.

She didn't hear anyone approach and started in shock when a twig snapped beside her and a voice asked, "Is something wrong?"

"Oh!" She brushed her hair away from her face with one dirty hand, hoping she'd not deposited any smears of dirt on her cheek. "Oh, you quite startled me, sir!" It didn't occur to her to be afraid of the stranger, for it wasn't in her nature to be suspicious of others, and besides, the gentleman had a very warm smile.

"I'm sorry about that." He knelt beside her. "I thought you must have heard me coming."

She sat back on her heels and smiled at him. "No. I was too busy trying to help poor Snowy."

"Yes, so I see. May I assist you?"

He was staring at her in undisguised admiration and she found herself blushing slightly. For a moment everything seemed to happen very slowly and she was conscious only of the stranger, with his blond hair and bright blue eyes smiling down at her. Then Snowy whimpered and she jerked back to the present crisis. "I'm having difficulty digging my dog out, for the earth will keep falling back in again. I'm afraid my poor little darling will be smothered if I'm not careful and I daren't go for help, because Snowy may bring the earth in on himself with his struggles. Or I may not find him again."

"Let me see if I can help."

Obediently she moved aside. The stranger was undoubtedly a gentleman, neatly, though not fashionably dressed, and he didn't seem to care that he, too, was dirtying his clothes. As he began to dig, she couldn't resist staying beside him and they worked together to hold back the earth and enlarge the hole.

Once or twice their hands touched and she was surprised at how she reacted, jerking away, almost afraid to touch him. And yet, how capable his hands were! He didn't seem to mind that he was getting very dirty and she liked that in him. She stole a glance or two sideways as they worked and when she caught him looking at her, for some reason she couldn't understand she felt herself blushing again, a reaction she had never experienced with any other young gentleman.

With the stranger's help, the puppy was soon released, but when Snowy tried to walk, he yelped and sat down again, nuzzling a back leg.

"Let me see!" Eleanor's companion picked up the wriggling little creature and examined it, seeming to know exactly what he was doing. "I don't believe the leg is broken, but he must have twisted the joint so it'll be sore for a day or two."

"Oh, thank you, sir!" Still on her knees, she kissed the puppy's face, but desisted when its effort to lick her nose in return made it yelp again. "Be still now, Snowy!" she commanded.

The stranger got to his feet, still holding the puppy, and held out his hand to help her up. When she took it, he pulled her to her feet and for a moment they stood close to one another, not speaking, just studying one another quietly. It seemed important not to disturb that silence with conversation, important too that she learn every detail of his appearance.

He was only slightly taller than she was, for the Graceovers were a tall family, even the women, but she decided that in spite of that defect – for all the heroes in her novels were over six foot tall – he was rather handsome. Not as handsome as the Duke of Hanmouth in *Cressida's Revenge*, of course, but he was quite the best-looking gentleman she had ever met in real life.

Not that she had met many eligible gentlemen, she thought ruefully, for they lived so quietly at Satherby. She hadn't even been allowed to become well acquainted with the few she did encounter from time to time at the hunt or at the houses of neighbours. They were, the Dowager invariably said when they called, not of sufficient consequence to be seriously considered as future conjugal partners for a Graceover. So they were not encouraged to call again.

It never seemed to occur to Grandmamma that one might just enjoy their company without wanting to marry them, but it did to Eleanor.

"I don't think I've met you before," she said now in her forthright way. "Are you new to the district?"

"Yes. I'm visiting some family friends at Treevers Hall. My name's – er – Lanby – Christopher Lanby."

She didn't notice his slight hesitation over the name, but held out her hand with her usual sunny smile, "I'm Eleanor Graceover. I live at Satherby Abbey."

When he took the hand in his, she couldn't help realising that he was holding it for a moment or two longer than was necessary, but she didn't mind that. Unlike Beatrice, she was quite prepared to flirt a little. Her only impediment so far had been the lack of gentlemen upon whom to practice that art.

"Yes, I've heard of you," he said after a minute, his eyes still devouring her. "You're the Dowager Lady Graceover's granddaughter, are you not?"

"Yes." She removed her hand from his and wondered what to do next. Of course, it wasn't quite the thing to talk to strange gentlemen in the woods, but he *had* arrived just in the nick of time to save poor little Snowy, and in fact was still carrying the puppy. "Oh, do give Snowy back to me! He's dirtying your waistcoat."

"It'll come clean. And if it doesn't, I'll buy another one."

She rather liked his indifference to his appearance. She was an unceremonious creature herself, for all the

Dowager's love of formality, and never minded when she muddied her skirts or tore them on brambles. She leaned forward to pat Snowy's head, well aware that this brought her own head nearer to Mr Lanby's. "He's been a very naughty boy, but he's sorry now. Are you not, young sir?"

The dog wriggled with delight, then yelped again.

"Oh, you poor little darling!"

"He'll need carrying, I think. Let me do that for you, Miss Graceover." The man was holding the little creature as if he were quite used to dealing with animals and Snowy was now trying to lick his fingers, so Eleanor knew that he must be a nice person, in spite of them not having been introduced properly. Anders said dogs could always tell a person's real nature.

She was still standing very close to the stranger and wondered why she should be feeling rather distant and breathless. Perhaps it was just the after-effects of the shock. She moved back a step or two, but it made no difference. "Well – all right, then. We're not far from home if we go in this direction."

As they walked through the woods together, they began to talk and found they had one or two acquaintances in common, notably the neighbours with whom he was staying, though she hadn't heard of Mr Lanby before. She soon grew comfortable enough with him to chat about her life at Satherby, telling him about her grandmother and poor Bea, who had been forced to undergo a London season when it was the last thing someone like her would enjoy.

"Not that you're to think that Bea is a boring sort of person. She isn't! It's just that she has little interest in fashion and gossip. Well, neither do I, actually."

"I thought all ladies were addicted to both."

She wrinkled her nose at him. "There are other things in life, sir. Not that I wouldn't like to visit London myself. I'd love to go to a few ton parties, even! But I prefer to live mostly in the country." In fact, she loved Satherby Abbey so much, she couldn't imagine living anywhere else, though when she had said that, her grandmother had told her not to be so foolish. A lady lived where her husband did.

"Why did you not go to London with your aunt, then?" he asked.

She made a moue, which made him suddenly want to kiss those soft pouting lips. "Because Grandmamma says I'm too young and rackety."

He stopped walking for a minute to stare at her. She was pretty, but better still she was frank and lively. He liked her and wanted to know her better. He realized she was looking at him in slight puzzlement and asked hastily, "Why did your – Bea, that is – go to London, then, if she doesn't like fashionable parties? Couldn't she have said no?"

"When Grandmamma decides on something, it's rather hard to refuse to do as she wishes. I think there was another reason for Bea going, but Grandmamma didn't confide in me." Eleanor didn't add that the reason seemed to concern her, for that might have sounded conceited.

"So Bea is not enjoying herself."

"Not completely. She writes that she is enjoying the theatre and seeing the sights, of course, but not so much the parties. As I could have predicted, if anyone had bothered to ask me!" She decided that Mr Lanby had a lovely smile and she enjoyed the way he listened to her with flattering attentiveness. Several times, she found herself responding to that smile in kind.

Once they had discovered they shared a passionate love for riding, they spent the rest of the walk exchanging tales of their favourite horses.

When they got to the edge of the woods, however, Mr Lanby hesitated. "Perhaps I'd better leave you now."

She paused beside him. "Won't you come in and meet my grandmother."

He looked down ruefully at his clothes, which were covered in black smears from the digging, as well as dribble from the puppy, which was now chewing happily away at the remains of one of his coat buttons. "I think I'd better not. I'm unfit to meet anyone, least of all a great lady like your grandmother."

"Oh, Grandmamma won't mind that! And she'll wish to thank you for helping me."

He shook his head, looking somewhat embarrassed. "I – look, I'm afraid there's no way of hiding it, Miss Graceover, but I don't think I'd better come in at all. Your grandmother was not on the best of terms with my parents and I think I might not be welcome in her house."

"Oh bother, if that's not just like her!" Eleanor exclaimed. "She has the strangest ideas of our family consequence and is forever snubbing perfectly nice people!"

She felt desperately disappointed. Now she wouldn't be able to pursue his acquaintance. And she wanted very much to know him better, for she liked him better than any gentleman she had ever met, as well as feeling herself under an obligation to him. "Perhaps when she hears how you've helped me, she'll change her mind?" she ventured, but not hopefully.

He shook his head. "I doubt it. The – er – disagreement is of long standing. I have not, of course, met the lady myself, but from what I hear of her..." Delicately he left the sentence unfinished, but shook his head again.

Eleanor's face fell. "I'm afraid you're right. If she takes a dislike to someone, Grandmamma rarely changes her mind." She sought desperately for a reason to detain him and her eyes fell on the dog. "But how am I to let you know about Snowy? You'll wish to know how he goes on, will you not, since you saved his life?"

He looked down at her with an even warmer smile than before, for she was as transparent in her intentions as any schoolgirl. In fact, she was one of the most delightful girls he had ever met, with the most beautiful eyes, dancing with life and laughter. "Yes, I would rather like to know how he goes on," he agreed with a straight face.

Eleanor started fiddling with the puppy's ears, wondering what to suggest.

He was more experienced. "Do you often go for walks in that part of the woods?"

She dimpled at him, quick to seize on this opportunity. "Oh yes, most afternoons if it is fine, for Grandmamma likes me to get some exercise and she always takes a nap then." She didn't notice that she was standing close enough for the puppy to chew happily on one of the ribbons of her dress. In fact, they had both quite forgotten the little creature which had brought them together. "I'm *very* fond of walking," she added.

He repressed a sudden urge to kiss the dirt-smudged bloom of her cheek. "I'm fond of walking myself." He decided that her eyes were hazel shot with gold and her hair was the most beautiful shade of russet brown that he'd ever seen, full of glinting golden lights.

She looked down, a little afraid of the sensations rising within her. What the Dowager had actually said to her was, "Get out and use up some of that dratted energy, child, for I can't abide people who fidget in their chairs! Go for a walk or a ride or whatever you young people like to do nowadays! But don't go off the estate. And take that silly little creature with you! It's not properly trained yet."

"The strange thing is," Mr Lanby said, his eyes filled with laughter, "that my hosts also like to rest in the afternoons. An amazing set of coincidences, is it not?" In fact, his hosts had been friends of his parents, not of himself, and were nearer to the Dowager's age than his own.

"Then I may see you tomorrow, perhaps," Eleanor said, toe tracing patterns on the ground as she avoided his eyes.

"I very much hope so. It's far more pleasant to have someone to talk to as one walks. I have no acquaintances in the district yet, apart from my host and hostess. Perhaps you could tell me what there is to see, the best rides and so on? I don't know this part of the world at all and I shall be here for a week or two."

She beamed at him with no attempt to conceal her pleasure. "Oh yes, I'd be happy to do that. It's a good time of the year for walks and we have some very beautiful rides in the district – if you don't mind taking a few fences, that is?"

"One can always dismount and look for a gate," he said, keeping his face straight.

She gave the most delicious gurgle of laughter. "Now you're teasing me. A man who knows as much about horses as you obviously do can have no fear of jumps!"

What a beautiful ingenuous creature she was! "We must pray, then, that it doesn't rain."

She examined the sky anxiously. "I don't think it will. I shall ask my groom when I get back. Anders always knows about the weather."

Crispin knew he must take his leave before anyone from the house saw them together, reluctant as he was to part from her. Don't get in too deep, you fool, he said to himself. You've only just met her. And they may already have plans for her, plans which don't include someone like you, from the poorer side of the family. Aloud he said, "Take your dog, then, Miss Graceover. There! Will you be all right now?"

"Oh, yes. It's not far."

It was really strange, she thought as she watched him walk away, how she felt whenever his hands touched hers. As if something was making them tingle. As if she wanted to hold on to one of those hands tightly and not let go.

She remained where she was at the edge of the lawns, watching him until he was out of sight, her head on one side. Her thoughts were in such turmoil that the puppy's wrigglings were completely ignored. She liked him. In fact, she might even be falling in love with him. Was that possible so quickly?

Anders was scandalized to hear of the encounter and would in no way hear of his young mistress going off on her own to meet a strange gentleman the following afternoon. In fact, he scolded her at length for having gone anywhere without an escort. "I thought you'd grown out of such tricks, young lady!"

She tilted her head at him and pulled a face. "Really, Anders, you can be as stuffy as Grandmamma sometimes!" She explained carefully the delicate situation between Mr Lanby's parents and the Dowager, but Anders was not to be moved.

"That's as may be, Miss Eleanor, but it still doesn't make it right for a young lady like you to go out for walks on her own and well you know it! Downright disobedient, you were today, and what her ladyship would say to me for not stopping you, if she knew about it, I dread to think! And as for you talking to strange gentlemen and arranging to meet them again, I don't know what the world is coming to when a young lady in your position does such things. Her ladyship would have a fit if she knew about it."

She laid her hand on his arm coaxingly, afraid he would tell her grandmother. "We only talked a little, Anders. Mr Lanby is a very well-mannered gentleman. No one, absolutely no one, could have faulted his behaviour toward me. And if he's staying at Treevers Hall, well, he *must* be respectable, because the Treevers are as ancient and as fussy as Grandmamma!"

Anders folded his arms and shook his head in a way he had when he was displeased with her, but his words showed he was softening a little. "Well, you can do your talking in my company next time, or you'll not do it at all!"

She looked at him pleadingly, but could see no sign of his relenting further. "Oh, very well!" she said crossly, then hesitated, before adding. "Please don't tell Grandmamma about Mr Lanby! You won't, *dearest*

Anders, will you? You know how unreasonable she can be when she takes a dislike to someone's family!"

"I'll meet the gentleman first, Miss Eleanor, and then we'll see. If he seems respectable, and if you promise me faithfully that you'll always take someone with you when you go to meet him, then perhaps, just perhaps, we need not inform her ladyship. But I'm making no promises, mind!"

She flung her arms round his neck and hugged him ruthlessly, in spite of his protests. "You're a dear and I don't know what I'd do without you, Ander-Panders!" It had been her childhood nickname for him.

"Give over, do, Miss Eleanor!" he said, quite failing to conceal his pleasure. "What would her ladyship say if she saw you a-hugging of me like that?"

"She'd say I was being over-familiar with a servant and give me a scolding about what's suitable behaviour for a person of my rank." She pulled a face. "But I don't care for such nonsense. Why, I've known you for longer than absolutely anyone else, even Bea, and if I can't hug you, who can I hug? And anyway, Grandmamma never comes down to the stables, does she, so we're quite safe."

She grinned at him cheekily and he shook his head at her again, trying without success to hide his own smile. A minx she was, a proper minx, but not a nasty bone in her body.

He stood and watched her run back to the house, leaving the dirty, yawning puppy sprawled across his boots, chewing at their laces. When she'd disappeared from sight, he bent down to pick the little animal up, sighing. Not for him to question her ladyship's ways, but it was a shame to keep a lively lass like Miss Eleanor shut away from other folk of her own age, a proper shame, it was! He wouldn't allow his young lady to make any unsuitable acquaintances, but it wouldn't hurt to look this fellow over. If he was visiting the Treevers, he must be a gentleman, and Miss Eleanor had been moping about ever since Miss Beatrice went up to London, in spite of that dratted puppy.

He would make inquiries of the grooms at Treevers Hall about this fellow Lanby. The servants' grapevine could yield a lot of information that would surprise the gentry. He picked the puppy up, looked it in the eyes and shook his head at it. "See what you've done now, little fellow! You'd better watch your step in future, or I shall give you a proper scolding!"

Snowy tried to lick his nose.

He cradled the small warm body against his chest. "Well, let's go and take a look at that leg of yours, shall we? And I dare say a bowl of bread and milk wouldn't come amiss, either, eh?" One rough fingertip tickled it gently under the chin, but a frown remained on his face as he ministered to the puppy. He wished very much that Miss Beatrice were here to take charge of the situation. She'd know what was the right thing to do and he had a great deal of respect for her judgment.

The idea of some strange gentleman taking advantage of his Miss Eleanor was a worry that even haunted his dreams that night.

As Mr Lanby haunted Eleanor's dreams.

Chapter 6

In London Justin Serle was not the only gentleman showing an interest in Beatrice. She might underrate her own attractions and insist she was here only to find a husband for Eleanor, but she was both charming and pretty, as well as having a substantial dowry.

Only the previous evening, Lady Clayrie had commented on this to Johanna. "That cousin of yours has got good manners, better than most young folk nowadays. When she got cornered by St John Hardinge at Amelia's rout, I tried to rescue her. Felt guilty, him bein' a connection of mine. You know what a bore he is."

Johanna raised expressive eyebrows. They had all been cornered by St John Hardinge at one time or another.

"Well, I couldn't get across the room in that crush, so I watched your cousin listening to him and you'd have sworn from her expression that he was a wit, instead of a half-wit."

Lady Clayrie guffawed so loudly at her own joke that she choked and by the time she'd recovered, she'd found another subject to pursue. But what she'd said left Johanna thoughtful. She, too, was finding Bea full of surprises and in more ways than one. She would never have expected her shy cousin to become quite so popular.

Lady Jersey said much the same thing about Beatrice, and Johanna had a hard time keeping her face straight as the garrulous woman known as "Silence" to her own generation absolutely lavished praise on the newcomer.

"One gets so tired of dealing with the caprices and fussations of the more dashing type of person," Lady Jersey declared. "Your cousin is the easiest guest imaginable, with impeccable manners and an elegant simplicity in her dress that has taken very well with the other patronesses. You must be sure to bring her to Almack's regularly." She raised one eyebrow. "Dowry?"

Johanna seized the opportunity to spread the news. "I believe my mother has settled twenty thousand on her."

"Indeed. Then it shouldn't be hard to find her a suitable *parti.*"

"I hope not." But she wasn't sure Beatrice would agree about what made a gentleman suitable.

The following day Justin, arriving late as usual for a musical evening, paused in the doorway to listen to a pleasant contralto, the sort of voice it was a pleasure to listen to, especially as it was singing something in English instead of one of those damned incomprehensible German *lieder* that always sounded like funeral dirges to him. He blinked in surprise when he saw that the singer was Beatrice Dencey, for he would have thought her too shy to perform in public.

When the song was over, she settled down at the piano, face slightly flushed at the applause, to accompany first one then another young lady. The Dowager had insisted on both her charges being able to entertain company – something the old lady considered a social imperative – but although Beatrice had learned to sing when requested, she would rather not have done so. She much preferred acting as accompanist, her skill at the pianoforte being such that the other young ladies present were able to show off their vocal prowess to the very best advantage.

From across the room Justin watched her encourage a rather bashful young lady, who was fluttering about with her music and who looked ready to burst into tears in her terror of singing for the first time before the London ton.

The terrified young lady drew in a deep breath and turned to face her audience, while from behind her Beatrice murmured encouragement. He smiled at the scene, nodding approval of Miss Dencey's kindness. No wonder she was popular with her own sex, for all her quietness and her self-effacing manners. And that made him wonder what there was about her that people took to so readily? He found himself trying to analyse this and forgetting to move on, so that another new arrival had to ask him twice to stand aside and allow others to enter the salon.

The other guests found Justin Serle very unlike his usual self that evening, so quiet and thoughtful. And it was noticed that he made a particular effort to speak to the young Harnston chit, who had overcome her nervousness to sing so prettily to them. Was he really looking for a bride from this season's hopefuls or did he have some other reason to be kind to the girl? He spent quite a bit of time chatting to Miss Dencey, too, but there was no sign of him flirting with her.

–

After that evening Beatrice found that several of the very young ladies took to confiding their hopes and fears to her, as they could not do to their own mamas. With them treating her like an elder sister or cousin and eagerly awaiting her arrival at parties, she no longer felt a stranger and enjoyed helping them settle into society. They reminded her very much of dear Eleanor – though they were not as pretty or lively, of course.

As Johanna expected, Lady Jersey let it be known that Miss Dencey had a very respectable dowry and was in the market for a husband. This set the seal upon Beatrice's success, though she would have been horrified if she had known about it.

Johanna took care that she didn't find out. It was the way things were done in their world and it was foolish of poor Bea to get upset about the money. You had to know your own worth and make the most of it. Why, Johanna would as soon have let one of her own daughters marry a penniless younger son as she would have shaved her head.

During the weeks which followed, brothers, younger sons and nephews were summoned up to London by various steely-eyed matrons and displayed to Miss Dencey in all their masculine glory. Beatrice studied everyone to whom she was introduced for Eleanor's sake, not her own, and didn't realize for a while how much interest there was in herself. The marks and notes against the names on the Dowager's list multiplied rapidly and the paper became quite worn from her anxious perusals of it.

The first proposal of marriage Beatrice received shocked her to the core, coming as it did from a gentleman whom she had only met three times and that briefly. When he drew her into an anteroom after a dance, she protested, "Mr Tarrow, I don't think we should…" She fell silent in horror as he fell to his knees before her, blocking her way out.

"My dear Miss Dencey," he began, seizing her hand and covering it with wet kisses. "My dearest lady—"

"Oh, please. Mr Tarrow, please do not!" She was scarlet with embarrassment by now.

"Miss Dencey, I must speak! I cannot wait any longer. Since the moment I first saw you I have longed to call you my own. Only say that you will marry me and I shall be the happiest man in town!"

He tried to kiss her again and in desperation, she pushed at his chest with both hands. Since he was on one knee at the time, this made him lose his balance and by the time he had scrambled to his feet, he was as red-faced as she was. He placed one hand on his chest and opened his mouth to speak.

Beatrice rushed to prevent him. "Please don't say anything else, sir! I have no wish to marry."

For a moment, his expression was anything but conciliatory. "Dash it all," he began, "what else are you here for but to find a husband? The word's out all over town about your dowry."

"*What?*" She took a deep breath, anger kindling her eyes into brilliance, then repeated firmly, "I have no desire to marry you, or anyone else." She retreated strategically behind a pot plant. "And I shall not change my mind. Please leave me now, Mr Tarrow!"

Seeing the implacable expression on her face, he could do nothing but bow stiffly, his movements constrained by the size and height of his now rather crumpled neckcloth, before striding out of the room.

She stayed where she was for a moment, hands pressed to her burning cheeks, then said aloud, "How did he find out about that dreadful dowry?" As she was waiting for the flush to subside, she caught sight of two legs behind another potted palm tree and gasped. "Oh, no! Who – who's there?"

Justin sighed and moved forward. He would have preferred to remain unnoticed, for he knew she'd be embarrassed that he'd overheard the incident. "I cry pardon, Miss Dencey! I had no wish to eavesdrop, believe me, but the gentleman was so eager I had no time to reveal my presence before he launched into his speech." He took the fan from her trembling fingers and began to waft it gently to and fro in front of her flushed face.

"He was only eager to gain access to my fortune! Even *I* have heard about his debts," she said bitterly. "As if I'd accept such a person!"

"He's a fool, and always has been," Justin said with rather more warmth than he had intended. Actually, he felt like pursuing Tarrow and knocking him to the floor for upsetting Beatrice like this.

She looked at him shyly. "He's – he's what I accused you of, Mr Serle, is he not? A dandy? So I'm more sorry than ever for my error. It was because you always look so elegant that I, well, I mistook matters."

He smiled, a smile as genuine as her compliment. "Tarrow is indeed one of the dandy set," he murmured. "All the crack, or so some people say, but to me he looks more like a fowl stuffed for the oven."

"Yes. And that ridiculous neckcloth! It must be at least a foot high! He can't even turn his head, but must move his whole body to look sideways!" She laughed suddenly.

"If some of our older villagers could see him, they'd be convulsed and he'd hear a few home truths!"

"Can we not arrange it? I have a few older tenants who have a similar frankness of speech."

"Oh, don't tempt me!" Her colour had faded to near normal and her expression still showed genuine amusement.

He returned the fan and offered her his arm. "Perhaps we should return to Lady Ostdene now? Are you feeling better?"

"Yes. And I do thank you for being so understanding."

"It was my pleasure."

Johanna was merely amused when Beatrice told her about the offer she'd received.

"Oh, Tarrow won't do for you!" she said, dismissing the man with a wave of her hand.

"But it was so humiliating!" Beatrice protested. "How can you talk about it so casually? He wasn't offering for *me*, but for my dowry! How did he even know of it?"

"Oh, these things get around. I may have mentioned it to one or two of my friends." She saw the anger in Beatrice's eyes and shrugged. "That's the way of the world, my dear, and you won't change it. And you *are* here to find a husband, are you not? I must say I thought even Tarrow would have had more address than to rush things. He must be badly dipped again. He's a known gamester."

Such frank talk disgusted Beatrice, but she could hardly complain to her kind hostess, who was going to inordinate trouble to take her around and introduce her to people.

–

The attentiveness of certain gentlemen continued to increase, to Beatrice's great embarrassment, and several times the watchful Justin Serle rescued her in the nick of time from what she considered to be an unpleasant situation. She began to feel so comfortable with him that she treated him like a cousin or a brother.

However, her blatant lack of interest in him as a man began to pique him. He wasn't at all sure he enjoyed the role of "safe relative", which was one he'd never played before.

Fortunately, not all the gentlemen were as blatant in their pursuit as Mr Tarrow, and Beatrice managed to enjoy herself some of the time, especially when they went to the theatre or the opera, or when they could attend a salon where the guests were expected to talk of literature or poetry in a more intelligent way.

Johanna pulled a face sometimes at the nature of the entertainments Beatrice preferred, but realized that she wouldn't be able to keep her cousin happy if they only attended the more frivolous functions which she and her daughter enjoyed most.

After a while, Johanna realized that Justin was watching the attention Beatrice received, often with a frown of disapproval on his face. And that frown became a scowl if he saw her several times talking to the same gentlemen.

He did not yet realize the reason for his own interest, Johanna thought, watching them both with growing amusement. But it could be only one thing. He was attracted to Bea. It was so diverting to watch him and so important to let things take their natural course that she threatened to murder her daughter if Jennice dropped so much as a hint to anyone else about the possibility of serious interest between Bea and Serle.

"If you do that, Beatrice will freeze and Justin will retreat," she insisted.

Jennice pulled a face, but for once held her tongue. She was quite fond of Justin and would be glad to see him married into the family.

Beatrice, more intent upon working through the Dowager's list of eligible suitors for Eleanor, treated all the gentlemen who did not displease her with a distant kindness that piqued others besides Justin.

Johanna watched this in puzzlement and decided after a while that it was not going to be as easy as she had expected to bring Bea to accept anyone, even Justin Serle. Her cousin was genuinely not looking for a husband for herself. Johanna could only be thankful that neither of *her* daughters had been so hard to marry off. They had both worked enthusiastically with her to find themselves husbands and had discussed the candidates at great length before settling on one.

She became so concerned about the situation that she discussed it with Jennice. "I really can't understand Bea. She makes no push to fix anyone's interest upon herself. I'm not even sure that she's really interested in Serle. Sometimes they seem very cozy together, but at other times, she doesn't even seem to notice him."

"Then she's a fool not to make a push to capture his interest, for he's very eligible." Jennice chose another sugar plum and popped it in her mouth. "Perhaps," she began, her mouth full and her words almost inaudible, "a clergyman would be more the thing for Bea? I mean, she's always so serious."

"Yes." Johanna looked thoughtful. "Who can we introduce her to?" She gave a knowing smile. "If we can set up another serious contender, maybe that will push Justin into action. I could swear he likes her. He certainly seeks her company often enough."

"And she his," agreed Jennice, licking the sugar from her fingers. "I thought when they were waltzing the other night how well they looked together. She never looks as relaxed in anyone else's arms. And did you see her face when he was flirting with Gwendoline Firsby?"

Johanna leaned forward eagerly. "No! Did she look upset?"

"Yes. For a minute or two, anyway. Then she turned away and didn't look across at him again."

"Hmm. That sounds promising. I wish I'd seen it myself. But I'd better not say anything to my mother yet. You know what she's like once she gets an idea into her head. I wouldn't put it past her to summon Justin down to Satherby and ask him his intentions – and that would drive him right away."

They both chuckled at the thought.

So although Johanna duly reported in her letters to her mother that one or two gentlemen were making a little progress with Bea, she didn't mention Serle.

As the days passed, Lady Marguerite Graceover's letters to her daughter became more and more querulous in tone and she complained bitterly about the delays in settling what was surely a very straightforward matter. Mama, Johanna told her daughter, always did expect people to obey her orders in an unreasonably short time.

In her response Johanna suggested that her mother consider extending the list of eligibles, which was very restricted. Why, Johanna could think of several gentlemen who might well be worthy of consideration for Eleanor. She mentioned one or two names as examples.

She received a stinging reply commanding her to do as she had promised and ordering her not to interfere with Beatrice's instructions. The Dowager was only interested in persons of rank and breeding for her granddaughter and niece, thank you very much!

After two more weeks had passed without any progress being made, Lady Marguerite wrote a very sharp letter to Bea that had her drooping all day. Guilt overwhelmed her. She had let her aunt down badly. But try as she might, she couldn't see any of the gentlemen she had met making good husbands for Eleanor.

By the evening of that day Johanna could stand it no longer. She sat her cousin down for a frank talk. "You mustn't let Mama bully you like this, Bea. She means well, but you know what she's like."

"She has a right to complain. I've been neglecting my duty quite shamefully and looking only to enjoy myself. I must stop going to so many concerts and – and…" Her voice faltered.

"You can't do much more than you are doing," Johanna pointed out reasonably. "You've met most of the people on that list who are up in town this season."

"I *must* do more!" Bea went up to her room and wrote an extremely detailed report on those gentlemen she had met so far and sent it off the next day to her grandmother.

When she received the report, the Dowager thumped her stick on the floor in rage and demanded of heaven why she was saddled with such feeble-witted descendants.

"Is something wrong with Miss Dencey?" her lady-ship's maid ventured to ask.

"Yes. She's turned into a timid, romantic nincompoop! Look at that!" She waved the letter in the air. "She doesn't think any of them are suitable for Eleanor, and on the most ridiculous of grounds. Too stupid. Too reckless. Not kind enough. *Not kind enough!* What does she think we're looking for – a saint? They're men of breeding, ain't they? Some of them must be presentable!"

Lippings knew better than to respond and merely stood attentively beside her mistress as the tirade continued.

After a sleepless night, Lady Marguerite decided not to take issue with Bea again about her failure to nominate some suitable candidates for Eleanor's hand. "However," she told her maid grimly, "if things don't improve soon, I shall take matters into my own hands. I am not yet too old or too decrepit to manage my family's affairs, and so they will find out."

Chapter 7

Johanna continued to puzzle over Bea's future while the pair of them worked their way through the rest of the eligibles on the list. It wasn't hard for Johanna to ensure that Bea got to meet and inspect all the unattached scions of those particular lines who were presently in town. Some of them, she warned, were quite young gentlemen, some of them not so young. The Dowager's instructions specified that all unmarried males up to the age of forty were to be considered in those families of whom she approved.

"Does Mama honestly expect," Johanna asked in frustration, "that a girl as young as Eleanor will even consider marrying a man of thirty or older?"

"She expects everyone in her household to do exactly as she tells them, whether it's reasonable or not. But I don't think Eleanor will obey meekly in something as important as this," Beatrice said thoughtfully. "She tries to avoid clashes with my aunt, but they're very alike and she has a will of her own."

From then onwards, the two ladies sat down after each meeting with a new gentleman from the list and compared notes in a way which would have horrified most of the young bloods concerned. Beatrice, unwilling to discuss her own suitors, was happy to discuss at length those

who were under consideration for Eleanor. She set ridicu-
lously high standards, though, in Johanna's opinion, and
to make matters worse, she was more concerned with the
gentlemen's personal qualities than with their station in
life and their fortunes.

"What about young Lord Haroldby? He's certainly not
ill-favoured and will come into a very respectable fortune
when he inherits," Johanna asked one day, feeling that the
latest candidate had been better than most.

"Young Lord Haroldby," declared Beatrice, lips curling
scornfully, "is far too daredevil in his ways and will
undoubtedly kill himself within the year. Did you see that
horse he was riding in the park yesterday?"

"Well—"

"And someone told me that he's ready to accept any
wager, *any wager at all*, and even makes it a point of honour
to do so, however ridiculous the bet."

"Well, most young gentlemen are like that. He'll settle
down once he's married."

"I have no wish to see my dearest Eleanor widowed
young. A man like that won't do for her at all."

Johanna rolled her eyes toward the ceiling, but didn't
waste her time arguing this point. "What about the
Barrowdene heir, then?" Johanna asked, reaching for an
apple tartlet. "He's rather handsome, don't you think?"

"If you like that sort of pale good looks. He's aping
Lord Byron in his mannerisms and he's far too moody.
That would never do for dear Eleanor. She's the most
affectionate, sunny-natured person in all creation, and his
moods would drive her to distraction in a fortnight." She
saw Johanna begin to open her mouth and said savagely,
"And if you're going to ask about the Honorable Fergus

Kitsby, I have to tell you that I've never been so disappointed in anyone in all my life."

Johanna could only sigh. The Honorable in question was making more than one young debutante act in a foolish way and dampen her pillow with fruitless yearning. "He's thought to be very stylish," she ventured.

"When seen at a distance on the dance floor or at the theatre, perhaps."

"And his smile is—"

"Is pleasant enough, I will admit, but that makes it all the worse when you find out that he has shockingly bad breath. He must eat nothing but onions! *And*," she paused before revealing the most dreadful tidings of all, "he not only wears padded shoulders, but also *a padded chestpiece* to his coats."

"It's all the crack for gentlemen to have a broad silhouette!"

Beatrice was not to be moved. "Falsity is a thing which I have always abhorred." The padded chestpiece had been the final straw in a long list of disappointments. She could just imagine what her aunt would say about that!

"You're far too demanding, my dear. You really can't condemn a man because he wears padding! He's only following fashion, after all."

"Well, I find I don't care for that particular fashion. And anyway, I think *that* amount of padding reflects a deviousness of spirit. I care too much about Eleanor's happiness to entrust her to a man who presents a false appearance to the world. Who knows what lies and deceits he would practice upon *her* after they were married!"

Beatrice was looking so desperately worried that Johanna was moved to cross the room and hug her. "Look, love, forget about Eleanor for a while! Let's turn our thoughts to your own future. You're also here to find a husband for yourself and you'll never have a better opportunity than this season."

Beatrice shook her head, lips tightly pursed. "I don't matter half as much. There's plenty of time for me to find myself a husband later if I so choose. And I do keep it in mind, I assure you. I've already come to the conclusion that I'd prefer to marry someone who lives mainly in the country. That's enough progress for now."

She fiddled with a fold of her skirt and added, "I know you think I'm being over-fussy, but your mother is very concerned about Eleanor's future, and it's not good for her to worry so. I just can't settle to thinking of myself until I've sorted something out for Eleanor. I promised Aunt Marguerite faithfully that I wouldn't fail her in this."

She hadn't told her cousin that the Dowager's health was deteriorating fast, and this omission was preying on her conscience, for it never seemed to occur to Johanna that anything *could* happen to her mother.

A spirit of mischief made Johanna say, "Then it must be Justin Serle, after all, Bea! His cousin is his heir now that his brother's dead, and Luke Serle is a gambler and reprobate. I never thought to see Serle brought to the altar, but Luke's going to do it if he goes on like this."

Beatrice tried to think of some other subject of conversation.

"I wonder whom Serle will choose," Johanna continued.

"Choose?" exclaimed Beatrice, in tones of great disgust. "*Choose!* You speak as though he had only to signal and any woman would come running!"

"Well, he *is* very eligible, you know, not to mention handsome. He's been much sought after for years."

"Handsome is not everything!" declared Beatrice, nose in the air. "Mr Serle is not as arrogant or trivial-minded as I had thought at first, I will admit, but although he may not be a dandy, he *does* spend a lot of time on his appearance and his conversation is frequently very frivolous. I cannot approve of that." Or so she tried to tell herself whenever she found herself thinking about him.

"My dear, what do you expect him to talk about at social gatherings? Riots and mayhem?" Johanna was watching her closely. "I like Justin. I'm sure he'd make an excellent husband for Eleanor. He's always very pleasant company and you must admit he's an exquisite dancer."

Beatrice couldn't disagree with that. She'd had the pleasure of dancing with Mr Serle at many functions and found him the perfect partner. Their steps matched so well she didn't have to think what she was doing, but could float away on the music. She did not, however, intend to admit that to Johanna. "Well, I think a man of his station and wealth ought to set a better example than he does! Fancy being famous for the way you tie your cravat! Or for the horses you drive! A man should stand on his own merit, not that of his animals! And him a great landowner, too! He should spend more time thinking about his tenants and about – about agriculture!"

"Oh, pooh! Agriculture! Who cares about things like that when one is in London? Agriculture is a topic only suitable for the country, and then in very small doses. The land he owns may be what makes Justin Serle so eligible, but to be prosing on about turnips would make him the greatest bore in town!"

Beatrice resolutely held her tongue.

"Anyway," Johanna continued airily, "Boris tells me Serle *is* seriously looking for a wife, so I can't help being interested in whom he'll choose. He's been impervious to a whole series of beauties who've set their caps at him over the years." She looked sideways at Beatrice and asked casually, "What do you say to the Metterleigh heiress? She might do for him, don't you think?"

"*Her!* I never met such an empty-headed featherbrain in all my life! She hasn't got an idea in her head, apart from clothes and dancing. Even Mr Serle would not choose someone like her!" Eleanor sighed and added half to herself, "Though I dare say he'll choose someone just as frivolous and they'll spend their time discussing clothes and the latest gossip and how to tie cravats!"

"You're very scathing. Don't you like Justin?"

"Oh, he's pleasant enough," Beatrice was avoiding Johanna's laughing, knowing eyes, "and my aunt thinks a great deal of the family, but well," her fingers were fiddling with a ribbon now, "there's not enough substance to him. Though I do owe him a debt of gratitude for saving me from those men, and I try not to forget it. But I couldn't think a man like him right for Eleanor, whatever you say. And I couldn't marry a man like him myself!"

She tossed her head at the mere idea, which no one had raised but herself, then changed the subject hurriedly. "Did I tell you how well poor Tom is doing? He's found himself some more respectable lodgings and his cough's completely gone."

Johanna raised her eyes to heaven and let the question of matrimony drop. She'd come to the conclusion that her cousin Beatrice, for all her sweet biddable ways, was as stubborn as the Dowager underneath.

–

After a few fruitless weeks, they had to take Jennice, who was still staying with her mother in town, more fully into their confidence. She entered into the search with real enthusiasm, for it was just the sort of thing she enjoyed. She was in blooming health, but was beginning to show her condition, so was making the most of what she called her "last weeks of freedom" by indulging in a frenetic round of social engagements and shopping. Her only concession to Boris's worries about the baby was to take a nap every afternoon. And that, she confided in her mother with a grimace, was only because she really did feel sleepy.

Jennice studied the Dowager's list carefully, for naturally she knew all the families on it. "Hmm," she said after a while, "Grandmamma is very choosy, isn't she? I can think of a dozen other gentlemen I'd have considered eligible – and several of them have nice juicy fortunes – yet they're not on her list. And why on earth have you crossed Justin's name off, Bea? You can't accuse *him* of being too fat or of having a sniff, and he certainly doesn't pad his coats! Why, he's easily the most eligible bachelor in town!"

She leaned back and smiled reminiscently. "I did consider him for myself at one time, you know, but I decided he'd be too hard to manage. My dear Boris suits me much better – though even he's getting a bit troublesome since we started having the baby!" She shook her head and repeated in puzzlement, "Why *did* you cross Justin's name off, Bea?"

"Beatrice thinks he's not serious-minded enough," explained her mother, eyes twinkling.

"Justin?" Jennice screamed with laughter. "Oh dear, I must tell him! Such criticism has never been offered to him in all his life before! Most people simply *fawn* over him, whatever he says to them!"

"Don't you dare say a word to him!" commanded her mother. "You'll only embarrass poor Beatrice and you'll put him in a fit of temper. In fact, if you breathe a word of any of this, we won't let you help us at all."

Jennice pulled a face. "Well, I wouldn't really tell him, of course I wouldn't – I'm not rag-mannered – but I can't help wishing I could tease him just a little about it." She sighed with regret at the delectable prospect of giving Justin Serle an unanswerable set-down, for he often teased her and usually won their verbal bouts.

After a few minutes' more perusal she handed the dog-eared sheet of paper back to Beatrice. "What are you going to do if you can't find anyone suitable?"

"I don't know. You've no idea how I worry about that! I've met everyone on the list, well, everyone who is in town. I can hardly go round the countryside knocking at the doors of the rest of them, can I?"

"Let me see this again, Bea." Jennice took back the list and studied it with a frown, counting something on her fingers, then she looked up at them with a triumphant smile. "I have an idea! A *brilliant* idea! Mama, you can't say that Beatrice is enjoying her Season, can you? Even though she's setting a new fashion in her own quiet way, I never saw anyone so uninterested in parties and balls. She might just as well not be on the market."

"Don't be vulgar, dear!"

Beatrice flushed. "Surely my feelings don't show so clearly!"

Jennice grinned. "They may not show to others, but *we* know you a little better, my dear and *we* hear what you say *after* the parties."

Beatrice turned to her kind hostess. "Johanna, it's got nothing to do with you or your hospitality, really it hasn't! You couldn't have been kinder to me! I'm just – I'm not cut out for this sort of life. I prefer the country and – and real things."

Johanna nodded gloomily, but reached across to pat her hand reassuringly. "I know, love."

"Well, then," said Jennice, positively beaming at them, "no less than three of the families listed here live near us, well, near enough to visit occasionally, and I know half a dozen other eligibles in our district alone who might suit Bea, even if Grandmamma didn't consider them good enough to put on her list for Eleanor. And Boris is growing so impatient for me to return home that I suppose I'll have to leave London soon. But it would be delightful to have some company, so why don't you and Bea come back to Lymsby with us, Mama? Stay for a while. I promise to introduce Bea to dozens of eligible gentlemen!"

Johanna looked at her thoughtfully, then eyed Beatrice sideways. What Jennice hadn't mentioned was that Melbury Park, the Serle demesne, was the next estate to Lymsby. It would be very interesting to see whether Justin followed them to the country – and how Beatrice reacted to that. "Why not?" she asked lightly. "What do you think, Bea? You keep saying you're not fond of town life. We could go and spend a week or two with Jennice if you like."

"Oh, I'd love that!" Bea exclaimed. Anything to avoid returning to the Dowager as a failure. The last missive from Satherby had contained another sharp query as to why none of the gentlemen on the list had yet been invited to the Abbey, not to mention why Beatrice had done nothing about herself, when Johanna reported a considerable interest being shown in her.

"We'll do it, then!" said Johanna, who intensely disliked country life, but who intended to see how this comedy played itself out.

They set off within the week, an impressive cavalcade consisting of a carriage large enough to carry four persons in extreme comfort, followed by the servants in another vehicle, among whom was an excited Tilly, who had to be told twice by Johanna's Sarah to sit still and behave like a proper lady's maid before she would stop jiggling around. The baggage followed in two more vehicles.

Lord Newthorpe, who had come up to town to escort them, chose at the last minute to ride with his groom in attendance, which Jennice said was a blessing since he was the most fidgety traveller in the world and never stopped criticizing the way the vehicle was being driven.

The journey into Hertfordshire was neither long nor onerous. Jennice sometimes talked as if she lived in a remote county, but actually, she was within less than three hours of the capital, and it was a pleasant drive at that. How pretty Hertfordshire was! Beatrice settled back to enjoy the scenery and allowed the others to gossip as they wished.

Lymsby Hall was a modern residence built by Boris's grandfather, who had indeed made his fortune in tea, to the Dowager's everlasting disgust, but who had also been the younger son of a perfectly respectable old county family. Boris's parents were now dead, but he'd inherited their love of Lymsby and was a passionate landscape gardener when he wasn't hunting, shooting or fishing.

Luckily for marital harmony, the neighbourhood wasn't short of families with whom the young couple might enjoy a varied social life and there was a very pretty assembly hall in a nearby town where balls were held, which were quite tolerable, Jennice said, if one took one's own party and kept away from the local shopkeepers.

Shown up to an elegant suite on the first floor, which looked out over the beautiful parklands surrounding Lymsby, Beatrice drew in a deep breath of pleasure. Surely no one could object to her going for long walks here? She could take Tilly with her, if necessary. She had by now grown quite fond of the girl and had to admit it was indeed necessary to have a lady's maid when one was involved in as many social events as she had been over the past few weeks. She'd already decided to ask Tilly to stay on with her after her return to Satherby. The Dowager wouldn't object, she was sure.

From what Jennice had been planning on the journey, there would seem to be no shortage of company near Lymsby. These plans had caused several squabbles with Boris before their departure, for he seemed to think his wife should take to her bed immediately upon arrival and stay there until after the baby was born.

Not until Johanna assured him that it was better for pregnant ladies' health if they took regular exercise did he desist from his plans to immure Jennice in an overheated chamber, with several attendants at hand to prevent her from lifting even a fingertip.

Johanna listened patiently when he went on to discuss what kind of exercise would be safe. No, riding would not be at all suitable, but regular walks in the grounds would be just the thing for a lady in a delicate condition and also regular outings in the carriage to visit their friends and neighbours, for this would prevent the expectant mother from moping. Moping was the worst possible thing for ladies in Jennice's condition.

Beatrice was obliged to hide her smiles as Boris was manipulated into agreeing to everything Jennice wished to do, while his young wife happily promised not to indulge in various activities she heartily disliked, such as tramping through the woods.

Jennice in the country was far more to Beatrice's taste than Jennice in the town. They found interests in common in the running of a large house and the vagaries of servants, though her staff seemed to give her far more trouble than the servants at Satherby had ever given Beatrice. But then, Jennice seemed to thrive on crises, and if one were lacking, she was quite capable of creating some drama or other to add interest to the day.

The first week they were a little short of company, Jennice complained, and she sulked about that until Boris coaxed her out of her mood with the gift of a pretty new bracelet. Their social life developed rapidly after that, however, and soon there was a dinner party somewhere most evenings, or an impromptu hop, or an al fresco luncheon, or some other outing to enliven the day.

These casual country affairs were much more to Beatrice's taste than the London events had been, but even so, she would have welcomed fewer of them and ventured to say so.

Jennice looked at her reproachfully. "Have you forgotten that one of the reasons we came here was so that you could meet some of the gentlemen on your list?"

Beatrice blushed and admitted that she had indeed forgotten it.

"Don't you *want* to find yourself a husband as well as one for Eleanor?"

"Not someone only interested in my dowry."

"Well what do you think of the Vicar as a potential husband? For you, of course, not for Eleanor. He'd be too old for her."

Beatrice realized guiltily that she had nearly forgotten her mission for a few days in her enjoyment of the beautiful countryside around Lymsby. Her heart sank and she felt suffused with guilt. She was letting her aunt down once more. "I'm sorry, Jennice. I was just enjoying being in the country again."

"And the Vicar?"

"No. I think he's too old for me as well, and besides, I've never liked men with red hair."

"No. That particular shade of bright ginger makes their complexions seem so washed-out, doesn't it? Well, it does if they're as pale as he is. Oh, well, we'll just have to look further afield."

Beatrice sighed.

It was several days before Beatrice found out that Serle was their closest neighbour.

"Be good to have old Justin back," said Boris one day over breakfast. He beamed at them all impartially, in the best of humours because one of his mares had just foaled.

Jennice nudged her mother.

Beatrice's fork froze in midair. "Mr Serle? I was not aware – does he live nearby, then?"

"Next estate, if you don't count the Thatchbule family," said Boris indistinctly, his mouth full of kidneys. "And we don't."

"I – hadn't realized he was so close."

"How did you find out he was expected, Boris dear?" asked Jennice, all sweet innocence. She'd already known about it, but had kept quiet, wishing to see Beatrice's reaction when surprised by the news. Actually, she'd have preferred Justin to have simply walked in on them one day. The shock of that would surely have caused Beatrice to betray her feelings. "I'd heard nothing."

"Oh, my groom heard it from one of the Melbury grooms yesterday evening in the village alehouse. Justin will probably be here today."

"Is he – has he brought anyone down with him?" asked Johanna, since Beatrice was rearranging the food on her plate very carefully and showing no sign that she wished to participate in the conversation.

"I don't think so. He doesn't usually. But I dare say he'll hold a dinner or two while he's here. He'll probably ask you to act as his hostess, as he usually does, Jen, but you could do it instead, Mother-in-law. Jen'd better not tire herself with such things."

Jennice pulled a face at him behind his back.

"We can get some shooting in, too," he went on, still full of enthusiasm. "Justin's woods are overrun by pigeons and he'll have to do something about them or they'll be moving into my coverts next! Of course they're not as good eating as pheasants, but the tenants like them well enough."

Beatrice grimaced, thus betraying the fact that she had been listening. She could never bear to see birds slaughtered, though the Dowager always gloated over the size of the bag and allowed favoured persons to shoot at Satherby during the hunting season, as long as they stayed elsewhere, for she detested holding house parties.

Boris turned to his guests, beaming. "You ladies may care to take a gun out with us one day, eh?"

Jennice looked pained. "Not in my condition."

"I wasn't considering you," her spouse told her. "It's obvious *you* couldn't do anything like that now." His eyes rested gloatingly on her stomach.

"Yes, I'm far too big to go clambering through the woods, aren't I?" Jennice looked down at her increasingly pear-shaped figure with immense satisfaction. "It's growing so quickly, I wouldn't be surprised if I didn't have twins."

Boris paled. "*Twins!* Have you asked Dr. Sangler about that?"

"Good heavens, no! I was just joking. He's such a fussy old bore I don't mean to see him for ages yet."

"What? Jennice, I gave strict orders that you were to consult him as soon as we returned!"

Jennice tilted her nose at him. "Well, I haven't, my Lord, so there! I'm feeling perfectly well, thank you, and I don't *need* to see a doctor!"

Boris stood up and thumped the table, shooting forgotten. "In that case, I shall fetch him myself this very day and make sure that you *do* see him! If you think, Madam, that I'm going to risk the life of my unborn son—"

"Or daughter," put in Johanna, unable to resist the temptation.

"Daughter!" exclaimed Boris, scandalized. "We Newthorpes *never* have daughters first, I'll have you know, or we haven't for generations! Though I wouldn't put it past my wife to do so, if only to spite me!"

Jennice tittered. "Well you can't do anything about that, My Lord! Even a Newthorpe can't dictate the sex of his offspring."

"No, but I *can* see that you get proper attention while you're in this condition. And what's more, if you try to avoid seeing Dr. Sangler, I shall bring him to your room and hold you down myself while he examines you."

"You wouldn't *dare*!"

"Oh, wouldn't I?"

"I shall lock the door."

He folded his arms and took up a melodramatic pose. "I'll break it down."

Tears suddenly sparkled on Jennice's lashes. "Oh, how can you be so cruel to me?" she asked, her voice breaking pathetically as she spoke. She sniffed delicately and applied a lace handkerchief to her eyes.

"*Cruel?* Is it cruel to care about your welfare?" demanded her outraged husband, not to be cajoled when such an important matter as his unborn son was at stake.

Johanna nudged Beatrice and they left the two lovers to continue their quarrel and reconciliation in peace and comfort. However, for once Boris had his way, and the afternoon saw the doctor's gig bowl up to the door and that gentleman shown straight up to my lady's bedchamber by Lord Newthorpe in person. Nor did the chamber door prove to be locked.

"Well," said Johanna, smiling broadly, "I never would have believed it! She doesn't usually give in so easily."

"I think I'll go for a ride," said Beatrice, who had been pacing about restlessly for a while. After receiving yet another peremptory missive from Satherby, she was suffering from another wave of guilt at having totally failed to comply with her aunt's wishes. She had dutifully allowed Jennice to introduce her to several gentlemen from the district, whom Jennice described as eligible, and these had included two more from the Dowager's list.

But Lord Whinber's son and heir had proved to be a red-faced, hunting-mad country bumpkin, however elevated his breeding, and he was so lacking in sensible conversation that he would have driven Eleanor insane within an hour. And as for Mr Standrey, well, he might look better when he had recovered from his cold, but she doubted it. A nose as large as that could not but intrude upon one's marital life.

–

A groom saddled a horse for Beatrice and would have accompanied her on her outing, but she waved him away.

"I'm only going for a gentle ride round the home park," she said. "You needn't come with me."

"But his lordship said that—"

She stared at him frostily. "I do not wish for company, thank you, Semsby. I shall be staying within the park. I can't possibly come to any harm there!" What she desperately needed at the moment was some time alone to think through her predicament, for predicament it was undoubtedly becoming.

She rode slowly along the leafy alleys cut through the woods by Lord Newthorpe's father to enhance the pleasures of just such outings. Gradually the peace of the day seeped into her and she began to relax. She was quite content to let the horse pick its way slowly over the soft earth so that her own thoughts could drift miles away.

After a while, she came to a quiet pool which she hadn't seen before on her outings. It was so beautiful there she decided to dismount and sit for a while on a fallen tree trunk. But although she continued to rack her brain, she could make no sense of her own feelings or come to any conclusion about a suitable husband for Eleanor.

Suddenly she realized that the sun was appreciably lower in the sky than she would have expected and when she looked at the little fob watch pinned to her waist, was startled to realize she'd been out for over two hours. They would be starting to worry about her and probably the groom would now be in trouble on her account, which was quite unfair, because Semsby had tried to do his duty. Hastily she put on her gloves and picked up her riding switch.

The mare was contentedly munching the lush grass at the edge of the clearing. Beatrice strode over to the animal and set her foot in the stirrup, but just as she was starting to mount, two birds screeched out of the undergrowth, erupting right under the mare's hooves, and the animal reared in fright. Unprepared, Beatrice lost her grip on the reins and was thrown to the ground, for which Anders would have scolded her roundly.

"Always keep hold of the reins, Miss Beatrice," he had told her times without number. "Whatever happens, don't let go of your horse's reins!"

She tried to get to her feet and found she'd twisted her ankle and couldn't stand, only sit and watch the mare vanish from sight, still whinnying in protest at the birds' unprovoked attack. She tried again to get up but could bear no weight on that foot and sank back to the ground, grimacing in pain.

"How stupid of me!" she exclaimed aloud. "Any idiot knows to keep a firm hold of the reins!"

"Careless indeed," a voice informed her. "You seem to be remarkably prone to accidents, Miss Dencey. And it appears I shall need to rescue you once again."

She blushed scarlet in embarrassment. "Oh no! Mr Serle!"

"None other," he said lightly. "And as I am myself on foot, I'm afraid I can't rush off to catch your horse for you. How came you to be riding alone? I'm sure Boris wouldn't approve of that. He is, if anything, overprotective of his womenfolk."

She could feel the warmth in her cheeks and she didn't know how to look him in the face. "I – I wanted to think about something, so I dismissed the groom." She moved incautiously and winced.

He knelt beside her. "You're hurt. Where exactly?"

"I've twisted my ankle."

"Let me see it."

She drew back "It's just a sprain. There's nothing you can do about it." The thought of exposing her leg to his gaze made her feel suddenly shy.

"I hadn't expected *you* to be missish. Let me see it. You may have broken something."

"Of course I haven't! I'd know if it were broken. It's just a sprain, I tell you!"

"Nonetheless, I prefer to check for myself." He pushed her hand aside and raised her skirt to remove her boot.

"I can remove the stocking myself, thank you." She could feel herself blushing furiously.

He grinned and averted his gaze, then, when she said she was ready, he turned to examine her ankle. With gentle fingers he palpated the joint, which was swelling rapidly. "No, you're right. It's not broken. But I think we should bathe it in cold water or it will continue to swell and become very painful. There's a rock by the pool that you can sit on while you dangle your foot in the water. Put your arms around my neck."

Without waiting for an answer, he picked her up.

For a second time, she found herself being carried in his arms, pressed closely against his chest. She was filled with the same urge to nestle against him, but this time resisted it sternly.

He walked across to the rock and set her down gently. The pain of moving her foot made her draw in her breath and forget everything else.

"It'll feel better when you've held it in the water, I promise you," he said encouragingly. He helped her to immerse her ankle, noting that she was rather pale and seeing how she gritted her teeth as the coldness of the water began to penetrate. "It's uncomfortable, I know, but there's nothing quite so good for a swelling. Bear with it for as long as you can, my dear."

She nodded, unable to speak, for the ankle had started throbbing and shock was now setting in. Had he really called her "my dear"? No, she must have misheard.

"Are you all right, Miss Dencey?"

"Yes," she managed after a while. But the pain was making her bite her lips.

"Of course you're not!" His voice was warm and sympathetic. "That ankle must be hurting abominably and will hurt more when we try to move you. Here, lean against me."

Before she could protest, he had put his arms around her, upon which she forgot everything but the closeness of him. Slowly she raised her eyes and found him gazing earnestly down at her. She couldn't seem to look away and when he bent to kiss her gently on her cheek, she couldn't even protest, for she wanted quite desperately for him to do it again.

"What were you thinking of to ride so far on your own?" he asked, his warm breath fanning her face. "You're in my grounds now, you know, not Boris's!"

It was an effort to speak. "I hadn't realized this was your land."

A picture of her lying there injured and alone made him suddenly say harshly, "You could have been killed and no one would have known!"

She was hurt by the tone of his voice and could only look down, blinking the tears from her eyes.

He didn't notice, but continued, still in a scolding tone. "Boris's guests don't usually behave in such a bacon-brained manner."

She burst into tears.

He was horrified. How could he have bullied her like that when she was in pain? Without thinking of the consequences, he took her in his arms and kissed her cheek again, then her lips. "Ah, don't cry, Bea! I'm sorry! I didn't mean to rip up at you." Neither of them noticed till afterwards that he'd used her pet name.

"I don't don't normally cry like this," she gasped, clutching him as if he were her only support in a harsh world. "I despise women who cry for nothing. It must be the – the shock." She tried to stop weeping, but the effort only made her sob harder, her worries having left her feeling very low. And the embarrassment of having to be rescued a second time by Justin Serle made everything worse, somehow, for she'd crossed his name off her list and he didn't deserve that insult.

When she had eventually hiccuped to a halt, still leaning against his chest and clutching his sodden handkerchief, she tried to apologize for making such a fuss, but he wouldn't hear of it.

"It's my fault. I was far too sharp with you. I should have realized you were in a state of shock. And that ankle must be hurting like the devil."

"It is," she said in a small voice. "But it's my own fault, after all. Getting myself into a scrape again! What an idiot you must think me!" She scrubbed furiously at her eyes and tried not to think of the way he'd kissed her.

"I don't think that of you in that way at all."

"Don't you?" She raised her eyes again and couldn't believe the tenderness she saw on his face.

Silence whispered around them and neither spoke, but the looks they exchanged said a great deal, as did the colour in Beatrice's cheeks.

In the end he was the one who broke the silence. "Let me look at that ankle again." He knelt to remove her foot gently from the water and hold it in his warm hands. The swelling had gone down, but the leg was blue with cold and the swollen ankle was now showing signs of bruising. He could feel her shivering slightly.

"How on earth are we to get you back to Lymsby?" he worried as he put his arm round her again.

She laid her head on his shoulder, giving in to temptation to lean against his wonderful masculine strength just for a moment more. "I – I can perhaps limp along – if you will help on one side and if you can find me a piece of wood to lean on."

"Impossible! That ankle will start throbbing once you begin moving around. We'll have to get you back to my house, but it's too far for me to carry you, so I must seek help."

She didn't want to see anyone else, just wanted to stay here with him, feeling safe and cherished.

"Mrs. Powis will be delighted to have someone to fuss over."

"Mrs. Powis?" Bea's voice was soft and dreamy.

"My old nurse." He raised one hand to brush a strand of hair from her eyes. "She's a tartar, but her bark is worse than her bite." Beatrice's eyes were, he decided, even more beautiful when bright with tears. He wanted very much to kiss the tears away, to kiss her properly this time, with the passion that was welling in him, but he was afraid of frightening her. "She – my nurse – is excellent with all manner of hurts. I gave her plenty of practice when I was young, as she never lets me forget. Now," he put temptation resolutely aside, "let me help you away from the water. Your ankle's quite blue with cold, but it has stopped swelling."

The rock was small and he was already balancing on its edge where water had dripped from her foot. As he helped her to rise, his foot started to slip and before either of them could do anything to prevent it, they had both fallen into the water. Luckily, it was only a couple of feet deep at that point, but as they both surfaced, Justin was betrayed into a curse and Beatrice couldn't help spluttering and splashing as she tried to right herself.

He caught hold of her almost immediately and held her head above the water. "Are you all right? My God, I'm so sorry! Of all the clumsy things to do!"

She was shaking in his arms as they sat there in the water.

"Beatrice! Miss Dencey! Please – it's all my fault – but I'll soon get help and—" He broke off as he realized she was laughing, not crying.

"Look at us!" she spluttered. "Did you ever see anything so ridiculous? What a comedy of errors! Oh, my goodness, you do look silly! Your hair, Mr Serle, is covered in green weeds."

The humour of the situation began to dawn on him. "And you, Miss Dencey, are also wearing a coronet of water weed." Chuckling, he knelt in the water beside her and helped her remove the clinging green strands. But what he really wanted to do was pull her into his arms and kiss her soundly, not those gentle touches he had risked before, but passionate kisses. The desire was so strong it shook him. Instead, he offered to pull her up on to the rock, and she burst out laughing again. How lovely she looked when her face was lit up with amusement!

"I hardly dare let you help me!" She chuckled again. "We'll probably wind up under the water. Oh, oh, my stomach hurts from laughing."

Very gingerly, he assisted her out of the water and drew her back to the rock. It was at that moment, with her cool wet hand in his, that he admitted to himself that he loved her. How splendid she was! What other woman would have seen the humour in this situation? Now, still standing on the rock staring at her, he realized that one could enjoy sharing one's life with a sensible woman like this. That one's life would, in fact, be blighted beyond redemption if one was not able to spend the rest of it with her.

Their laughter tailed off as they both began to shiver. "I think it'll be best if I run back to the house for help, rather than expecting you to limp along." He looked at her in anxiety, for she was quite pale now and was shivering violently. "You mustn't jolt that ankle. Will you be all right on your own for a few minutes?" He helped her to sit down.

"Yes, of course." The ankle was throbbing again, she was freezing cold and her urge to laugh had completely faded, but she saw no use in complaining. She watched him run off through the woods, her expression bemused.

The memory of his laughing face as they sat spluttering in the water made her smile briefly, then the smile vanished again as she remembered the kisses and realized how attractive she found him. And that was followed by the further realization that he was the one man she had met whom she could love. Did love, in fact.

No! She mustn't think of that! She had no *right* to love him! He was Aunt Marguerite's first choice for Eleanor. He was the only one on the list whom Beatrice herself could think at all suitable as a husband. She had made a promise to the Dowager, a most sacred promise to a dying woman. One couldn't betray such a promise.

She drew a deep breath and began to give herself a severe talking to. By the time he returned with help, she was able to face him with reasonable calm, relieved that her shivering hid any feelings she might betray, relieved that the presence of others prevented him from saying anything personal.

Deep within herself, she felt like weeping. But that would come later, when she was alone. For the moment, she allowed them to help her but tried to avoid meeting his eyes. Those kisses had meant nothing, could mean nothing. Justin Serle was not for her.

Chapter 8

At Satherby, the day following Snowy's adventure dawned sunny and bright. Eleanor shivered with happy anticipation as she jumped out of bed and went to stare though the window. Since the Dowager was still a little lethargic, no impediment arose to prevent Eleanor from keeping her rendezvous with Mr Lanby, though it seemed a long time until luncheon was over and the Dowager safely back in her chamber.

After the meal, Eleanor dressed in one of her prettiest gowns and spent a long time fussing over her hair, till her maid started to stare at her.

When at last the clock showed it was time to leave, Eleanor went down to the stables to meet Anders as arranged, not daring to disobey him, for she knew that he'd keep his promise to inform the Dowager if she tried to leave him behind. Anders always kept his word.

She spent a minute or two petting Snowy, who was still convalescing in one of the stalls, then suggested they leave, trying not to sound too anxious.

Anders shook his head, sighing. "Aye, I suppose we can go now. But I doubt I'm doing the right thing, letting you meet this man."

"You said you would!"

"Yes, well, that was yesterday. Today, I'm not so sure. Mind now, if I don't like the looks of him and say we're to return, then you must do as you're told straight away. Promise me!"

"Well, I will promise, but only because I'm sure you'll find nothing to object to in Mr Lanby." She danced along the woodland path beside the elderly groom, chattering happily about the progress of the latest foal and speculating as to how soon Snowy's leg would be better. "Perhaps I can take him up to the house when we – Oh, Mr Lanby! You quite startled me!"

He had been waiting there for nearly an hour, annoyed with himself at how afraid he was of missing her. When he saw that she'd brought someone with her, he looked toward the man questioningly, for he was obviously a servant. Servant or not, the fellow looked disapproving and when their eyes met, he didn't lower his or look away, but stared steadily back.

Eleanor found the sight of Mr Lanby so splendid that it was a minute or two before she could speak. "This is my groom, Anders, come to keep an eye on me."

The older man was at his most wooden. "You'll pardon me for coming along, sir, but her grandmother doesn't approve of her walking in the woods alone."

The younger man nodded, but looked disappointed. "It's only to be expected that a young lady should have proper guardians."

"Oh, pooh!" Eleanor exclaimed. "As if I need guardians on our own land."

"I have to look after her," Anders continued, determined to get things clear, "for she's as trusting as a kitten." His tone implied that he was not.

"Well!" exclaimed Eleanor, setting her hands on her hips. "What an awful thing to say, Anders!"

"It's true, though, Miss. Anyway, I'll just drop behind a little and leave you two to choose our path. It's a pleasant day for a stroll, and no mistake."

When Anders was out of their hearing, Mr Lanby smiled at Eleanor and said softly, "So you brought your guardian angel along to look me over!"

"I didn't bring him," her tone was a trifle sulky. "He insisted on coming. The trouble with servants who've known one all one's life is they never recognize when one has grown up."

"I have a butler who feels just the same about me and sometimes treats me like a naughty schoolboy."

Her dimples returned. "Well, then, Mr Lanby, you will understand my feelings precisely."

He offered her his arm. "Where shall we go?"

She took the arm, feeling suddenly shy. "There's a very pleasant walk through the woods to the right here, which comes out at a bit of high ground. You get a lovely view of the village from there. It's one of my favourite places."

And after that, the time simply flew and she soon relaxed again. She couldn't have said what they talked about, only that they'd been comfortable together. It was as if they'd known one another for years. He'd made her laugh and they'd never been at a loss for a topic of conversation.

But all the time there had been shivers of something else running beneath the words, some unspoken communication between them. And she knew it meant something important, knew she wished to see much more of him.

At the end of the walk, Crispin clasped one of her hands in both his and said simply, "May we meet tomorrow?"

She didn't hesitate. "Yes, of course."

"I shall look forward to it."

She stood and watched him walk away, repressing the urge to run after him. Not until Mr Lanby had disappeared from sight, did she turn and march back toward the stables, not saying a word, trying desperately to understand her own feelings.

When they arrived, she turned to confront Anders. "Well, do you think he's a proper enough gentleman?"

"He does seem pleasant enough, I will admit. But proper is as proper does. You still can't go a–meeting him without your grandmother's knowledge."

"I can and I will."

He shook his head.

"Anders – please." Her voice broke on the word.

He sighed deeply, saw the desperation in her face and said, "Well – as long as you take me with you each time. Promise!"

"I promise." She closed her eyes in thankfulness.

When she'd gone, he shook his head. There had been something in the way the two of them behaved – something that was going too deep too fast. He'd have to try to find out more about this Mr Lanby. He didn't want his young mistress getting hurt.

Eleanor met Mr Lanby four times that week, with Anders accompanying them doggedly each time, in spite of all her protests and pleading. He could see the love growing between them as if it were something tangible, even if they themselves didn't yet realize it.

The old groom lay awake at night worrying about his young lady, for she'd told him her ladyship had some disagreement with the gentleman's family, and it seemed certain that only trouble could come from that. Yet he had to admit that the two of them did seem made for each other. Even an old bachelor like him could sense that.

But how was he to find out about the gentleman's circumstances? All his inquiries so far had led nowhere. Mr Lanby might be staying with the Treevers, but nothing seemed to be known by the servants there about his home, his finances. Could the man offer Miss Eleanor enough to satisfy her ladyship?

Anders also began to suspect that there was some sort of secret being kept, for although Mr Lanby would talk about his home and his horses all afternoon, nice as you please, every now and then he would catch himself up in the middle of a sentence. Could he be an adventurer? He didn't seem like one, but perhaps he was setting a trap for Miss Eleanor, who had a tidy fortune waiting for her?

These suspicions faded whenever they were with Mr Lanby, for a more open-looking face you couldn't wish to find on anyone, but the worries came back to Anders many times in the dark hours of several anxious nights.

When the groom laid his fears squarely before Eleanor one day, she sat frowning and pulling Snowy's ears. "He can't be hiding anything bad," she said eventually. "I just know he can't, Anders!"

"So you suspect something, too, Miss?"

She hated to agree but she wouldn't lie to him, so nodded her head.

"Miss, *please* be careful!"

"Yes. I will. I'll be very careful indeed, I promise." Then she walked away, lost in thought, heedless of the little animal left whining behind her.

Which was not, Anders decided, watching her, at all like his Miss Eleanor.

On the tenth day of this idyll, after a rainy day had prevented them meeting and left Eleanor fretting, she and her young gentleman went again to the lookout and sat there on the grassy knoll on a horse blanket, staring across the valley.

"I think," he told her, face very solemn, "I had better confess something to you before we before this goes any further."

Her heart jumped in her breast, for he looked so serious, and a cold feeling crept up her spine. She knew she couldn't bear it if anything were to separate them now, but she managed to say more calmly than she felt, "Go on."

"I – I haven't been quite honest with you."

She could only stare at him. "About what?" she asked, panic filling her.

He took a deep breath. "Well, first of all – my name isn't Christopher Lanby." He seemed to be having trouble continuing.

"What is your name?" she prompted at last.

"It's – Crispin."

She gasped aloud. It was such an unusual name that she asked immediately, "Not Crispin Herforth?"

"I'm afraid so."

"But why didn't you tell me that at once? Why did you need to come here incognito?"

"I wanted to see my future inheritance. A few weeks ago your grandmother invited me to stay so that I could get to know Satherby. It was a – well, a rather condescending letter. That made me angry, so I refused to come straight away. But I asked the General if I could come and stay with them. I wanted to see Satherby. I'd heard so much about it."

"Grandmamma was very angry that you didn't come here straight away."

"Yes. I meant her to be. I grew up hearing how fearsome she was, so apart from anything else, I didn't want to risk a snub, or worse treatment, not in a house which would be mine one day."

"No. I can see that. She can be difficult. Is that," she began to fiddle with the material of her skirt, avoiding his eyes, "all you have to confess?"

"Isn't it enough?"

Her heart lifted and she dared to steal a glance sideways. When she caught him looking at her, she said simply, "That doesn't seem so very terrible a thing to me." She smiled and he smiled back at her. For a moment, she would have sworn they were the only people in the whole universe. Then her expression became serious again and she added, "I realized something was worrying you, of course. You've been a bit quiet the last day or two."

"Yes. And you've been very patient with me."

"I was waiting for you to *reveal all*," she said demurely, eyes glinting at him, "as they say in novels."

"Minx!"

She smiled. "So now we know where we stand, do we not, Crispin?"

"Not quite. There's something else which needs setting right." Forgetting the attendant groom, he pulled her into his arms and kissed her soft lips, as he'd been longing to do since the first day they met.

She made no protest, only raising one hand shyly to stroke the crisp blonde hair.

"I think I've fallen in love with you, Eleanor Graceover," he said abruptly, staring anxiously into her eyes.

"I should hope so, Crispin Herforth." She smiled at him, not shyly, but showing her own feelings quite openly. "I wouldn't like to think you kiss all the young ladies you meet in the woods in that manner."

For answer, he kissed her again, so that the world spun crazily around her and she had to cling tightly to him. He held her close for a moment, then growled in her ear, "Nor that you kiss all the gentlemen you meet – whether in the woods or elsewhere."

"No," she said, with one of her very direct looks. "I've never kissed anyone in this way but you. And I shall never kiss any other gentleman again."

All thoughts of flirtation had left her mind days ago and she was more concerned to verify the exact moment when he'd known he loved her and to tell him how she herself had known it as early as the second day, when she saw him waiting for her in the woods.

Neither of them remembered Anders, sitting on a fallen log some twenty paces behind them and he remained where he was, doing nothing to stop them kissing one another. His mind was greatly relieved, for he had unashamedly eavesdropped upon their conversation, not moving away until he had heard who "Mr Lanby" really was.

The heir to Satherby wasn't out to gain Miss Eleanor's fortune, for he would have a greater one himself. And anyway, Mr Herforth was a nice young gentleman, just right for Anders' young lady. The only thing that really worried the groom was what the Dowager's attitude would be to this whirlwind romance. Her ladyship had a lot of high-nosed notions about what was right and even the servants knew she considered few gentlemen remotely worthy of her granddaughter.

Still, Anders mused to himself, chewing on the stem of his unlit pipe, it was Miss Eleanor's happiness that mattered most, not that of a bossy old woman nearing the end of her life. And so he would tell Lady Marguerite if she made trouble for these two – even if he lost his place because of it.

The lovers spent a precious half-hour telling each other exactly what had made them fall in love and stealing a kiss or two at intervals.

It was Eleanor, nothing if not practical, who said thoughtfully in the end, "I don't know what Grand-mamma is going to say to this, Crispin. She's not at all fond of your family, you know, and she intends me to marry a gentleman of the highest breeding." She pulled a face at the thought. "In fact, she's been discussing marriage settlements secretly with the lawyers for months and I'm sure that's why she's sent poor Bea up to London, to look over the eligible suitors for me."

She spoke rather hesitantly, for he'd said nothing to her of marriage yet, but surely she couldn't be mistaken about where this was all leading?

The arm around her tightened. "I must see her ladyship at once, then, and tell her how we feel. You will marry me, will you not, my dearest girl? I don't think I could bear it if you didn't."

She smiled radiantly at him. "Well, of course I will, silly, but," the smile was replaced by a puckering of the brows, "I don't think you should go and see Grandmamma! Not just yet, anyway."

"Why ever not? Surely, even Lady Marguerite will see that it's a very good solution to the inheritance problem? It'll keep her precious Satherby Abbey in the family."

Eleanor wrinkled her nose in thought. "Well, Grandmamma's not quite like other people. She may approve eventually, if things are put to her in just the right way, but there again, she may not. You can never tell and she rarely changes her mind about people, so we must tread carefully."

"She will *have to* change her mind about us."

"Oh yes, I know that! But it's better to tread softly with Grandmamma and let her think something is her own idea. Not just because you can never force her to do anything, but because I don't want to make her unhappy. She's very autocratic, but I love her dearly and I won't have her hurt."

"What do you think we should do, then?"

She frowned and began tracing the lines on the palm of his hand, "I think you should go home and write to her that you've been thinking things over. Say you feel she was right about your visiting Satherby and the sooner you come the better."

"Will she still welcome me?"

"I don't think she'll welcome you at all, but she'll probably wish you to come. She thinks you'll need showing how to run the estate."

"As if I haven't been running my own for years!"

"Oh, how many years? I had thought you were only twenty-four."

"I am, but my father was never much interested in such matters, so I've been more or less managing things since just before I was sixteen." He raised one of her hands to his lips and kissed it gently, his eyes holding hers and promising so much more. "Go on, my love. Once I get here, what must I do? Pretend to fall in love with you all over again?"

"Under no circumstances! Grandmamma strongly disapproves of people who fall in love. She considers it vulgar. We must pretend to be completely indifferent to one another."

"I don't think I can do that!" He gave in to the temptation to plant a kiss on the tip of her nose and that led them into a more lingering embrace.

When they had drawn apart again, she said severely. "You *must* hide the fact that you love me, Crispin! Believe me, I know her! The important thing is to persuade Grandmamma that you're worthy of inheriting and really will care for the estate. We can't confuse her by falling in love! Not at first. She'd likely send you away again and tell you to wait until she's dead to claim Satherby, then find me another man to marry – not that I would, of course."

"She sounds fearsome."

"She can be! Make no mistake about that, Crispin! She's had a hard life, lost nearly everyone she loved, and yet she's survived and not given in to her grief."

"You're very fond of her, aren't you?"

She looked rather surprised, saying slowly, "Yes, I am. I hadn't realized quite how fond until now. I should hate to be at odds with her." When she looked at him, she had tears in her eyes. "And especially now."

"Why now, my precious one?"

"Because I don't think she's got much longer to live. She seems weaker lately. She hasn't said anything to me about it, well, she never would! But you can tell by the way she moves and by how long she has to rest if she does anything. So it would be nice to do this in a way that would please her. Do you understand?"

"Of course I do, my darling. And it will be no trouble to show her how much I care about the estate. It's the loveliest place I've ever seen. I'm afraid you've agreed to marry a man who's a farmer at heart. I could only be happy in the country, dealing with the land. So if you hanker after the fashionable life…"

"Oh, no! I'm a country girl, too. Both Bea and I are. And I love Satherby." She looked at him shyly. "That's not why I want to marry you. I would want to, anyway, wherever we had to live, but it does make things quite perfect."

"Then we're particularly well suited."

She looked at him, her head on one side. "You know, it may sound strange, but I understand now what Grandmamma meant when she said that marriage was a business arrangement. I don't think I could easily contemplate marriage with a man who wished to live in town, however handsome he was, or however engaging his ways. Does that sound mercenary?"

"No, for I feel the same. That's yet another reason why you're the perfect woman for me. But Eleanor, you're mine now and I mean to keep you. Whatever I have to do to achieve that, I shall! Even if your grandmother doesn't approve. Even if it means abducting you."

She could see that he meant every word and a thrill went through her. "Good," she said, somewhat breathlessly. "Because I don't think you'll really like what I'm going to say." She was back to tracing patterns on his hand.

He raised her chin and kissed her very gently on the lips. "Tell me, then, adorable one."

"Well, while you're learning about the estate, I think I must find an unsuitable gentleman to fall in love with, or at least, to flirt with."

He stiffened. "No! I couldn't bear that! Even in pretence."

She sighed in exasperation. "I told you you wouldn't like it. But it's the only way I can see, so you'll just *have to* bear it."

"But why?"

She answered him obliquely. "Crispin, I'm the only person in the world, I think, who can manage to get my own way with Grandmamma, and even then, it doesn't always work. Bea just does as she's told, well, most of the time, anyway. Even the lawyer is terrified of Grandmamma! And the bailiff creeps in like a quivery little mouse to see her. So you absolutely *must* promise to do as I say, because it's our only hope. I won't go against her wishes, not openly, anyway. And I won't make her final years unhappy, if I can help it. She's had too much unhappiness in her life already."

"You have no doubts about marrying me, though?" he asked, surprised to see how resolute she could be when she wanted something. He began to wonder whether she did not, perhaps, resemble her grandmother more than anyone realized. But he decided she was not the only one with a stubborn streak. He was bred from Graceover stock, too. He would go along with what she said for now, even though he didn't like it, because she clearly knew Lady Marguerite better than he did. But he wouldn't follow her suggestions meekly for ever. If they didn't work, if he had to, he'd whisk her away and make a runaway match of it.

"Of course I don't have any doubts! I always know my own mind." She beamed at him.

"I think I must be the most fortunate man on earth."

She sighed in delight. "That's the nicest thing anyone ever said to me! Say some more!"

He spent the next ten minutes telling her how beautiful she was and how he longed to make her his wife, and she sat leaning against him, chuckling with delight at his more outrageous compliments.

This dalliance was much superior to the behaviour of the heroes in novels, who never seemed to have any sense of humour at all, just as her Crispin was far superior to the various counts and marquises about whom the tales were built. He might not be tall or wonderfully handsome, but somehow he was just what she wanted.

And if it was necessary, she would defy the world to marry him.

Chapter 9

By the time Justin's grooms had helped him to carry Beatrice back to the house, her teeth were chattering uncontrollably, in spite of the horse blankets he'd snatched from the stables to wrap round her.

Mrs. Powis had been warned to prepare for them and the minute they entered the house, they were both swept away to separate bedrooms, where hot baths and even hotter cups of chocolate awaited them.

The housekeeper was amazed to hear that her master had been meeting unknown ladies in the woods. Her curiosity about this mysterious Miss Dencey led her to tend the stranger herself and to abandon her nurseling to the ministrations of his valet. She hoped desperately that the stranger would prove to be a lady and not *the other sort*, though she couldn't see Master Justin bringing an immodest female back to a respectable household. She was also praying that the lady was indeed the object of his affections. He'd been feeling very low since his brother's death and let alone it was time he got himself an heir, she would like to see him happy again.

A very little time with Miss Dencey served to convince Mrs. Powis that this was no scheming harpy, but a sensible lady with whom it was a pleasure to chat, or it would have been had the lady not been shivering so violently. When the shivering continued, Mrs. Powis decided to reinforce the cup of hot chocolate with a brandy toddy made to her own special recipe. This she insisted on Beatrice swallowing, in spite of the latter's protests.

"Never shall I forgive myself," declared Mrs. Powis, arms akimbo, "if I let you catch a chill when it can be prevented! Nor will Master Justin – I mean, Mr Serle – forgive me, either. We have a better regard than that for our guests at Melbury." She spoiled this high moral tone by adding, "Though how he came to be so clumsy as to tip you both into the water, I cannot imagine! I thought he'd grown out of that sort of escapade years ago! I shall have a word or two to say to him later about it, I promise you!"

In vain did Beatrice protest that she wasn't given to taking chills and that she hated brandy.

"Nor should I think you're given to immersing yourself in icy water on a nasty chilly afternoon, Miss! Middle of April and still as cold as February!" declared Mrs. Powis, eyes alight with the fervour of one who had devoted her life to looking after the health and welfare of others. "We'll not risk the chill, thank you, so I'd be grateful if you'd just swallow this down while it's hot."

"But—" began Beatrice.

Mrs. Powis swelled up to twice her normal size and asked, with awe-inspiring dignity, whether Miss did not trust her to know her own business.

Quite cowed, Beatrice swallowed the toddy and allowed herself to be tucked into a bed which had just been thoroughly warmed by a bustling maidservant with a warming pan filled with hot embers. She lay luxuriating in the warmth, and before long fell asleep.

"Ah," said Mrs. Powis to herself, as she prepared to leave the room half an hour later. "That's more like it!" She gazed down at the stranger, admiring her russet hair and healthy complexion. She and Master Justin would make some handsome babies together and Mrs. Powis was still young enough to help rear them. Turning to the maid who had been posted discreetly in a corner away from the bed, she ordered in a whisper, "Continue to keep an eye on Miss Dencey, if you please, Mary, while I check that the master is all right."

Mrs. Powis then strode along the corridor to find out from Master Justin just what this lady was doing in his grounds and just what *he* had been doing to tumble them both into the water. Downright careless, that was! But Miss Dencey didn't seem to bear him any ill will for it, which was another good sign.

–

When Beatrice awoke, it was to find the day well advanced and the room half in darkness, with Johanna sitting by her bed. "Oh! I didn't mean to fall asleep," she gasped, still confused.

"If Mrs. Powis meant you to sleep, then you had no choice, believe me, Bea! How are you feeling now, my dear?"

"Embarrassed!"

Johanna chuckled. "You do seem to make a habit of getting into scrapes and letting Serle rescue you from them, don't you?"

Beatrice was thankful the room was dark enough to hide her blushes. "It was an accident. And it was *his* fault we fell into the pond, not mine!" Honesty compelled her to admit, "Though it was my own carelessness which left me without a horse."

Johanna just chuckled again, well pleased by what had happened and hoping it would bring them together.

"I'll get up at once," Beatrice said, very much on her dignity. "I'm sorry to have caused all this trouble. I don't know why they sent for you! I'm perfectly all right now, except for my foot."

Johanna's hand pressed her back against the pillows. "Don't you dare get up!"

Beatrice stared up at her in astonishment.

"If you set one foot out of that bed, you'll bring Mrs. Powis's wrath down upon me and that's a fate I'd rather escape, thank you very much! I have strict instructions to send for her the minute you wake up and not to let you leave the bed under any circumstances until she's seen you, and, my dear, I dare do nothing but follow those instructions to the letter. No one who is at all acquainted with Mrs. Powis would dare to defy her!"

"But Johanna, I'm perfectly all— Wait! *No!*"

But it was too late. The bell had been pulled and not long afterwards, Mrs. Powis surged in. She immediately felt Beatrice's forehead and tutted to herself. "Just as I thought! Feverish!"

"I'm perfectly all right, Mrs. Powis! Really I am!" Beatrice protested.

"Ah, but will you be all right tomorrow and the day after if we let you get up so soon?" demanded the domestic tyrant. She turned to Johanna. "It's a good thing you sent for your things, Your Ladyship, so that you can stay with us tonight. Miss Dencey will be sneezing by tomorrow and in no fit state to travel if we don't look after her now." She tucked the blankets firmly around her patient.

"I've told Master Justin what I think of him for tumbling into a pond on a freezing spring day at his age," she went on. "And as for pulling a lady into that nasty dirty water with him, well did you ever hear of such a careless thing?" She smoothed the covers, smiling reminiscently. "Mind you, he was even worse when he was a boy! If he couldn't find something to fall into, he'd find something to fall out of, with equally bad results. He'd only to see a tree to want to climb it! The number of times I've had to nurse him better, and Master Peter with him. It's a wonder I'm not in my grave already!"

"This time it was partly my fault," ventured Beatrice, not wishing Justin Serle to bear all the blame. "I'd sprained my ankle and he said it would be better if it were soaked in cold water."

"The master has already explained what happened, thank you, Miss. And I'll say to you what I said to him: it's one thing to soak an ankle – which I'll allow is the sensible thing to do in the circumstances – but it's quite another to soak the whole person! Master Justin loses any sense he ever had when he gets near water. I couldn't count the number of times he's fallen into that very same pond and come home covered in nasty green weed. You should hear what the laundry-maid said about the state of his shirt today!"

"Yes, but it was only because he was trying to help me," pursued Beatrice, still trying to protect her rescuer, "so we can't *blame* him!"

"What I would like to know is why you were out riding without a groom in the first place," said Johanna. "What on earth got into you today, Bea?"

She could feel her colour rising. "I just – wanted to have a think. Somewhere quiet."

"Well, Lymsby's anything but quiet today, I'll grant you that!" Johanna sighed. She turned to Mrs. Powis and said with feigned casualness, "There is some question of whether my daughter is expecting twins or not, you see, so Boris has sent for the doctor – and Jennice doesn't like fusses."

Mrs. Powis's eyes brightened. "Twins! Now, that *is* good news."

"Yes, but we shall have to look after her. I would," Johanna avoided meeting Beatrice's eyes, "certainly value your advice on that."

Mrs. Powis beamed at her. "Any time, your ladyship. The Newthorpes and the Serles have always been good neighbours to one another." Then she turned back to eye Beatrice. "I'll go and order a light meal now for you now, Miss. And afterwards, when you've eaten it – every scrap, *if* you please! – you are to go to sleep again. There's nothing like a good long sleep for reducing the chances of a chill."

She marched majestically out of the room, tossing over her shoulder. "By tomorrow, she'll be able to limp on that foot – *if* she does as she's told now, that is, Lady Ostdene – and I'll find a walking stick to help her."

When she'd left, Johanna put her hand over Beatrice's. "My dear, I'd be extremely obliged if you did as you were told while we're here."

"But Johanna—"

"*Please!* You see, Boris is going to ask for Mrs. Powis's help with the birth – though what Jennice will say to that, I don't know. Mrs. Powis is the best midwife hereabouts, even if she does terrify everyone."

Beatrice muttered to herself, but gave in and did as she was told. She was surrounded by well-wishers who were driving her mad and who were all in league against her. Besides, she didn't wish to cause more trouble for Mr Serle, with Mrs. Powis or with anyone else.

Just as she was drifting off to sleep, however, she jerked upright and clutched at her cousin's arm. "Johanna! You won't tell anyone about this, will you? Promise me! I couldn't bear people in town to know!" They would say she'd been throwing herself at Mr Serle and insist he was not for her. As if she didn't know that.

"My dear girl, surely you've lived in the country for long enough to realize that we won't need to tell people anything. The news will already have wafted around the district and by tomorrow it'll have crept across the county without any help from me."

"Oh dear! You're right. It's just the same at Satherby." Beatrice stared into the distance, then said firmly, "That settles it, then! I'm *not* going back to London! I can't face what people will say after having *him* rescue me again! I just can't!"

"We'll think of something," Johanna said soothingly, patting her hand. "There's no need to do anything drastic. Now, go to sleep, do."

–

In the morning, Mrs. Powis reluctantly conceded that the danger of chills had probably been averted and gave permission for Beatrice to leave Melbury, though not until after luncheon, when the day would have warmed up a little.

Beatrice found her ankle to be much better and was able to move around quite easily with the stick, if more slowly than usual.

When she limped downstairs, she was met by her host, with a rueful smile on his face.

"I do hope you're all right now, my dear B— Miss Dencey? Can you ever forgive me for tipping you into the water?" His smile was particularly warm, begging her to share his amusement.

Aware that both Johanna and Mrs. Powis were watching them with great interest, Beatrice said stiffly, "It was an accident. I'm perfectly all right, thank you, Mr Serle."

Justin also became aware of the two spectators and said in a low voice, "Look, I need to talk to you, Beatrice. Alone." He raised his voice and added, "Would you care to come and see my father's collection of oil paintings, Miss Dencey? They're on this floor, so you won't have any more stairs to climb."

After a moment's hesitation and a doubtful look at her cousin, Beatrice accepted Mr Serle's arm and allowed him to escort her along to the gallery. Now would be as good a time as any to cut short his attentions. She would then have the satisfaction of knowing that she was doing her duty to her aunt and it must be just the aftermath of the accident which was making her feel like bursting into tears at the mere thought of what she must do.

When Mrs. Powis came back a little later with a light snack for the guests, she found only Lady Ostdene sitting thoughtfully by the fire.

"They're still looking at the paintings," Johanna said, yawning and stretching like a well-fed cat. "I don't think we should disturb them just yet."

"We'll leave them to come back of their own accord," Mrs. Powis agreed. "If I might ask, your ladyship, has Master Justin known Miss Dencey for long?"

"For a month or two. They seem to get on well, most of the time, anyway, but don't get your hopes up, Mrs. Powis, for there's been nothing lover like about them so far. In fact, they very frequently argue with one another."

Mrs. Powis's eyes brightened. "That's a very good sign, if you don't mind my saying so, your ladyship. He would never be happy with a lady who didn't stand up to him. He's like his father there."

"We'll see. My cousin's not really interested in finding a husband for herself, though it's what my mother wishes."

"Even better. Master Justin hates ladies who chase after him."

Johanna shook her head but didn't continue the discussion. With any other couple, she would be sitting here expecting an interesting announcement. With Bea and Serle, she had no idea what to expect.

She looked at the clock, sighed and decided to take advantage of the moment on her own behalf. "I shall be glad to return to Lymsby, for I don't mind telling you, Mrs. Powis, that my daughter is rather upset at the possibility of twins."

Mrs. Powis frowned. "And Master Boris?"

"He's delighted. But I fear Jennice is not the maternal type. I don't quite know what to do about that."

"You make sure they put the babies into her arms the minute they're born. It never fails!"

"The trouble is," Johanna confided, "the doctor also said that Jennice has been racketing about too much and he advises her to take things more easily from now on. Boris is determined to see that she does so, and the two of them have done nothing but squabble about it ever since the doctor left."

"She needs a good talking to! The idea of it, and her probably carrying The Heir to Lymsby! Still, I dare say she'll grow accustomed to it. Do twins run in your family, then?" Mrs. Powis had a hungry expression on her face.

"Oh, yes! In both the Dencey and Graceover lines. My grandmother bore twins." Johanna's face clouded. "Unfortunately, they both died, poor things. But I believe there have been several other cases with happier outcomes. We'd have to ask my mother for details. She knows everything about the family history."

"Twins do need careful rearing, that's for sure," agreed Mrs. Powis. "If I can be of any assistance to Miss Jennice at the birth…"

"Oh, Mrs. Powis, if only you would! I'm sure that with *you* to help her give birth and to look after them all afterwards, Jennice would cope very well. A stranger is never the same. The doctor is talking about bringing in a month-nurse from Watford, but how do we know what she'd be like?"

"We don't know. And I shall be delighted to help, Lady Ostdene. Delighted."

In the picture gallery, Justin stole a glance at Beatrice, wondering how to start. Strange that he'd thought her silly on first acquaintance! She was probably the most intelligent woman he'd ever met. And the bravest. Not to mention being beautiful. And who else would have been able to laugh at their misfortunes yesterday?

He walked on for a few paces pointing out some of the better paintings as he wondered whether to press his suit immediately or whether it would be better to lead up to the declaration with a few compliments. He felt horribly uncomfortable and as nervous as any callow young man at his first ton party. And Beatrice, who had a distant air to her today, wasn't contributing much to the conversation, or even looking at him, which didn't help matters.

"Perhaps it might be more pleasant to sit outside in the sunshine?" he ventured, offering her his arm again.

She jumped back as if he were poisonous. "Oh, no! Thank you, but I'd much rather study the paintings." She stopped in front of a landscape and perused it earnestly, though it might have been a page of algebraical equations, for all she noticed about it. "Lovely," she said in a faint voice and as he moved toward her, she limped hurriedly on to the next painting.

"I'm glad you like them. We share several interests, do we not?"

Her heart lurched at the warmth in his eyes. If only she didn't feel so— she would not allow herself to finish that thought. She stared at another blur of colour. She could hardly be so rude as to cut him short and flee back to her cousin's protection, so she continued to move along the wall of paintings, jerking on to the next every time he drew too near or took a deep breath, as if about to speak.

After a few minutes of this, he stepped forward quickly and with a firm hand turned Beatrice round so that she was forced to look at him. "I rather get the impression that you're trying to prevent me from speaking, Miss Dencey."

Her face flamed. "Oh, no, I – I just – I'm still feeling a trifle out of sorts. That's all. What did you wish to s-say to me?"

He tried to take her into his arms and she pushed him away quite roughly, letting her walking stick fall to the ground in her agitation. "Oh pray don't! We mustn't!"

He picked up the stick and handed it to her, frowning. "Why must we not? I had thought we were getting on well together – more than well. You've seemed to enjoy my company over the past few weeks. As I have yours. Even when I pushed you into the pool you didn't seem to hate me."

"No! I mean, yes, but it's not right! We can never..."

She wrung her hands and turned on him eyes so full of anguish he was startled into asking, "Have I offended you in some way, Miss Dencey?"

"No. Oh, no!" How could it offend her for a man like him to pay her attention? But she mustn't allow it. He was marked by the Dowager for Eleanor. He was the only one suitable on the whole list. If anyone deserved a good husband, dear Eleanor did. And Beatrice owed so much to her aunt, that she couldn't let her down out of sheer selfishness.

He looked at her earnestly. "The last thing I wish to do is distress you, Miss Dencey, but I had thought this a suitable time to talk about ourselves. Perhaps, though, if you're still feeling a little under the weather, we should postpone our discussion until tomorrow?"

"Oh, yes! Yes, that's a very good idea." She hardly knew how to stop herself from bursting into tears at the pain of having to prevent his proposal, and she found herself quite incapable of telling him to his face that she didn't wish to marry him. She wished very much to marry him. She could imagine nothing better in the whole world. "I'm f-feeling a trifle dizzy. If I could just s-sit down and be quiet…"

"Certainly. There's a couch over here. Let me help you to it."

"*No!*" The violence of her rejection surprised them both. "Actually, what I'd really like is to retire to my room, if you don't mind, Mr Serle. Mrs. Powis was right. An immersion in cold water can lead to a chill. I must be a trifle – a trifle feverish."

He realized there was something else wrong, something she was concealing from him, but he didn't feel he could press her when she was looking so desperately unhappy. He remembered the feel of her in his arms when they danced, the good sense of her conversation, the beauty of her eyes – why, there were a dozen things about her which had grown upon him gradually, so that he was now quite determined to make her his wife. He didn't feel her to be indifferent to him, either. Indeed, her expression always revealed more about her true feelings than she realized.

He smiled at her, feeling quite overwhelmed with love for her.

She looked as if she was about to burst into tears.

They turned as one to walk slowly back along the gallery, neither speaking.

Justin was both perturbed and puzzled. He hadn't expected to fall in love, not after all these years on the town, and he was feeling rather hesitant about it. Perhaps Beatrice was experiencing similar feelings? She was older than most women looking at marriage and probably afraid of ridicule. Perhaps she'd given up any thought of marriage and now needed time to grow used to the idea again?

For the moment, he could only escort her to her bedchamber, then go down to let Lady Ostdene know that her cousin was feeling unwell.

–

Once in her room, Beatrice threw herself upon the bed and gave way to the tears. A touch on her arm made her catch her breath on a sob and stare up at the worried face of her maid. "Oh! Tilly! I d–didn't see you."

"Is there anything I can do, Miss, anything at all?"

Beatrice shook her head. "No. No one can help me now. Please, I can't talk about it. Will you just pack my things for me?"

"Are we leaving now, then, Miss?"

"Yes. I – I can't stay here. He will… I must get away from him!" She could see Tilly's astonishment at this dramatic statement and went on quickly, "I think it's time for me to return to Satherby. Tilly, would you consider coming to work for me as my maid – permanently. I think we might deal very well together."

The young maid broke into a beaming smile. "Oh yes, Miss! Oh, I'd love to!"

"It'll mean you moving away from London. I could never live in a city. I don't think I'll ever return."

"Oh, I don't mind where I live, Miss. It's the people as count in life, isn't it?"

Beatrice's eyes filled again. "Yes. The people." And the main people in her life were, had to be, Eleanor, whom she had helped raise, and the Dowager, who had taken her in when she was destitute, and who had so little time left to live. Their wishes and their happiness were far more important than her own.

There was a knock on the door and Johanna poked her head inside. "May I talk to you for a moment, my dear?"

Beatrice nodded dismissal to Tilly, dragged in a deep breath and prepared for the first onslaught. She took the initiative by immediately declaring her intention of returning to Satherby the very next day and refusing to give her reasons, refusing also to explain why she'd been weeping.

"But my dear, there must be something wrong. Is it Serle? How has he upset you?"

"Mr Serle? Upset me? Of course not. Please don't think that. He's been extremely k-kind to me. It's not him, it's *me*! I'm just – homesick. You know I don't like all this – this fuss and sociability. And I haven't really enjoyed London, either, though you've been quite wonderful to me."

"But why rush off home like this? Why now, so suddenly?"

"I told you. I feel homesick. And as for now, well, at the moment you have Jennice to look after. How proud you'll be to become the grandmother of twins!"

"Bea, dear—"

171

"Oh, Johanna, please don't try to stop me! I need to go home!" Tears welled in Beatrice's eyes. "*Please*, just let me go home!"

She sounded so agonized that Johanna stopped trying to argue, merely clasping her hand and saying quietly, "I don't know what's upsetting you, my love, and I'm not going to pry into your private affairs, but please believe me that if I can ever help you in any way, I shall be very happy to do so."

That started Beatrice's tears falling again and she threw her arms round her cousin and sobbed incoherently into her shoulder. But she still wouldn't say what had happened between herself and Serle.

And she was still insistent on returning home.

Chapter 10

As the carriage bowled along the highway in the early summer sunshine, Tilly tried to make herself invisible in the corner so as to leave her mistress in peace with her thoughts. She didn't know what Mr Serle had done to upset Miss Dencey, but whatever it was, he shouldn't have done it and the trouble must be his fault, because Miss Dencey was the kindest mistress as ever lived, and why she wasn't married, with a home of her own, Tilly didn't know, for she was as pretty as she was kind.

When they arrived in Satherby village, she saw Miss Dencey take a deep breath, as if pulling herself together, then turn to her.

"You cannot help but have noticed, Tilly, that I – well, I'm not feeling very happy at the moment and – and you've perhaps guessed that it concerns Mr Serle. I'd be grateful, very grateful indeed, if you would not discuss my problems – not even to hint about things – with the other servants."

"I hope I know how to behave better than that, Miss."

"Thank you." Miss Dencey put her hands up to check her bonnet. "Is this straight, Tilly?"

"Just a minute, Miss. Let me tie the ribbons again. There you are! And a proper treat you look, too." But how sad her mistress's expression was!

When the carriage pulled up inside the front portico, Tilly got out and looked round, trying to take in everything, absolutely determined to do credit to Miss Dencey. The front doors were so enormous she couldn't help staring up at them in awe. And Borrill, the butler, was flanked by two tall footmen, with superior expressions.

Tilly clasped her hands in front of her, which Sarah said was the best thing to do with them if you had nothing to hold, and followed her mistress inside, trying not to show her own nervousness.

Miss Dencey was just turning towards the right when there was a shriek of joy and a young lady in pink almost tumbled down the stairs in her haste to fling herself into the newcomer's arms and pelt her with questions.

That would be Lady Eleanor, Tilly guessed, the niece Miss Dencey had brought up, the one she was so fond of. She watched with great interest as the two ladies embraced, seeing a distinct resemblance between them: both were tall, with lovely hair of exactly the same shade, though Miss Dencey's was more stylishly cut.

When the younger woman gestured towards the stairs, Miss Dencey shook her head. They younger one pulled a face then they went off in the other direction together. Miss Dencey didn't want to be alone with her niece yet, in Tilly's opinion.

An older woman in rustling black, with a massive key chain at her waist came round the corner just then and made straight for the newcomer.

"I'm Mrs Inchby, the housekeeper."

"Yes, Ma'am."

"You're Miss Beatrice's new maid, I believe? Tilly, isn't it?"

"Yes, Mrs Inchby. I'm Tilly Hulls and I used to work for Lady Ostdene before Miss Dencey took me on." She knew that housekeepers preferred staff who had been with the family for a while. In some country houses, only relatives of staff or offspring of tenants of the estate could get jobs at all.

The housekeeper's expression relaxed slightly. "Our Miss Johanna, as we still think of her. Is she keeping well?"

"Oh, yes, Mrs Inchby, very well."

"And how long did you work for her?"

"Since I was fourteen, Ma'am. Eight years. I started off as a junior housemaid, but her ladyship's maid, Sarah, has been training me up for a lady's maid and now I'm to work for Miss Dencey."

"We call her Miss Beatrice here."

"Yes, Mrs Inchby. I'll remember that."

"Well, you seem to know your manners. Are you good at your trade, Tilly?"

She hesitated, then decided the truth would be safer. "I'm still learning it, Mrs Inchby, but Miss Den— Miss Beatrice, I mean, seems pleased with my work and I'll do my best not to let anyone down, I'm sure."

Mrs Inchby nodded again. She'd already guessed that the girl wasn't a properly-trained lady's maid. She was too cheerful and honest. Experienced lady's maids often had an exaggerated notion of their own worth, which was probably why Miss Beatrice had chosen this one, because likely she just wanted someone cheerful and pleasant to look after her clothes, as one of the young maids had done before she left.

"Well, Tilly, I'll take you up to your mistress's rooms now and you can unpack her things while I'm having a bedroom prepared for you. We're well housed and fed here. The family looks after its own, so see you serve them well in return. And if you have any problems or questions, come to me with them."

Tilly followed Mrs Inchby upstairs, very impressed by the size of Satherby, but amazed at how old its furnishings were. You'd think they could afford new curtains and some more modern furniture than these dark old things! As for the suits of armour, they fair gave her the creeps, for they looked ready to leap out at you. And it wasn't very nice to stick swords and spears all over the walls, was it? Plain unfriendly, if you asked her.

–

Downstairs, Beatrice was endeavouring to answer the questions her aunt threw at her. She thought she was doing quite well, but after a while, Lady Marguerite dismissed Eleanor.

"Now, give me a round tale, Beatrice. Why have you returned so unexpectedly? Has something happened? Have you received an offer?"

"No. I just – I was homesick, Aunt Marguerite, and – and I think I've completed your commission with regard to Eleanor, though I haven't f-found a husband for myself – and well, I wanted to come home." She had to gulp back a sob, she felt so desolate still.

"Hmmph! What about the chit, then? Whom have you decided upon?"

Her aunt's fragile appearance only emphasized that Beatrice had made the right decision, but even so, she had to force the words out. "I thought – Mr Serle. He is superior in every way to the other gentlemen I met."

"Aha! I thought he would be! Good stock, the Serles, except for that worthless cousin of his, and *he* must take after his mother's side! Pity young Peter Serle got himself killed at Waterloo. Why they didn't execute that murderer, Bonaparte, when he started all the fighting up again, instead of sending him to live in comfort on another of those islands, I'll never know. He'll find some way of escaping again, you mark my words!" She sat back and looked smugly at her niece. "Anyway, I've already invited him down for a visit."

"Who?" Beatrice was still thinking of Bonaparte.

"Serle, of course!"

Beatrice felt the blood drain from her face and the room wavered round her, so that she had to clutch the arm of her chair. But her aunt's eyesight wasn't good and the old lady didn't seem to notice anything amiss.

"I didn't want to wait any longer and you were shilly-shallying about, so I took matters into my own hands. Serle should receive the invitation today. I sent one of the grooms across country with it. I don't trust those mails. Never have. I knew Serle's grandmother quite well, you know, because we came out together, but she didn't make old bones, poor Elizabeth. Knew her son, too, Serle's father. And his mother. I should have just trusted in his breeding in the first place and sent for him."

Beatrice swallowed hard and forced some words out, "Well, then, we shall – shall have to s-see whether he accepts your invitation or not." But she prayed fervently he would not. She couldn't imagine how she would ever face him again without giving herself away.

A smile flickered over the Dowager's face. "Oh, I think he'll come! But I won't tell him why he's been invited until he's met Eleanor and I've had time to look him over myself." She frowned. "But what about you? Why haven't you got yourself engaged? Wasn't the dowry large enough?"

Beatrice blushed bright scarlet. "It was *more* than enough! Far too much for me! They – some of the men I met, that is – were only interested in the money. I just didn't, I—" She fumbled to a halt for a moment, then managed to find the strength to say bluntly, "Aunt, I tried, I really did, but you know I never liked the idea of your buying me a husband. It makes me feel very uncomfortable. And besides, I think I'd prefer to remain single."

"Hmm. We'll see about that. But not now. You look tired, girl. That's what London does to you. Too many late nights and too much racketing around. I must say you're well turned out, though. That colour suits you. Trust Johanna for that. She has an excellent eye for style and colour." She waved one hand dismissively. "Anyway, we'll discuss your future another time."

Beatrice managed to mutter some platitude.

Almost as an afterthought, the Dowager asked, "Oh, before I forget, how's that younger daughter of Johanna's? Breeding, ain't she?"

"Yes. And the doctor told them just before I left that she was probably expecting twins."

"Twins, eh? Good girl! That's doing your duty with a vengeance." She chuckled at the thought. "Of course, twins run in the Graceover family. And in the Denceys, too."

"Good heavens!" said Beatrice faintly. "On both sides?"

"Oh, yes. Good stock, you see. Mind, twins do give you a bit more trouble and they're harder to rear. I had twin brothers myself." Her expression became sad for a moment, then she sniffed and banished those memories. "Well, as it turns out, I'm not displeased that you've come home. I was going to send for you anyway. I should have known better than to expect you to manage things for me, though I'm sure you did your best. You're too gentle for your own good, Beatrice, and always have been. Like your father. Never could stand up for himself, poor Warren. And you're exactly the same." It didn't seem to occur to her that she flew into tantrums with people who did try to stand up to her.

Beatrice bit her lip, but said nothing.

"So," continued the Dowager with great cheerfulness, "I've decided to take a hand in things myself."

Beatrice closed her eyes and prayed for patience. Whatever her ladyship said or did, she didn't intend to marry a man whom she didn't respect, just because her aunt had arranged it. Or one she didn't love, a voice whispered in her head, but she refused to listen to that. Love was out of her reach now.

"I've got myself a maid at last," she announced, trying to divert her aunt's attention from the subject of husbands.

The Dowager allowed herself to be diverted and listened to the story of Tilly's trial and appointment, approving the idea of a lady's maid in principle, but reserving judgment until she'd met the girl. She then allowed Beatrice to guide the conversation toward clothes and listened with an appearance of interest to a description of the ravishing ensembles Odette had designed for her, not to mention the elaborate court dress and its accompanying feathers. "…though I'm afraid Odette was very expensive," Beatrice wound up apologetically.

Lady Marguerite dismissed that with a wave of her hand. "Persons such as ourselves must dress to suit our station in life and to set an example to others."

"I think," said Beatrice, when she had run out of clothes and bonnets to describe, "I'd like to go and change my clothes now, Aunt Marguerite. Travelling always makes one feel so grubby."

"Yes, you do that, girl!" The Dowager watched her go, still with that affable smile on her face, but it faded once the door had closed behind her niece.

"I should have known that she was too shy to look after her own interests," she said aloud when she was alone. "Well, I still have a few surprises up my sleeve, Miss, as you'll shortly find out. Lippings, bring me my writing materials and tell them I need another groom to deliver a message."

–

To her dismay, Beatrice found Eleanor in her bedroom, getting acquainted with Tilly and examining the new clothes.

"I hope you don't mind, Bea. I couldn't wait to see your London things!"

"Of course I don't mind. Thank you, Tilly. You may leave us for a while."

Eleanor started fiddling with a pair of gloves. "Was Grandmamma pleased with what you did in London, Bea?"

"What do you know about that?" Her voice came out more sharply than she'd intended.

Eleanor opened her eyes very wide. "Nothing much, Bea, just that Grandmamma wished you to undertake some commissions for her in London, did she not?"

Beatrice forced herself to stay calm. She was seeing problems where there were none, she told herself firmly. "Well, I think I did what she wished, more or less, anyway. Though she really wanted me to find myself a husband."

"I thought so. And was there no one you liked?"

"Not enough. Anyway, I doubt I'm the marrying kind." Beatrice was pleased that she had managed to speak lightly. "How do you like my new clothes?"

Like the Dowager, Eleanor allowed herself to be diverted from the dangerous topic, but she, too, had noticed that Bea had avoided answering her question directly. She had also noticed how sad her aunt was looking. "I adore them! Before I'm very much older, I intend to go up to London myself and have some clothes made for me by a fashionable modiste. These are ravishing! I like the apricot one best. It's such a pretty colour."

Beatrice fingered it wistfully. That was what she had been wearing the first time she'd really talked to Serle, the day Boris came up to town to confront his wife. She'd always liked the gown, but didn't think she could face wearing it again for it would stir up all her memories of *him*. She tried to smile. "Yes. It used to be my favourite, but I've worn it too often, I feel. And what do you think of Tilly?"

"She seems nice enough. I'm going to introduce her to my Betty when she gets back from the village. They're bound to become great friends, just as we are. Why, I dare say they'll tell each other all their secrets – just as we do."

Beatrice looked at her with narrowed eyes and Eleanor smiled with such an innocent expression that she at once became suspicious. However, she didn't wish to probe any subject deeply just now, so she continued to show off the new garments and bonnets, and talk about London parties until it was time to get changed for dinner.

She didn't allow herself to think of Justin Serle coming to Satherby. Well, not much. That prospect was too difficult to face at the moment. And anyway, surely he would refuse? Yes, of course he would. She was counting on that.

—

During dinner, Eleanor asked casually, "What's Mr Serle like, Bea?"

Beatrice choked on her fish and it was a moment before she could respond. "Why do you ask?" She saw that Eleanor was wearing her most guileless expression, which definitely meant she was up to something.

"Well, you've invited him down to stay, haven't you, Grandmamma?" Eleanor turned to the Dowager again, "And I knew you'd met him in London, Bea."

Beatrice had regained control of her emotions, if not of her colour. "Yes, I have met him once or twice. He's about thirty. Elegantly dressed, but not — not a dandy. Tall, dark, not handsome exactly, but very," she sighed and gazed into the distance, "very distinguished looking." After a pause, she added without thinking, "And he's a marvellous dancer. The easiest person I've ever danced with, I think."

Eleanor said nothing, but did not fail to notice every nuance of that description. Or the sighs that accompanied it.

"Is he a man of sense, though?" demanded the Dowager, who had also been listening carefully. "Does he know what's due to his position in society?"

"Oh, yes. He's very – very—" Beatrice wanted to say autocratic, but thought this would not appeal to Eleanor. "Yes, he does," she finished lamely.

The Dowager nodded, only partly satisfied, but diverted by the reference to dancing. "I like a man who can show a neat leg. Your grandfather was an excellent dancer, Eleanor, as I was myself in my younger days." She looked down at her twisted hands and sighed briefly.

Beatrice's heart was wrung for her. Her aunt never complained, but was obviously in a lot of pain. She *must not* let the old lady down.

Eleanor kept her own counsel about certain suspicions that were beginning to form in her mind about Bea. She would see what she could get out of Tilly. She rather prided herself on her ability to elicit information from people without their realizing it. Finding out would keep her mind from her own problems.

She was missing Crispin quite dreadfully, though he'd only been gone a few days. However, she'd already received a letter from him, sent via Anders, and that had cheered her up greatly. Her first love letter! She knew it by heart already. And it was much more satisfying than the flowery language used in novels, for it talked of real things and of their future together. As well as his love for her. Tears of joy had come into her eyes when she first read it.

Whatever it took they were going to spend the future together, she vowed. She and Crispin would find some way to win her grandmother's consent to their marriage.

The next morning, the Dowager joined them for breakfast, which showed she was in fine fettle, for she rarely left her own suite before eleven o'clock. She uttered a crow of triumph as she opened her mail. "I thought he'd come round!" she exclaimed gleefully.

Her two young relatives looked at her questioningly.

"That Herforth fellow. The one with the silly name. Crispin. The heir. You know the one I mean!"

"Yes, Grandmamma." Eleanor kept her eyes down and started to butter a piece of toast. "I remember you mentioned him."

"I wrote to him while you were away, Bea, inviting him to come here for a visit and learn about the estate, and do you know, the fellow had the impudence to turn the invitation down! Well, he's come to his senses now. See!" She read from her letter. "*Conscious of the honour of your invitation… regret that I was unable to accept immediately, but have now arranged matters to be taken care of in my absence… quite see the necessity for getting to know Satherby… happy to be with you as soon as I receive word*".

"That's a bit more like it! He shows some proper feelings, at least."

"And shall you send him word to come, Grandmamma?"

"Of course! He can come next week. We'll make up a house party. Serle won't refuse me, and the Smeathleys are going to be staying here as well."

Beatrice and Eleanor exchanged puzzled glances. Who were the Smeathleys? Lady Marguerite rarely invited people to stay. She had been declaring for years that she was too old for house parties. Who wanted to face strangers over breakfast? she always said scornfully. Who wanted to spend all day entertaining people who would be better off staying at home and keeping their own houses in order?

"Who are the Smeathleys, Grandmamma?" Eleanor thought it best to change the topic, afraid she might betray how happy the news of Crispin's coming visit had made her if she tried to speak of him.

"What? Oh, yes. Better tell you about 'em. They're connections by marriage, relatives of your Uncle Alfred – the one who died so young. Pity I ever allowed him to marry my poor Harriet, but there you are. How was I to know he'd get himself killed without producing an heir? No use crying over spilt milk. *She* didn't live very long, either. Nice girl, my Harriet, but she was never strong. She was a bit like you, Bea, not one to look after her own best interests. Good thing she had me to sort her life out. Good thing you've got me, too! I can still hold my team together and don't you think otherwise!"

She was obviously in high spirits and was just as obviously plotting something. "The Smeathleys," she went on with a smug smile, "are a church family. It was Johanna who put it into my mind that a cleric might be just the thing for Beatrice here. She likes looking after the poor, helping the sick, all that sort of thing. Might as well do it to some purpose."

Beatrice stared at her in horror.

"The Smeathleys have a son," the Dowager continued. "He's turned thirty now. Good age for an ambitious cleric to marry. And this one's ambitious. They've got some hopes he'll end up with a bishopric. He's apparently well

185

regarded. So I told them to bring him down here to meet Bea."

Beatrice, who had been growing steadily paler, could keep quiet no longer. "Aunt! I told you I have no wish – none at all! – to marry. I'm too set in my ways. And – and I'm happy here."

"Well, you won't be able to stay on here after I'm gone, will you, so you'd better make up your mind to give this fellow a serious looking over. I won't force you to marry him if he turns out to be a nick-ninny or a mealy-mouthed Bible-spouter, but you owe it to me to look him over, at least." She paused, stared at her niece and added quietly, "Don't you think?"

Recalling the way the Dowager had once begged for her help and how she'd let her down, Beatrice could only swallow and nod miserably. "I'll be happy to – to meet him," she said in a low voice. "But don't expect too much of me. *Please.*"

"We'll look him over together," her aunt said sooth-ingly.

Eleanor intervened to keep the Dowager's attention away from poor Bea, who was looking terrible and who was definitely hiding some guilty secret. "Grandmamma, if the Smeathleys are coming here so that Bea can look their son over, why is Mr Serle coming?" she asked, judging her time to a nicety.

Lady Marguerite choked over her cup of tea and had to have her back patted before she could respond. She fixed a stern gaze upon her granddaughter. "Hmm. I suppose you'll have to be told some time. Sit up straight and pay attention."

Eleanor did as she was told.

The Dowager chewed her lip for a moment, then said, "Well, Eleanor, I'm thinking of finding you a husband as well – a good match, mind. Someone worthy of a Graceover. You're the right age for marriage. That's why Bea went up to London, to look over some of the eligibles. As I'd expected, she thought Serle the most promising. Good family, that! I'd also hoped she'd find a husband for herself while she was at it; I settled a decent dowry on her, least I could do, and Johanna says that there was some interest, but it seems no one *caught her fancy*."

The last was said with heavy sarcasm and a look which made Beatrice feel as if her aunt were heaping coals of fire upon her head. She could only stare down at her plate and long for the meal to end.

Eleanor clapped her hands, still intent on diverting attention from her poor aunt. "What fun! You'll have to tell me everything you can remember about Mr Serle, Bea! Every little detail. I shouldn't at all object to being married, Grandmamma, as long as he isn't ugly, or too old, or unkind."

She sat back with the air of one willing to oblige and she remained in a highly cheerful mood until the meal ended. If her grandmother believed it was time for her to marry, that was one hurdle got over. The fact that it was Crispin she intended to marry need not be mentioned as yet.

Watching her aunt surreptitiously, Eleanor decided poor Bea needed some time alone, so she talked about the beautiful display of lily-of-the-valley in the South Wood, not to mention the fritillaries along the water meadows, until Beatrice said she thought she would go for a stroll and look at them. "And I hope you don't mind, Eleanor," she ended, "but I'd like to be alone for a while. I did nothing but meet people while I was away, and – and quite frankly, I'd welcome the chance for some peace and quiet."

"Oh, you go, Bea. I don't mind at all. I've got a new piano piece to practise." Eleanor turned to leave, then swung back again. "But would you mind if Betty and I asked Tilly to show us all your new clothes again first, so that we can study the latest fashions? I shall want to look my best for Mr Serle, shan't I?"

"Do what you like!" Beatrice fled for the woods, horrified at the jealousy which had seared through her at Eleanor's innocent words. She couldn't think how she'd face him and her only hope was that he would refuse the invitation and stay well away from Satherby.

Surely he would?

Chapter 11

The day after his abortive attempt to propose to Beatrice, Justin went to Lymsby to see how she was recovering. He'd decided that if things didn't go well with his attempt to propose this time, he'd confide in Lady Ostdene and ask for her help. He didn't come to this conclusion without considerable thought, for he disliked betraying his vulnerability to anyone.

Beatrice was not indifferent to him! Surely he couldn't be mistaken in that? The way she reacted to him. The way she felt in his arms. The way their bodies moulded together when they were waltzing. But he couldn't understand why she'd become so agitated when he tried to press his suit.

He remembered the way they'd sat and laughed together in the icy water of the pond and his confidence rose. Then he recalled the way she'd avoided his eyes the previous day, changing the subject and generally rendering it impossible for him to declare himself, and his confidence sank again.

At Lymsby he handed his horse to a groom and walked up the steps to the front door, feeling nervous. Inside, he was shown into a salon and left to wait. Several minutes dragged by and he began to prowl around the room.

It wasn't like the Newthorpes to keep a visitor waiting. Perhaps something was wrong?

When Lady Ostdene came in at last, looking worried, Justin's heart lurched. "Is Miss Dencey all right?" he asked before he could prevent himself.

Johanna looked surprised at the abruptness of this greeting. "It's kind of you to call, Serle, but I'm afraid you find us at sixes and sevens today."

"Miss Dencey?" he prompted, his voice harsh with anxiety. "She hasn't taken a chill, has she?"

"Bea? Oh, didn't she tell you? She left this morning. She decided to go back to Satherby, said she was homesick."

"*What?*"

Anger had made his voice over-loud, and Johanna blinked and stared at him, jerked out of her own worries. "Is something wrong, Serle?"

"I came to see Miss Dencey," he said stiffly. "I expected... she *knew* I was coming and she made no mention of any plans to leave."

"Her decision was rather sudden," Johanna agreed, studying him closely.

"She's taken no hurt from her drenching, though?"

"Oh, no. Bea's never ill. She has the most robust health of anyone I know, and Eleanor is much the same. My mother ascribes it to the excellence of Satherby's air and general situation."

"I'm glad to hear that." He began to fiddle with the braid on the arm of the chair on which he was sitting, wondering what to say or do next.

Johanna's attention was now fully engaged. "I think you'd better tell me about it," she said softly. "I've never seen you like this before, Serle."

He smiled at her ruefully and gave in to the temptation to confide in someone. "I've never felt like this before, Lady Ostdene."

"Like what?" She held her breath and watched indecision and worry flit across his face. She was glad to see that he'd lost that cool detached look he'd worn for so long. "It often helps to talk to someone," she coaxed, "and you've known me long enough to trust me, surely? I'm almost like an honorary aunt by now."

"I don't quite know how to start," he confessed, staring down at his hands, unable to face her.

When he didn't continue, she asked quietly, "It's Beatrice, isn't it?"

"Yes." He stood up and went to stare out of the window, tossing the words over his shoulder at her in short bursts. "I've come to love her. I thought, no, I was *sure* she felt the same. But yesterday when I tried to speak, to ask her to marry me, well, she prevented me. She looked so upset I couldn't press the point. And yet," he fumbled in his pocket and threw down a crumpled piece of paper, "that came this morning. And well – I don't know what to think now."

Johanna read her mother's invitation to stay at Satherby. "Aaah,"

"What do you mean by 'Aaah'?" he asked irritably. "If Beatrice has no feeling for me, as she implies, why am I being invited to stay at Satherby?"

"I doubt Beatrice knew about this invitation. It's from my mother. She sometimes takes the bit between her teeth. She can be a very determined woman."

"So can your cousin Beatrice!"

"We're not a family of ditherers," she agreed smugly. "Well, not usually."

She was trying to make up her mind as to how frank she dared be with him when the door crashed open and Boris strode in.

He didn't notice Justin, and even if he had, would have paid him no attention. "You'll have to come and talk to her, Mother-in-law!" he announced loudly. "She's determined to get up and *I will not have it!*"

"Boris, dear, go away!"

"She has no right to— What did you say?"

"I told you to go away. Serle and I are discussing something important and private."

A shriek of anger from upstairs made Boris growl under his breath and stalk out of the room again, banging the door behind him.

Johanna ran her fingers through her hair distractedly, quite ruining Sarah's expert handiwork, a thing she would never normally have dared do, then turned to Justin. "Look, I can't talk now, everything is in chaos here today. Jennice isn't at all herself. Could you possibly come back tomorrow? I'll have time by then for a long talk with you. I can't deal with anything else at the moment, not until I've sorted Jennice and Boris out. He's being unreasonably protective and she's throwing hysterics at regular intervals."

He gave a grunt of frustration and stood up to leave.

Johanna went over and laid one hand on his shoulder, gazing earnestly into his eyes. "It's not as bad as it seems,

Serle. I, too, am sure Beatrice isn't indifferent to you." There was a loud burst of sobbing from upstairs and she closed her eyes in despair. "I don't know what's got into that daughter of mine. She's done nothing but scream and weep today. Would you, could you possibly lend us Mrs. Powis for a few days? I'm beginning to think she's the only one who can talk sense into those two idiots upstairs."

He hid his disappointment. "Of course. I'll ask her to come across immediately." There was nothing for him to do, but bow gracefully and leave.

He rode home slowly and thoughtfully, but as he approached his home, he couldn't resist the temptation to turn aside and visit the pool in the woods. There, he sat on the rock for nearly an hour, thinking hard, before coming to some conclusions of his own.

—

"Ha!" said the Dowager triumphantly over breakfast the next day. "He's coming. Told you he would."

"Who's coming, Grandmamma?" asked Eleanor, suspending her enthusiastic demolition of a juicy piece of ham and some coddled eggs.

"Serle."

Beatrice, at the other side of the table, tried to continue eating as if nothing special had been said, but her cheeks turned first red, then white, and the stricken expression which passed fleetingly across her face betrayed her.

Only Eleanor noticed, however, the Dowager still being engaged in gloating over her triumph. "When is he coming, Grandmamma?"

"In two days."

Beatrice dropped her fork with a clatter.

The Dowager frowned at her. "It ain't like you to be so clumsy, girl! Are you feeling all right? We can't have you going down with something when there are guests to be entertained."

"I'm sorry, Aunt Marguerite. I was just, um, just thinking about something and didn't watch what I was doing."

"Well, be careful what you're thinking about over the next few days! You won't be able to breathe without someone watching you once they arrive! House parties are tedious beyond belief and *I* am far too old to manage things, so it'll be up to you two to keep the guests entertained."

She looked round the oak-panelled room and nodded in satisfaction at its appearance. "I shall go back to breakfasting in my rooms while they're here, I think. I never could face people on an empty stomach."

Eleanor saw that Bea was still struggling to appear normal, so stepped in quickly. "Very well, Grandmamma. We'll look after the guests for you."

"You'd better arrange a few picnics and dinners and invite the neighbours, too. Those worth inviting, that is! I won't have curates and farmers at Satherby, whatever the occasion. You can start making your plans today. I've told Mrs. Inchby to get the rooms ready and she can confer with cook about what to feed 'em, but you'd better keep an eye on what she's doing as well, Beatrice. She hasn't had a house full of visitors to look after for years."

She chewed a piece of ham thoughtfully, then waved her fork at her niece. "Not that I don't trust Mrs. Inchby – she's a good housekeeper and knows her job – but we don't want anything going wrong, do we?" She put her fork down, pushed her plate away and rang the bell. "I'll leave it to you to oversee the preparations, Beatrice."

She waved a hand to signify that the footman should start pushing the wheeled chair she was moved around in.

Beatrice sat and watched her aunt leave, too upset to hide her feelings. Closing her eyes for a moment, she tried desperately to think what to do, but her mind seemed utterly blank. All she could think of was his name. Serle. Serle was coming. *Serle!* And she didn't know how she was going to face him.

"What's wrong, love?" Eleanor asked softly.

"Wrong? Nothing!" Beatrice caught the other girl's eye and realized that she couldn't hope to keep up this pretence with someone who knew her as well as Eleanor did, so added hastily, "Well, I do have just a bit of a headache, but it's nothing."

"Perhaps you're starting the influenza?"

"I wouldn't dare!" Beatrice managed a wry smile. "No, I just – well, to tell you the truth, Eleanor, I don't wish to get married. And certainly not to a stranger who wouldn't look at me twice if I had no money. I wish Aunt Marguerite hadn't invited these Smeathleys to visit us." She paused for a moment, then offered a distraction, "Did I tell you that your grandmother has settled twenty thousand pounds on me as a dowry."

Eleanor clapped her hands. "Why, that's marvellous! And you've certainly earned it! Think of the way you've looked after her all these years. And after me, too." She went over to hug her young aunt, who had been looking very down in the mouth since her return from London.

"It's too much," Beatrice protested.

"Nonsense! Don't you think that a woman should bring something of her own to a marriage? I do."

"But that's the whole point!" Beatrice cried. "I don't want to get married!"

Eleanor stared at her, head on one side. "What's made you change your mind? You always said you'd love to get married when we talked about it. And you said you'd like to have several children too. We even used to draw up lists of names for them. I think you'd make a *splendid* mother, Bea. Just see how well you've done with me!"

There was no response to her little joke, not even the curve of a lip in a token smile, and she frowned again as she stared across the table. Bea must be feeling really bad. Whatever had happened to her in London?

Beatrice spoke emphatically, articulating every word with the utmost care. "I don't want to marry someone who's only interested in my money and breeding capacity, Eleanor! That's all those gentlemen in London cared about and that's all this Smeathley person is coming here for! If he's an ambitious cleric, he wouldn't even consider a wife who brought him nothing. And I won't be sold like that! *I won't!*" She stormed out of the room, something she had never done before.

Left alone with the remains of her ham, Eleanor shook her head. "There's definitely someone in London she's interested in," she murmured. "She wouldn't get so upset if it were just a question of finding herself a husband. I think she's already found him, only something's stopping them getting married."

She waved the fork to and fro trying to work it out, the food forgotten. "She gets very agitated whenever Grandmamma talks of the house party, yet she's never even met the Smeathleys, or my Crispin, so that only leaves Mr Serle. Mmm. I must definitely speak to Tilly."

After checking that Beatrice was out of the way conferring with the housekeeper, Eleanor went to look for the maid. Under the pretence of studying one of the London dresses again, she managed to elicit a considerable amount of information from the maid about Bea and Mr Serle, including the involuntary dunking in the pond, which Beatrice had somehow quite failed to mention.

Without realizing what she was doing, Tilly also revealed the fact that Mr Serle had upset her mistress greatly just before they left Lymsby.

Humming to herself, Eleanor then went away to have a serious think about that and her own situation, which was not going to be easy to resolve, either. Her grandmother hadn't even thought of Crispin as a possible husband for her, presumably because she didn't approve of that branch of the family. It was Serle whom Eleanor was supposed to marry, while Mr Smeathley was clearly destined for Bea.

If Eleanor were to carry out her plan to make the Dowager accept her marrying Crispin, she would have to pretend to be attracted to someone unsuitable first. But who? There was only Mr Smeathley and how on earth was she to persuade anyone who knew her that she'd fallen in love with a middle-aged cleric of turned thirty? Her grandmother and aunt were certainly not stupid enough to believe any such thing!

She did not, however, allow herself to become downhearted about this dilemma. Problems were there to be solved. There was always a way through them if you looked hard enough, and she knew herself to be a very enterprising person, not to mention being utterly determined to marry the man she loved.

–

Three days later, the household was on tenterhooks and the Dowager was alternating between extreme satisfaction at her own cleverness and querulousness at the thought of her privacy being invaded and her infirmities paraded before strangers.

In the afternoon on which the guests were due to arrive, she summoned her niece and granddaughter to attend her and sat bolt upright in her wheeled chair in the Chinese Salon, waiting for the guests to arrive.

When Crispin Herforth was shown in, the Dowager said "Hmph!" quite audibly and her expression as she studied him didn't seem to Eleanor to augur well.

"How kind of you to invite me here, your ladyship," he said, bowing over her hand.

She allowed him to touch the hand briefly, then repeated, "Hmph!" in a disapproving tone.

He remained where he was, a slight smile on his lips, quietly confident of himself. Eleanor, watching him, thought how attractive he was looking, with his neat country clothes and his blue eyes set so steadily and fearlessly upon the Dowager. Her heart swelled with pride. He wasn't afraid of anyone, her Crispin! After a moment or two, she lowered her eyes again in case her expression betrayed her. You couldn't be too careful with Grandmamma.

"You don't take after the Graceovers!" declared the Dowager, still eyeing the newcomer. "One would think you'd show *some* sign of the blood. We *never* have blond hair!"

"I believe I take after my mother's family in looks, your ladyship."

"Pity! Still, there's nothing we can do about that now."

He managed not to smile. "No, your ladyship."

The stick rapped the floor for emphasis. "I can't have you saying "your ladyship" every other minute like that, because you *are* one of the family, whether we like it or not. So you'd better call me Aunt Marguerite from now on, though I'm not your aunt, just some sort of second cousin. Still, Aunt's more respectful to a woman of my age."

"I shall be honoured, Aunt Marguerite."

"Hmph! That's as may be. Now – this is my niece, Beatrice Dencey, my brother's daughter. And this is my granddaughter, Eleanor. It'll be best if you address them both as cousins."

He gravely shook the hands of the two younger ladies, one of whom gave him a roguish wink.

The stick was rapped again, but not in anger. "We need to plan what to do with you. You'd better sit down first. I'm getting a crick in my neck looking up at you, for all you don't carry the Graceover inches. I don't think one of *my* menfolk was under six feet tall." She shook her head sadly.

"I'm very sorry to disappoint you, Aunt Marguerite."

"No use crying over spilt milk. You're the heir now, and that's that! At least you don't dress like a coxcomb. The bailiff will explain to you how the estate is run; I've told him to expect you tomorrow in the estate office. It's in the stable block. Eleanor or Beatrice can show you round the house when they have time."

Another moment's thought and she added, "We're expecting other guests, so there are bound to be plenty of riding parties in the district. You might as well go out with them, because it'll help you get to know the estate. You'll join the rest of us for meals and in the evenings, of course, but you'll be busy with the bailiff during the day, otherwise. At least, you will if you do your duty." She sounded rather dubious about this.

He inclined his head. "I shall be happy to get acquainted with Satherby, Aunt Marguerite. And it may comfort you to know that I'm quite used to managing an estate already, for I've been doing it since I was sixteen, though not one as big as Satherby, of course."

She stared at him suspiciously. "But your father only died last year!"

"He'd left the management of things to me for several years before that. He infinitely preferred his books. He was quite a noted medieval scholar, actually, something of an authority on the Code of Chivalry."

"He was always burying his head in his books when he was a lad, too. I was surprised he bothered to marry at all. And what good are Latin and Greek to a landowner? I'll tell you what good – none! Do you think Satherby would be in such good heart if my John had sat in the library reading old books and spouting Latin? No, it wouldn't!" She spluttered to a halt and stared at him, sighing that he should look so healthy while her own sons were long dead.

When she spoke again, it was more moderately. "Well, your father's dead now, and you seem to have more idea of your duty than he did, at least, so I'll not say any more about it."

"It isn't duty," he said simply, "but love of the land."

This time the look she cast him was more friendly. "Well, young man, we'll have to wait and see whether you can feel the same way about Satherby." She remembered a further point of grievance and glowered at him abruptly. "But with a name like Crispin, you never can tell. What on earth got into your father to call you that?"

He couldn't repress a quick smile. The old lady was just as rude as his father had always said, but Crispin rather liked her spirit. Most women of her age did little but sit and gossip, or hug their fires. She was still doing her duty, even though she was confined to a wheeled chair and twisted with arthritis. Besides, she was the grandmother of his darling, so he owed her a great deal of respect and tolerance, for Eleanor's sake. "It was my mother's choice of name, I believe. I dare say you'll grow used to it."

Feeling it would be better to change the subject, he gazed around him with appreciation. "This is a lovely room."

The Dowager nodded, accepting this tribute as natural, rather than taking it for flattery. "M'father-in-law did it. It was all the vogue in his day. I haven't cared to change it and hope you won't, either. People should treasure their inheritance."

"I wouldn't think of changing it. That's the most beautiful Chinese carpet I've ever seen. Their colours and designs are always so restful, don't you think? And this is a superb example of lacquer work." He moved over to a cabinet and began to stroke it with knowing fingers. "My own great-grandmother was rather taken by the Chinese vogue and I was able to preserve her belongings, though my aunt wished to throw them out when my mother died. I have them carefully stored in the attic at home. There's a cabinet which is almost the twin of this one, but smaller. It would look well in that corner."

The Dowager blinked. She had thought of training him to preserve Satherby and its treasures, but had never even considered the possibility that he might be able to add to them.

"I'd be very grateful if someone would spare the time to show me round the house, whenever it's convenient," Crispin continued, not looking at Eleanor. "I've heard a lot about it from my father. I believe that the remains of the old abbey are still standing?"

"Piles of old stones! Should have been cleared away years ago. Watch your step if you go there. It's dangerous and you're the only male left to the family now. How long are you staying here?"

Another of his neat bows. "I'm at your disposal for as long as you wish, Aunt Marguerite."

"We'll have to see, then." She was slightly mollified by his remarks, but wasn't going to show any softening of her attitude toward him until she had got to know him better. She rang the silver bell by her side and a footman answered. "Show Mr Herforth up to his room, if you please, Robert."

She turned back to Crispin. "I've had them prepare the master's suite for you." That decision had cost her a wakeful night, but she'd come to the conclusion that she could do no less than give him the respect due to the heir, even though he wasn't worthy. "It's yours by right, after all. You can go for a walk in the gardens once you've unpacked."

Eleanor watched him leave, then turned to her grandmother, eager to hear what she said about him.

"He can't be more than five feet ten. Pity he's so short. I prefer tall men!" declared her ladyship. "Still, he don't dress like a man-milliner, I'll give him that. And he looks you in the eye, as a gentleman should. I can't abide fellows with shifty eyes. But there's no hint of Graceover in him, none at all. I'm disappointed in that. Your grandfather would have been heartbroken to see the estate pass from the true line."

"Yes, what a pity!" agreed Eleanor. "Why!" she smiled as if the idea had only just occurred to her. "I'm the only one left of the true line now, aren't I?"

The Dowager treated her to a puzzled stare, as if she'd said something strange.

Satisfied that she'd planted a seed, Eleanor asked innocently, "What did you think of him, Bea?"

"He seemed pleasant enough. Good looking in a quiet way, I suppose." She spoke only to fill the silence, but was surprised to receive a beaming smile from Eleanor.

"Well," declared the Dowager, "the fellow talks sense, at any rate. Which is more than his father ever did." For her, that was tantamount to an admission that Mr Herforth had made a favourable first impression upon her.

They continued to sit in state in the salon, awaiting their other guests. Beatrice tried to occupy herself with her embroidery, but the stitches went sadly awry. Eleanor chatted to her grandmother, encouraging the old lady to tell them about her youth, which usually put her in a good humour, but though her ladyship obliged automatically, it was plain that her heart wasn't in her reminiscences today.

They had not long to wait for the next arrival. Beatrice's heart lurched at the sound of wheels on the gravel, and she gripped her embroidery tightly. Was this *him*? She was both longing and dreading to see him again.

"Shall I go and peep through the window to see who it is, Grandmamma?" asked Eleanor, winking at Beatrice.

"Certainly not! A lady never peeps through windows! A lady maintains a calm decorum at all times."

But it was to be seen that the Dowager's own mouth was tense and her hand was fidgeting on the silver handle of her cane.

After a while, the door opened and the butler appeared. "Mr and Mrs. Smeathley, your Ladyship, and Mr Augustus Smeathley."

The Dowager's face briefly registered disappointment then became calm again.

The trio who entered were rather a surprise to everyone. All three were very tall and stately, with dark hair and pale complexions. They moved like a matched set of carriage horses. The two older Smeathleys showed a certain embonpoint and the darkness of their hair was touched with silver, but this in no way detracted from their massive dignity or from their startling resemblance to each other.

As for the son, he was not only tall, but handsome, though in a restrained sort of way. His face had the clearly-etched profile and alabaster complexion of a Greek statue, his dark hair curled immaculately across his brow and his movements were graceful and studied. He looked like a man who expected life to serve him with many favours and who had not yet been disappointed.

Beatrice's heart sank at the sight of him.

Eleanor, on the other hand, brightened visibly as the full glory of Augustus Smeathley burst upon them. What a piece of luck! He was so handsome she could pretend to have fallen in love with him on sight, in spite of his advanced age. She waited for the trio to salute the Dowager, which they did with the air of imperial ambassadors greeting a minor king, and continued to observe them carefully as they were presented to Beatrice.

She noticed that Augustus Smeathley studied her aunt very shrewdly indeed as he took her hand. That man has come here to see if he can get a bargain for himself, she thought. He wouldn't do for Bea, even if she didn't love someone else. She studied his calculating expression again. She didn't like him very much, however handsome he was. There was something *oily* about him.

As he turned from Beatrice and took Eleanor's hand, however, she allowed her eyelids to flutter and gazed up at him with a dazed expression on her face, as if she were quite stunned by his magnificence. He bowed over her hand and for a few seconds the calculating expression showed itself again, to be quickly wiped away and replaced by a smile. "My *dear* Cousin Eleanor, how *very* delighted I am to meet you!" he said, in a caressing, mellifluous voice.

You, sir, are a calculating hypocrite, she thought to herself, as she fluttered her eyelashes at him. I shall have no qualms about deceiving you.

"Oh, I'm delighted to meet you too, Mr Smeathley," she whispered shyly, making her voice soft and silly like that of Caroline Bunnington, who lived down the road and became quite idiotish at the mere sight of an eligible male. "I've heard so-o-o much about you!"

It was very hard to keep her face straight as she said this, but by dint of thinking of Crispin and imagining she was addressing him instead, she managed it.

Mr Smeathley patted her hand, which he still retained in his own. "And I've heard a lot about you, too, my dear Cousin Eleanor."

The Dowager harrumphed loudly.

He at once relinquished the hand and turned to give Lady Marguerite his very best attention.

When he stole another glance sideways, Eleanor dimpled at him and was pleased to see him pause in mid-sentence for a moment, before continuing to speak to the Dowager. Heavens, would he never stop talking? And why was her grandmother looking so pleased, nodding so often? Not many people could have her smiling like that.

When at last the second set of visitors was dispatched to their rooms, Eleanor managed, by means of picturing the time when she would be married to Crispin, to maintain a dreamy expression on her face, which had both the Dowager and Beatrice staring at her and then exchanging puzzled glances.

"What do you think of 'em, Bea?" asked her ladyship. "Good looking, ain't he, young Smeathley?"

"I suppose so, Aunt Marguerite."

"We'll have to see what he's like to get along with, though. First impressions aren't everything, not where husbands are concerned. That voice will sound excellent in a church, but it might be hard to live with. He's born to be a bishop, though, with that voice and face."

"I'd just *love* to hear him preach!" sighed Eleanor.

The Dowager frowned at her and said pointedly. "Bea, you'd better make sure *you* sit next to him at dinner. Start getting to know him. His parents haven't changed a bit. Always were full of their own importance, but they won't give us much trouble as long as we feed 'em well and supply 'em with plenty of newspapers and journals. That side of Alfred's family always was a little dull. Surprised they even managed to produce someone like this Augustus."

The parents might be dull, but the son is a sharp customer and the way he was toad-eating Grandmamma made me feel quite nauseated! thought Eleanor. It's going to be hard to pretend to be in love with him, especially with Crispin in the same house. And I'll have to find a way to get Crispin alone and tell him what I'm doing.

Beatrice was staring down at her lap, wishing desperately that her coming ordeal were over. She kept thinking she heard carriage wheels on the gravel of the drive, then wondering whether it was disappointment or gladness she felt at the thought of seeing Justin Serle once more.

"Did you not hear what I said, Bea?" repeated the Dowager sharply.

Beatrice jumped. "What? Oh, yes, Aunt Marguerite. Sit next to Mr Smeathley at table." She had taken a violent dislike to the man on first sight, for all his polished address, but dared not say so yet. His ordered curls and well-manicured white hands filled her with revulsion and besides, he had lingered over Eleanor's hand, as if she were the one he had been brought there to meet. Perhaps he had other game in view?

But what she simply could not understand was why had Eleanor been looking so soulfully at him. Surely she couldn't have been taken in by a stuffed shirt like him? But then, she had met so very few eligible gentlemen that anything was possible. They knew nothing of how susceptible she was to good-looking gentlemen.

Oh, heavens, this nightmare of a house party was growing worse by the minute!

–

It wasn't until just before the dressing gong rang that the third carriage arrived and by this time, the Dowager was twitching with annoyance and fatigue. "About time, too," she grumbled as the sound of wheels and trotting horses came closer and closer.

When Justin Serle was shown into the Chinese Salon, Beatrice's heart started to thud, in spite of her resolve to remain calm. He was as handsome as ever, and even after a journey, he managed to look supremely elegant. But his expression, when he looked at her, was inscrutable – or was she reading too much into it? What did he think of this visit? Why had he come? How was she to make him realize that it was Eleanor he was there to meet, not her?

He was bowing over her aunt's hand. "I must apologize, your Ladyship, for coming in to greet you without changing my clothes, but your butler insisted on it, since you dine early."

The Dowager took his hand and stared up at him. "You look like just your grandmother," she said in a shaken voice. "I hadn't expected that. Same hair. Same eyes. Elizabeth's smile."

It wasn't often the Dowager allowed her vulnerability to show, and Beatrice's heart went out to her. How terrible it must be to be the last survivor of your generation and to see all your friends and relatives die before you! Well, Aunt Marguerite should not have her dying wishes thwarted, if her niece could help it. Serle was still smiling down at the twisted figure in the wheeled chair. How genuine his smile was compared to Smeathley's!

Beatrice didn't realize that her own expression had become as dreamy as that of her niece when facing Augustus Smeathley, but Eleanor did not miss a single nuance. Fancy Bea feeling like Crispin and I do, she thought in awe. At her age! I hope Mr Serle feels the same way about her.

"I'm honoured that you think I resemble my grand-mother, your Ladyship." Justin's voice was gentle. "I have no recollection of her, unfortunately, but her portrait hangs in our picture gallery and it's always been one of my favourites. She looks as if she smiled a lot."

"She did smile a lot. She did indeed." The Dowager took a deep breath and recollected herself.

"Hrmph. You know my niece already, I believe?"

"Yes, of course I do. We're old acquaintances. Good day, Miss Dencey." He strode over to clasp Bea's hand and felt it shaking in his. As he looked down into her eyes, his own softened involuntarily. "Are we not, Beatrice?" he added softly, so that the Dowager didn't catch the words, which were a caress in themselves.

For a moment, Beatrice forgot herself and smiled back at him, her eyes betraying the love she was trying to deny as clearly as if they had spoken it aloud. "How do you do, Mr Serle?"

"I hope your ankle is better."

"It's quite recovered now, thank you."

Goodness! Just look at them! marvelled Eleanor. Well, I don't need to worry about what to do with Serle. He loves her, too. Bea's being very noble, keeping him for me, so I must find out why, but I'll be better off with my Crispin. What fun this visit is going to be!

Beatrice swallowed hard and forced herself to stand back. "I don't think you've met my niece, Mr Serle. This is Eleanor." Her voice had become cool and impersonal again, as if he were a stranger or a distant acquaintance.

He turned at once to greet the younger lady with a smile.

Smiling back at him, Eleanor decided she would have to get on good terms with him as soon as possible. He might make a very useful ally. After all, there was a lot to arrange and her only hope of success lay in making the Dowager believe that a rearrangement of partners was her own idea. "I'm very pleased to meet you, Mr Serle," she said cheerfully. "I hope you had a comfortable journey here."

"Delightful. This is quite the pleasantest time of year, don't you think, Miss Graceover?"

"Oh yes, very pleasant. The gardens are so pretty one cannot help but enjoy being out of doors." But she could see his eyes stray back to Beatrice, who was deliberately looking the other way. What had got into her aunt? If she loved him, she should be doing all she could to get herself married to him, not throwing him at her niece. Eleanor intended to fight for Crispin tooth and nail. But no – Bea was just the sort to be noble and self-sacrificing about everything.

Well, that wasn't going to be allowed.

The Dowager rapped her cane on the ground. "I bid you welcome to Satherby, Serle, but as it's late, we'll have to pursue our acquaintance over dinner. It's time we all changed. We don't keep town hours here. We dine at six sharp."

"I shan't keep you waiting, your Ladyship. My man will have unpacked my things by now." He followed the footman out, tossing over his shoulder for Beatrice's benefit, "I'm no dandy!"

Beatrice blushed scarlet and deliberately upset her embroidery silks onto the floor to cover her confusion.

"Good looking fellow," said the Dowager before he was out of hearing.

Beatrice saw him cast a laughing glance at her over his shoulder and once again she averted her eyes.

Eleanor observed with approval that Mr Serle had a good sense of humour. "He is very good looking, Grandmamma, but not as good looking as Mr Smeathley, do you think?"

"Smeathley?" The Dowager blinked in surprise. "I suppose the fellow's all right, but he can't compare with a Serle. Don't like the way Smeathley does his hair, either. If those curls are natural, I'll eat my walking stick."

"Oh, I'm sure you're wrong!" declared Eleanor, clasping her hands at her bosom and sighing. She wondered for a moment if she were overdoing things and she had great trouble holding the pose, but had the satisfaction of seeing both ladies staring at her in puzzlement. To her relief, neither said anything.

As she and Beatrice walked up to their rooms, she managed to prattle only of Augustus Smeathley, though she was hard put to keep the eulogies going all the way upstairs.

Dinner wasn't a comfortable meal, for several members of the party had too much at stake to allow themselves to relax. The Dowager sat at the head of the table, flanked by Mr Serle and the elder Mr Smeathley. Eleanor was set at Mr Serle's right hand, with Crispin next to her. Beatrice sat on the other side of the table, between the two Mr Smeathleys, which made it very difficult for her to avoid Justin's eyes. Beyond Mr Augustus Smeathley was his mother, who said very little to anyone, but smiled a lot and partook of every dish offered to her.

They were served in state by both footmen and the butler. Eleanor was the life and soul of the party, prattling on about this and that, and fluttering her eyes at Mr Smeathley in a way that soon had Crispin frowning.

Beatrice sent her niece one or two warning glances, which were totally ignored.

The Dowager, whose hearing was not of the best, maintained a dignified silence most of the time, for she hated to mistake what someone had said and thus betray her own weakness, but she threw sharp questions at her guests every now and then to show them she was still in charge.

Beatrice spent the whole meal wishing the floor would open up and swallow her. She had always considered those words, when she read them in novels, to be as stupid as they were trite, but they exactly expressed her wishes at the moment. She didn't think she could maintain her composure over several days spent in his company and wondered whether she dared pretend to come down with the influenza.

The elder Smeathleys were, as the Dowager had prophesied, no trouble to entertain, for they maintained a dignified silence for most of the meal the better to concentrate on their food.

Their son proved himself not only an accomplished trencherman, but also one who was capable of contributing more than his fair share to the conversation. His unctuous utterances formed a regular bass counterpoint to Eleanor's bright prattle.

Within a short time, the sound of his voice had set Beatrice's teeth on edge. That man is a practiced sycophant, she thought indignantly, and if this is the way he intends to make his way up through the ecclesiastical hierarchies, then the church is welcome to him. It amazed her to see Eleanor hanging upon his every word and treating his threadbare utterances like pearls of wisdom.

And Eleanor was making little effort to converse with her other neighbour, Mr Serle, though he'd addressed several extremely intelligent remarks to her, to which Beatrice had felt compelled to respond herself.

Crispin Herforth was very quiet during the meal, observing everything very closely. He wasn't enjoying the sight of Eleanor hanging upon that buffoon's words and he meant to have some sharp words with her about it afterwards. Already he was deeply regretting that he'd agreed to be guided by her in winning her grandmother's consent to their marriage. To his mind, deceit never paid. If it were up to him, he would seek an interview with the Dowager the very next morning to let her know how he felt about her granddaughter.

Serle was also quiet, for his attention was focused on Beatrice, who was looking so strained and weary that his heart ached for her. She'd kept herself in the background and tried to avoid meeting his eyes ever since his arrival, though he'd managed to gain several responses from her, thanks to Eleanor's inattention. What puzzled him was why the old lady had invited him here? He had a faint hope that the invitation had been prompted by Beatrice, but now he couldn't believe that.

His eyes strayed to his neighbour. Surely the Dowager didn't think to match him with her granddaughter? Eleanor was a lovely young thing, but he was too old for her, even if his affections had not been engaged already. He rather thought the chit was up to some sort of mischief and he meant, if he could, to find out what, in case it was something which might upset his poor love. He turned his head and watched with some amusement the way the young minx was flattering Smeathley. The man was taken in by it, behaving like the veriest greenhead, for all his massive clerical dignity.

When the ladies eventually rose to leave the gentlemen to their port, the Dowager announced firmly that she would expect to see the gentlemen in the drawing room within the half hour. "I do not," she stared round, "approve of immoderate drinking."

"Nor would we wish to stay away from the ladies for too long," Augustus Smeathley said, throwing a languishing glance toward Eleanor.

Crispin was hard put not to punch him in the face.

In fact, it was barely twenty minutes before the gentlemen abandoned their port, because each of the three younger ones was so careful to guard what he said that conversation in no way flourished, while the elder Smeathley's attention was solely on his wine glass.

That port wine, Justin thought regretfully, was some of the best he'd ever tasted and should have been treated more respectfully than being gulped down as it was by the elder Mr Smeathley and ignored by Mr Augustus Smeathley, who was visibly fretting to rejoin the ladies. Herforth seemed a decent enough fellow and, in different circumstances, Justin would have been pleased to pursue a closer acquaintance with him, but for the moment, until he had summed up exactly who was playing which game, he would keep himself to himself.

He complimented the butler as he left the room on the way the port had been cellared and decanted, and made himself a staunch ally, because if Borrill had one passion in life, it was the proper management of good wines.

The ladies, having ensconced themselves in the Blue Drawing Room, passed a rather uncomfortable twenty minutes waiting for the gentlemen. Beatrice saw her aunt settled, noting that the old lady was already displaying signs of fatigue, then sat down next to her and pretended to embroider, putting in some more crooked stitches.

The Dowager and Mrs. Smeathley made desultory conversation about mutual acquaintances and the foibles of long-dead relatives. Eleanor, after twitching about rest-lessly for a few minutes, went to the piano and began to play.

It was there that Crispin saw her as he entered, her hair aureoled by the candelabrum behind her and her firm little hands caressing a delicate melody from the keys. She seemed for the moment to have forgotten that there were other people around her and her eyes were half closed as she played. Without thinking, he went to stand behind her to turn the pages and with a start she realized that the gentlemen had returned.

Under cover of the music, she was able to instruct him to meet her on the terrace half an hour after everyone had retired and to stay away from her until then. Further confidences were prevented by Augustus Smeathley, who loomed up beside them and began to hum the melody in a rich fruity voice.

Eleanor kicked Crispin on the ankle, which he correctly interpreted as an order to remove himself.

He did so most reluctantly, his lips tight with annoyance.

"Do you sing, Cousin Augustus?" Eleanor was cooing behind him.

"I delight in it, my dear young lady, delight in it."

Within minutes they had found some suitable music and were entertaining the company with a duet that proved Smeathley's boasted love of music to be no lie. It was the one good thing about him, Eleanor thought.

The Dowager watched them for a while, tapping out the tune with a wrinkled, twisted hand, but she didn't allow the tête-à-tête to continue beyond three duets. "Excellent!" she called. "Now go and find me that sketchbook of Beatrice's, child. I want to show Crispin the perspectives of the house and grounds."

Old and half deaf she might be, but within minutes she had them organized into the pairs she wanted. Crispin with herself, Serle with Eleanor and Smeathley with a very silent Beatrice. The senior Smeathleys were allowed to entertain themselves by dozing in a corner.

To Beatrice, the evening seemed to last for ever.

Chapter 12

At the prescribed time, when everyone seemed to have gone to bed, Crispin tiptoed down the dark staircase, wishing he dared light a candle. It was all very well for Eleanor, who knew the house like the back of her hand, to suggest they meet outside on the terrace, but he would have preferred to wait until early morning, when he could see where he was going. He fumbled his way to the bottom of the stairs, praying that everyone else was sound asleep, and with some trepidation made his way across what seemed a vast expanse of hallway.

A door at the back of the hall opened suddenly and a shaft of light stopped him dead in his tracks. He waited where he was, heart pounding, to see who had caught him behaving so strangely.

"Did you wish for something, sir?"

Crispin sighed with relief at the sound of the butler's voice.

"Yes." He sought desperately for an excuse. "I wanted to go outside to smoke a cigarillo. Not the sort of thing Lady Marguerite would appreciate one doing indoors, I suspect, and I didn't want to disturb the rest of the house. Now that you're here, perhaps you'd tell me which is the best place to go. The terrace, I thought?"

"Yes, sir. If you'd follow me. I would suggest you go out through the library."

Crispin followed him, hoping the man wouldn't wait to see the fictitious cigarillo being lit. Damn! He'd better get hold of some, just in case he needed to repeat the excuse. That's where deceit got you, into tangles! "Thank you."

"Would you like me to light you a candle, sir?" Borrill gestured with his own candlestick toward an unlit candelabrum.

"Yes. Thank you. I'll leave it inside, though, and just use it to light the cigarillo in a little while and guide me back to my room when I've finished. The moon's rising now and it's full enough to provide me with all the light I need. You needn't wait. I'll lock up when I come in again. You – er – won't mention my little weakness to Lady Marguerite, will you?"

Borrill smiled. He had already decided that he approved of The Heir. "No, sir, for it's one I share."

Crispin waited until the door of the library had closed behind Borrill before going outside. He didn't dare call out and could only wait for Eleanor to find him.

A rustle of skirts and a low chuckle heralded her appearance, and before he could take another step, she had thrown herself into his arms and was raising her face to be kissed.

"Oh, how I missed you!" she sighed, when at last they tore themselves apart and went to sit on a bench.

"And I you, my darling. But what the devil you mean by playing up to that fellow Smeathley! I came very near to calling this whole sham off tonight, I can tell you!"

She giggled. "He is rather a fool, isn't he? I've not had much experience of men, but he seems very gullible in his conceit. Am I doing it well, the flirting, I mean?"

"Much too well!" he growled, and kissed the tip of her ear, which was temptingly close to his lips. "If he continues to drool over you in that disgusting way, I shall wind up punching him in the face! Stupid windbag!"

"Well, I have to encourage him a little, so that Grandmamma will think I'm falling in love with him. I can't pretend to like Mr Serle, for he's the one she wants me to marry. He seems quite nice, though, don't you think?"

"Hang Serle! Look, love, let's be done with this play-acting and just tell your grandmother straight out that we've fallen in love and wish to get married."

"Oh, how I wish we could!" she sighed. "But I promise you it wouldn't work. Firstly, she doesn't believe that persons of our rank should allow themselves to fall in love. When she caught Bea and me reading a novel once, she threw it on the fire and read us a dreadful lecture about only housemaids falling in love." She smiled reminiscently. "And I was just about to find out whether Melissa escaped from the evil count and managed to be reunited with her childhood sweetheart, too."

"Dreadful. Tell me the damned book's name and I'll buy you another copy."

"Oh, there's no need. I got my maid to purchase another for me the very same week."

He shook with laughter. "I might have known." And of course he had to kiss her again, she was looking so beautiful in the moonlight. Then had to stop at a kiss or two in case he shocked her with his passion, because for all her talk, she was clearly an innocent where men were concerned.

"Aah," she sighed as he pulled away. "I missed you so much, Crispin!"

"And what else do you wish to tell me about your grandmother, my love?" he prompted, keeping firm hold of her hand.

"Well, I think if we told her the truth, she would probably send you away again. Believe me, she can be very autocratic at times – especially if her will is crossed. No, I've got to show *disinterest* in Mr Serle and a *fascination* with Smeathley," she grimaced at the prospect, "until she decides to do something about it. She's determined to marry me off, for some reason."

He sighed and they both sat there quietly for a while, hand in hand, her head against his shoulder, staring at the moonlit gardens.

Eleanor broke the silence, aware that she shouldn't linger there too long, in case someone saw her. "You'll be glad to know that you've made an excellent first impression on her, in spite of being called Crispin, and you must continue to woo her favour. And—" she pushed him away, "*Stop it!* I can't think properly when you're kissing me!"

He chuckled and pretended to pull his hand away from hers as well as his lips, but she wouldn't allow that.

"My master stroke is that I've planted an idea in Grandmamma's mind about me being the last of the true Graceovers and I rather think she'll decide to let me marry you in the end to keep the family breeding from the true line, even if the title has lapsed."

"You're a devious little schemer, and I doubt I'll be able to call my soul my own after we're married. But flirting with that fellow sticks in my gullet!" His voice rose a little with the vehemence of his feelings.

"Shhh! Someone will hear us!"

Justin, whose bedroom window looked out onto the terrace, was lying awake trying to work out how to get Beatrice on her own, so that they could have a frank discussion. As Crispin's voice rose, Justin realized that the whisperings he had put down to night animals and rustling leaves was the sound of people talking outside. He couldn't resist getting out of bed to see who they were.

By the time he'd managed to open the window, the couple below him on the terrace were once again entwined. Looking down, he could only see the tops of their heads, half obscured by some damned creeper which grew in profusion upon the old walls and by the branches of a tree which ought, he thought angrily, to have been better trimmed.

As the couple drew apart, Eleanor brushed her hair back behind her ears. Justin sucked his breath in sharply. He had seen Beatrice tuck her hair out of the way in just that manner. He tried desperately to make out the features of the people below him, but the lady, who could have been either Beatrice or Eleanor, was now sitting with her head on the gentleman's shoulder. By leaning perilously far out of the window, he managed to confirm that the man was Crispin Herforth, but he could neither confirm nor deny his fear that the woman might be Beatrice. He remained there, feeling murderous, trying to see more clearly and failing.

Eventually the two people below stood up and went indoors, but that was no help to the watcher above, for as soon as they moved away from the bench, they were hidden by the building itself.

Justin sighed and went back to toss around until the small hours of the morning on a bed which seemed to be full of lumps. If that had been Beatrice on the terrace, it would explain a lot. She might have been attracted to him in London, but she was presumably already promised to another. And it was clearly a secret attachment, for Crispin had shown no signs of paying her attention during the evening. In fact, Mr Herforth had been remarkably self-composed.

It might pay, Justin decided grimly, to get to know that gentleman better. He wasn't going to give Beatrice up without a struggle. And of course, the woman might turn out to be Eleanor. He prayed it would.

The following morning, the younger members of the party decided to ride out to look at Eleanor's favourite view, a place where she had spent many happy hours.

Crispin caught her eye for a moment and smiled at this way of describing their previous rendezvous spot.

Augustus Smeathley proved to ride very heavily and to have little skill at managing even the sluggish mount he'd brought with him, which made the other four members of the party, all accomplished horsemen and women, look at him in disgust.

Crispin, finding himself next to Serle, couldn't help exclaiming, "That damned fellow shouldn't be allowed to mount a camel, let alone a horse!"

"A heavy gentleman in every way," agreed Justin. "Had you met him before? He's some sort of a connection of yours, isn't he?"

"Good heavens, no! And even if he were a relative, I'd never admit it in public. No, as far as I can make out, he's a connection of Lady Marguerite's younger daughter's husband." He looked with loathing at Mr Smeathley's broad shoulders. "No," he repeated, almost to himself, "that fine gentleman will never be invited to put his legs under *my* table, I can promise you! Do you know, he recommended some verses from the Bible to me this morning, as being suitable for those whom the Lord had favoured with excessive worldly wealth! The impudence of the fellow!"

"Did he, now?" Justin grinned. "What did you say to that?"

"I recommended him to read Proverbs Three, Verse Seven."

"Did you, by heavens? I wasn't aware that you were deeply religious, Mr Herforth."

Crispin chuckled. "I'm not, but I was forced to learn verses of the Bible many times in my youth as a punishment. Never thought they'd come in useful, which just goes to show."

"Might one ask what that particular verse says?"

The grin broadened. *"Be not wise in thine own eyes: fear the Lord and depart from evil."*

Justin let out a shout of laughter that made the others turn their heads to stare at the two men. He decided that he definitely liked Mr Herforth and realized ruefully that he would not blame Beatrice for having formed an attachment to him.

"Is that your own mare?" he asked after a few moments. "She's a neatly-built creature."

"Yes." Crispin leaned forward to pat her neck. "But I shan't be riding her for much longer, shall I, old girl? It's about time I bred from her. Be a pity to waste this line, just because I'm fond of riding her."

The two of them went on to discuss horses and found a common interest in the breeding of suitable mounts, which both held to be more reliable than chancing one's luck at the sales, since you never knew what sort of temperament a strange horse might have.

During the course of the conversation, it became apparent that Crispin knew the countryside round Satherby rather better than a man should who had only arrived the previous night. Justin looked at him in puzzlement.

Realizing that he'd betrayed himself, Crispin grimaced. "I'm no good as a conspirator, am I? I must beg you not to betray me to Lady Marguerite, Serle. I've been staying with friends in the neighbourhood, spying out the land before I came to stay at Satherby itself."

"Did you not meet any of the family while you were here? That was a little risky, surely?"

"Oh, she will not betray me!" Crispin broke off again. "Hell and damnation! Can't I keep anything to myself?" He stared at his companion. Justin Serle was a great deal more dangerous than he had at first appeared. Crispin decided to terminate the conversation at once before he betrayed all. "I think someone had better rescue Miss Dencey from that bore," he said and spurred his horse forward.

Justin watched him go, frowning. Had it been Beatrice meeting Herforth on the terrace the previous evening? Surely she wasn't in love with him? He was a pleasant enough fellow, without guile or malice, but much too young for her. Then he realized, with a huge lightening of his spirit, that it was far more likely to be Eleanor whom Herforth had met if he'd been staying near here recently, for Beatrice had only just returned from London.

He beamed around him, certain he'd hit upon the correct explanation, then studied what the others were up to with renewed optimism. That young minx Eleanor was giving no sign of any attachment to Crispin, for Justin had been watching her and Beatrice surreptitiously. Eleanor hadn't even glanced his way, chatting to her cousin mostly.

As Crispin joined them, Beatrice looked up with a smile so warm that Justin muttered something under his breath and began to doubt his own conclusions again, in spite of their unassailable logic. He wished bitterly that she would smile at him like that, as she had done in London. He wished he could get her away from the others.

"They say it's the first sign of madness, you know," said a voice beside him.

He looked round to find that Eleanor had dropped back to join him. "I do beg your pardon. I didn't see you join me, Miss Graceover. I thought you were with Mr Smeathley and Miss Dencey."

"Yes, I was. How interesting Mr Smeathley's conversation is!" She sighed and rolled her eyes.

"Don't try your tricks on me!" he said deciding on shock tactics. "You're no more taken by him than I am!"

She stared at him open-mouthed for a moment, then inclined her head in a salute. "How very perceptive of you, Mr Serle! Pray don't tell Grandmamma!"

"May I know why you're doing it?"

"Oh, just funning," she said lightly. "Beatrice said I couldn't fool Augustus Smeathley into believing I was attracted to him and I wagered I could. I think I've succeeded, don't you?"

"Yes, you have. But to what purpose?"

She looked at him sideways, debating with herself how much to reveal. "Why, to show Grandmamma he's not a suitable husband for poor Bea, of course." A spark of mischief made her add, "Particularly now." She gave him a quizzical look.

"Why now?" His tone was harsh and the words came out more sharply than he'd intended.

"Because her affections are engaged elsewhere, of course," she answered lightly, then, as Beatrice turned to call some query about which route they should take, Eleanor left Mr Serle's side and cantered forward to join the rest of the party, leaving him no alternative but to follow suit.

Once again Serle began to doubt Beatrice's feelings and for a moment felt despair surge through him, then his expression became grim. Even if Beatrice did have an understanding with Herforth, he didn't intend to give her up without a struggle. He couldn't be mistaken about the way she reacted to him, the way she looked at him sometimes. He couldn't!

He rode the rest of the way to the lookout in grim silence, making no attempt to converse with any of the others.

Once there they dismounted, the gentlemen tied up the horses and nearly everyone sat down to enjoy the view from the shade of some trees.

Only Augustus Smeathley remained standing. He began to wander to and fro, as if admiring the view and after a few minutes, he called out, "Miss Graceover, I wonder if you could tell me what that landmark is?"

As the landmark in question wasn't visible from where the others were sitting, Eleanor was obliged to join him. "You ought to look at this too, Cousin Crispin," she called over her shoulder, not wanting, for some reason she couldn't fathom, to be on her own with Smeathley. "Grandmamma wishes you to get to know every bit of the estate. Why don't you join us?"

He jumped to his feet. "Certainly, Cousin Eleanor."

Beatrice started to rise and follow them, but by the simple expedient of setting his hand on her skirt, Justin managed to prevent her from moving.

"We need to talk," he said quietly.

"We can have nothing private to say to one another."

"Can we not? I had thought that—"

"*No!*" She pulled futilely at the skirt.

"I think you'd better explain why you say that. I believe we have a great deal to say to each other. And I also believe I received some encouragement from you in London." He reached out and seized her hand.

"Let me go!" she whispered furiously, trying in vain to pull away. "You have no right." She cast an anxious look at the rest of the party, but their backs were turned and they were concentrating on the view.

"Why did you run away from me at Lymsby, Beatrice? Why couldn't you explain your feelings to me then?"

She hung her head, very conscious of the warmth of his hand on hers. "I – I was cowardly. I shouldn't have let my interest be engaged. It conflicted with…" Her voice faded away. She could find no words to explain it which didn't betray the depth of her feelings for him.

"Conflicted with your other interest," he finished harshly. To hear it from her own lips seemed so final. "You should have remembered *him* sooner, should you not?" He released both hand and skirt, and began to stand up. "Don't be afraid that I'll pursue where I'm not wanted, Miss Dencey! I'll find an excuse to leave Satherby at the first opportunity."

It was her turn to catch hold of him. "Oh no! Please, you mustn't!"

"But you've just told me that my suit is hopeless!" he said, still speaking angrily. "Why on earth should I stay here?"

She flushed and avoided his eyes. "Because of Aunt Marguerite. Oh please, please stay for a while longer!"

He threw up his hands in bafflement. "*Why?* I wish your aunt no harm, but why in heaven's name should I wish to please a woman whom I've only just met? She has no claim upon me. Give me a reason in plain words, if you please, Miss Dencey!"

She took a deep breath and summoned up all her courage. "Because – because she wishes you to marry Eleanor. That's why she invited you here."

He stared at her, amazed. "Do you think me so fickle as to change my affections overnight?"

"N-no, but, but she – Eleanor, I mean – she's superior in every way to me. Once you get to know her, you cannot fail to like her better than me." She didn't know how to look him in the face.

"And that would please you?"

"Yes." But she turned her face away as she spoke.

He was now feeling even more bewildered.

She stole a glance sideways. "I beg you to be kind to my aunt, Mr Serle. She's growing old, wishes to see Eleanor established and has a great regard – a very great regard – for your family. I must – must follow her wishes in this."

"That's quite gothic!" he declared. "I have no intention of marrying to please someone else, especially when my affections are engaged already." He paused, then added softly, "With *you*, Beatrice, and only with you."

She could only stare at him and wish desperately that she could follow the dictates of her own heart.

As the silence continued, she raised her eyes to meet his.

What he saw in them looked like love, he was sure it was love – but it was mingled with despair and – something else. "I think," he said slowly, "you're concealing something from me, Beatrice."

She could only shake her head and turn it away again, knowing that if he looked at her too closely, he would see the tears she was having trouble keeping back.

When she didn't speak, did not look at him, he realized he could push her no further at this stage, not in such a public situation. "Come, this is fruitless. I suggest we rejoin the others!"

But he would, he vowed, find a way for them to speak more privately. He reached out and pulled her to her feet before she had time to move of her own accord and they stood for a moment, close together, with him still holding her arm while she found her balance. "Beatrice, Beatrice, I don't understand you at all," he said pleadingly. "And I wish you would tell me the whole truth."

She stepped backwards and said in cool tones, "I've said all I wish to, Mr Serle. Please better your acquaintance with my niece." Her voice broke on the last word and she started walking blindly toward the others.

He shook his head in utter bewilderment as he followed her across the grassy hillside.

Eleanor at once noticed the tears trembling in Beatrice's eyes and managed to stand between her and the others to shield her from their gaze for next few minutes while she fought for self-control.

She was feeling quite exasperated by her aunt's behaviour and longed to give her a good shaking. Especially when she saw Serle looking equally upset. What could possibly prevent Beatrice from accepting his attentions? From welcoming them? She clearly loved him.

It was almost time for luncheon when they arrived back at Satherby and there was no time to do anything but rush upstairs to wash and change their clothes. She would, Eleanor decided, speak sharply to Serle later. Surely he could see how much Bea loved him? He certainly gave the impression that he loved her? Had he asked her to marry him or not?

–

After the midday meal, Crispin reluctantly left the others to meet with the bailiff, while they went to sit in a pleasant room next to the library.

While the older Smeathleys passed on to Eleanor one or two items of interest from the newspapers which they had been perusing during the morning, Augustus described their outing to the Dowager in glowing terms.

Beatrice sat silently by her aunt's side, the maltreated embroidery lying untouched on her lap. She said yes and no at intervals, or nodded her head, which was all Mr Smeathley seemed to expect of her. But she had little idea of what he was saying, because she kept seeing Serle's face, hearing him plead with her to marry him, hearing him say he still cared for her. But every time she saw how frail her aunt was, it made her realize that she mustn't upset the old lady or deny her this last wish.

She saw the Dowager's expression became more a little glassy-eyed as Mr Smeathley continued to pontificate about the benefits of healthy and rational exercise. Her aunt didn't like to be talked at for too long but was obviously studying Mr Smeathley. Once she rubbed her head, as if it was aching and gradually her expression turned to one of open disapproval.

When Eleanor joined them and started to encourage Augustus to describe the architecture of Wells Cathedral, on the subject of which he had already bored Beatrice to tears, he was allowed to talked about it uninterrupted for about ten minutes. Then, as the Dowager began to grow visibly restless, Eleanor broke into the peroration with an offer to show him the flower gardens.

He rose with an alacrity which left the Dowager frowning. She turned to her niece. "Why didn't you go with them, Beatrice?"

"I'd rather not. And anyway, I wasn't asked, was I?"

"Haven't taken to Smeathley, have you?" her aunt asked abruptly.

"N-no, I'm afraid not. I did try, but… well…"

"He's setting his cap for Eleanor, unless I'm much mistaken," the Dowager said. "The impertinence of it! Who does he think he is?"

"But I don't think she – surely she wouldn't..." Beatrice's voice trailed away, as she remembered the rapt attention with which Eleanor had listened to Mr Smeathley's no doubt erudite but tedious monologue on church architecture.

The stick quivered as the twisted old hand tightened on it. "He's good looking, in his own way. And the trouble is, the chit's not had any experience of men. It's my fault. I've protected her too much. I'll have to speak to Serle about her before this gets out of hand. Perhaps..." She did not finish her sentence, just fell silent for a moment, then said curtly, "Ask Serle to come and see me in my rooms in a quarter of an hour, if you please. And then go outside and join those two. I'm not leaving Eleanor alone with Smeathley. He won't do for her and anyway, he's only interested in her money."

"Or mine," Beatrice said, trying to smile, but knowing she'd failed.

"Hmph. Well, as you don't like him, he'll not get that, either, will he?" She reached out to pat Beatrice's hand. "I would never force you into marriage with someone you disliked, child. You should realize that. Now, ring for my footman."

Beatrice did as she was bidden then moved across to speak to Serle and pass on the Dowager's request. "Lippings will come to fetch you when Lady Marguerite is ready." She turned away before he could say anything personal to her and went outside, her emotions in turmoil again. She had only to get close to him to forget all her good resolutions.

Justin watched her go bleakly. Once he'd spoken to the Dowager and explained that he could not accede to her wishes with regard to Eleanor, perhaps he should leave Satherby? It would be the most dignified thing to do.

No sooner had he made that decision than he changed his mind. Why should he not stay and fight for Beatrice's affection? Why give in so tamely?

His thoughts seesawed from one decision to another in a way he wouldn't have believed possible a month previously. He'd never been in love before and was finding it a most frustrating experience. Even his own reactions bewildered him, and until now, he'd prided himself on being a rational man.

He was relieved when Lippings arrived to take him to the Dowager.

–

He found the old lady sitting by the window, sunk in thought, and when he moved across to join her, he saw that she was staring at the three people walking up and down in the rose gardens. He cleared his throat and she turned her head.

"Ah, there you are, Mr Serle."

She must have been very beautiful once, he thought, rather like Eleanor. Her spirit still shone undaunted in her eyes, though her body was clearly failing. "The gardens at Satherby are very beautiful at this time of year," he said aloud.

"What do I care about gardens," she snapped. "Sit down, will you, Serle? I can't abide looking up at people. Now, what do you think of my granddaughter?"

"She's a nice child," he said carefully.

"*Child?* She's nineteen."

"She seems a child to me," he reiterated, hoping to avoid a confrontation.

"I'd rather hoped you'd find her attractive," she said. "In fact, to be plain, I'd welcome a match between our houses, and that's why I invited you here."

There was a moment's silence, then he shook his head. "I regret to disappoint you, your ladyship, but it's not possible."

"Not spoken for, are you? Beatrice said nothing about any other attachments."

"It's not generally known. She won't look at me, anyway."

"She's a fool, then!" The Dowager sighed and they both remained silent for a few minutes.

"You look very tired, ma'am," he ventured after a while, for she was white as a sheet and her hand was trembling visibly on the arm of her chair. "Allow me to send for your maid."

She sighed again and crumpled forward suddenly.

He caught her before she could fall to the floor, then managed, without letting go of the frail old body, to ring the hand bell that stood on the table beside her. She was as light as an autumn leaf in his arms and her skin had something of the same texture. Her body seemed a dried-out husk with its life juices nearly gone, which made him feel sad and protective.

Lippings came hurrying in and called out, "Oh no!" before examining her mistress with the air of one who knew her business. "Can you carry her through into the bedroom for me, sir?" she asked. "I think she's just fainted. I thought for a moment that – well, she has a bad heart, you see – but it's just a faint, I think."

They got the Dowager onto her bed, then Lippings asked, "Please, sir, don't tell the other guests about this, just send Miss Beatrice in. She's the only one who knows how bad her ladyship is. That's why she was sent to London. Her ladyship was relying on her to…" She broke off and stared at him in horror. "I do beg your pardon, sir."

"Please don't stop there," he said, scenting an answer to his worries. "Why exactly did Miss Dencey go to London?"

"To find a husband for Lady Eleanor, I believe. And for herself as well, if she could, but mainly for Lady Eleanor. Her ladyship gave her a list of suitable families."

Hope began to dawn again in Justin. "Did she, now?"

"I shouldn't be telling you this, sir. It was the shock. Please don't mention what I said to her ladyship. The slightest upset could kill her. The doctor said she hasn't long to live now. That's why she begged Miss Beatrice not to let her down."

"No, I won't tell her." He left the room without seeing anything around him and once he'd fetched Beatrice, made his way instinctively to the peace of his bedroom to think things through. If his darling – and for the first time since his arrival, he called her that in his head with some hope for the future – if his darling knew that her aunt hadn't long to live, knew that the old lady had set her heart on him marrying Eleanor in order to keep her precious granddaughter safe when she was dead, then she would try to fulfil her aunt's last wishes – even at her own cost!

He tried to remember his exact conversations with Eleanor and Crispin. Neither of them had actually said Beatrice was in love with Crispin, or he with her. And the figure he'd seen from the bedroom *must* have been, Eleanor. *That* was what the minx was plotting about, though he couldn't think why! If the Dowager wished to see her granddaughter married, surely the heir to Satherby was a good enough match for anyone?

His face brightened and his heart began to thud as he realized that very possibly he had mistaken the whole affair – no, not possibly, *probably.* Beatrice did love him. She did!

With joy flooding through him, he moved toward the door, intending to confront her with this at once, then he stopped as he realized she would still be with her aunt. After twitching around for a while, he went out for a walk, unable to sit still until he'd spoken to Beatrice.

Chapter 13

The doctor was summoned and pronounced Lady Marguerite to be suffering from exhaustion. Since he'd persuaded the Dowager to take a draught that sent her to sleep, Beatrice was not able to discuss with her aunt what to do about the guests, so she simply told them that their hostess was overtired and must rest.

Justin caught her on her own afterwards. "Do you wish me to tell everyone to leave?"

She stared at him, unable to think clearly. If she said yes, she would get rid of the Smeathleys, but Justin would go too, and if he stayed, her aunt might be happier. And there was also Crispin to think of. He should definitely remain here at this dangerous time, in case… her thoughts faltered. Somehow, she couldn't imagine Satherby without her aunt.

She realized dimly that someone was supporting her and making her sit down. "Put your head on your knees for a moment, Beatrice!" commanded a firm, but gentle voice. "I think you're feeling a little faint yourself. It's probably delayed shock." She obeyed him because it was easier to do that than argue.

The same voice told Borrill to fetch a glass of brandy for Miss Dencey, who was feeling faint. Then the voice's owner helped her to sit up and sip it. She found she was once again leaning against Serle's chest, but hadn't the strength of will to pull away. Oh, that she might have the right to lean against him every day of her life! Despair filled her.

"Take another sip, if you please, my dear foolish girl, and don't try to speak for a minute or two."

Dear girl! He'd called her *dear girl*. Her heart began to pound. When she ventured to look up at him, he planted a very fleeting kiss on her brow, which sent warm feelings running through her body. She couldn't help clinging to his hand.

"You've been making a mountain out of a molehill, Beatrice," he said softly, his expression tender.

He planted another kiss on her cheek before adding, "We'll find a way through this tangle without upsetting your aunt, I promise you. I'm not giving you up. And you *are* going to marry me."

She stared at him for a moment, then gave in to temptation and leaned against him, putting one arm round him in the most shockingly familiar manner, feeling amazed at how natural that felt. "You keep coming to my rescue," she said, with a ghost of a chuckle.

"You obviously need me around, then, or who knows what other troubles you will fall into." He could see her lips curving gently into a smile and put a finger under her chin to make her look up at him again. "We shall be married as soon as possible," he continued in a voice that brooked no argument. "You can't possibly manage everything here on your own." He put a finger on her lips to prevent her from speaking as he added, "I can't bear to live without you for much longer, my darling."

Tears overflowed from her eyes. "Oh, Justin, how can I be so selfish as to accept?" she whispered.

'How can you think I'd marry anyone else? But I do see that you care deeply about your aunt.'

"Especially now."

"She's failing, isn't she?"

"Yes."

"Blame it all on me. And never forget that I need you, too."

Her hand stole up to caress his soft, dark hair. "Do you? Do you really?"

"Oh, yes. Life would be unbearable without you."

"And – and do you really think we can do this without upsetting my aunt?" Hope was growing in her and joy was beginning to sing along her veins.

"I'm sure of it. *Will* you marry me, Beatrice? You haven't replied to my proposal and I'm feeling rejected and forlorn."

"Oh, Justin! I—" She did not seem able to breathe properly when she was so close to him.

His grip tightened. "No more prevarication. Yes or no?"

She looked up at him with a radiant smile. "Yes. Yes, of course I'll marry you, dearest Justin." She was suddenly surprised that she'd even considered any other course of action. A great weight seemed to fall from her shoulders as she spoke.

A cough from the doorway made them both turn round. Eleanor came in, shutting the door behind her and saying with mock severity, "Dear me, Beatrice, a lady should never show her feelings in public! Or allow herself to be alone with a gentleman to whom she is not related."

Justin wouldn't allow Beatrice to move from the shelter of his arms. "You may be the first to congratulate us, Miss Impertinence."

Eleanor squealed and rushed to plant a kiss on Beatrice's face, hesitated, then hugged Serle as well. "Oh, I'm so glad! I was at my wit's end as to how to bring you two together!"

Two faces gaped at her and she said airily. "Well, I couldn't help but see how you both felt. I know Bea too well and your feelings showed sometimes when you looked at her, Mr Serle."

"Impertinence is not a strong enough word for you, young lady!" He said with mock severity. "And my friends and relatives usually call me Justin."

She pulled a face at him. "Justin, then."

"Eleanor, you won't say anything until we can tell Aunt Marguerite, will you?" Beatrice begged. "Not to anyone. Promise me! The slightest shock could kill her."

The laughter left Eleanor's face. "Is that why you were being so noble about Serle and me? Is she – really bad?"

Beatrice nodded. The two of them clasped hands, for the thought of losing the old termagant who'd looked after them both for the past ten years caused a pain too deep for words.

The door started to open and Justin moved away from Beatrice as Mrs. Smeathley sailed in. "I came to see how you were, Beatrice," she said. "We were worried about you, and it's not seemly to stay here alone with a gentleman. Surely your maid should have been summoned to attend you by now? In fact, I think you should go and lie down until you have recovered from the shock of your aunt's illness."

Eleanor cleared her throat. "You don't seem to have noticed, Mrs. Smeathley, but Beatrice is *not* alone with a gentleman! I'm here, too."

"*You* are an unmarried lady."

"It's very kind of you to worry," Justin said, frowning at Eleanor to make her keep quiet, "but I think we can leave Miss Dencey to her niece's tender care. Allow me to escort you back to the drawing room."

He held out his arm in so imperative a manner that Mrs. Smeathley obeyed him meekly. At the door Justin turned to smile briefly across the room at his love, his heart lifting at the answering softening of her eyes, then he led the older lady inexorably out.

Beatrice, who was still looking pale, agreed to go and rest for a while, so Eleanor escorted her to her room, left her in Tilly's devoted hands and then went to look for Crispin. She couldn't tell him Bea's glorious news yet, but she wanted to be with him for a while, until she had grown accustomed to the thought of losing her grandmother in the near future.

Instead she met Augustus Smeathley, parading majestically to and fro on the terrace. He hastened toward her. "My dear, my very dear Miss Graceover, how is your grandmother?"

"Sleeping. The doctor gave her a draught and told us to stop her from doing so much. It's exhaustion, he thinks."

"She wishes to see you safely established before the Lord calls her to Him. One can see that she knows the end to be near." He said this perfectly calmly, with no hint of regret or sorrow sounding in his voice.

Eleanor found that by digging her nails into the palms of her hands she could prevent herself from speaking sharply. Taking a deep breath, she managed to say calmly, "Do you think so? She's said nothing to me about it."

"A clergyman has some experience of the types of things which cause concern to those whose days are numbered," he intoned, as loudly as if he were preaching in church.

A passing gardener stopped to stare at them in surprise.

"Pray come for a walk among the roses," she said hastily. "I want to pick a bunch for Grandmamma's room. Flowers always cheer one up, don't you think?"

"Indeed, yes. Flowers are one of our Lord's most beautiful gifts to mankind." He escorted her with measured steps to the rose gardens and as soon as they were out of sight of the house, he fell upon one knee before her. "Miss Graceover, I cannot keep quiet any longer. Words cannot express how I feel. Suffice it to say that one glance was enough to show me that you were the one above all others whom I should wish to take as my wife."

"It was Beatrice you came here to meet," Eleanor could not resist pointing out.

"I believe that was mentioned as a possibility. But as soon as I saw you, I knew the Lord had destined us for one another. And I could see you felt the same."

She stared at him in amazement. Did he really think this was the way to propose to someone? Or to speak to the woman he was supposed to be in love with?

"Although our fortunes are not equal," he continued, hardly seeming to look at her, gazing mostly up at the sky, "I can offer you a high position in the world, for I have every expectation of being offered a bishopric in the not too distant future."

"Oh," she exclaimed, clasping her hands and giving way to her sense of the ridiculous, "I am not worthy of such an honour!"

He rose from his knee and carefully dusted his trousers. "Have no fear on that score, my dear girl. You may be young and inexperienced, but under my guidance, you will learn all you need to know to support me in life as a wife should."

He seemed to take it for granted that she'd accepted him and went on to describe the house he currently occupied, a most superior type of residence, though smaller than he liked, and then detailed the glories to be expected of a bishop's palace. He made no attempt to take her into his arms or even to kiss her cheek, but expounded with immense enthusiasm upon the topic of his own dazzling future in the ecclesiastical hierarchies.

She soon grew bored with this and decided that she couldn't keep up the pretence any longer. "I must retire to my room. I'm quite overset by your offer, Mr Smeathley."

"The female mind is easily thrown into turmoil," he said in a kindly tone, nodding at her. "Fear not! Once we are married, I shall protect you from all problems and guide you carefully through the mazes of life."

"I haven't accepted you yet."

"I beg your pardon?"

She raised her voice. "I said: I haven't accepted you yet."

He stared at her through narrowed eyes, and then blinked, as if seeing her for the first time.

She stared back at him and shook her head decisively. "Nor shall I!"

"*What did you say?*"

"Nor shall I accept you." She enunciated each word slowly and clearly. "You're too old for me and far too mercenary. And," she added, carried away by the pleasure of giving him a well-deserved set-down, "I shall tell Bea about your proposal and beg her not to marry you, either. Well, she wouldn't marry anyone I disliked and besides, I don't think she's taken to you herself."

When she saw his furious expression, she realized she'd gone a bit too far and wished she'd just offered him a simple rejection. He took a step forward, looking so menacing that she took a hasty step backwards, feeling suddenly afraid of him.

"Why, you little—"

To her relief, she saw Crispin at the other side of the rose garden and fled to his side, calling, "Cousin Crispin! Will you please escort me to my grandmother's rooms?" She laid her hand on his and nipped his arm imperatively. Taking the hint, he inclined his head to Smeathley and led her away rapidly.

They did not, however, return to the house, but went and walked up and down near the ornamental pool.

"What was all that about, might I ask?" he asked curtly. "What has that damned fellow been saying to you?"

"Well – um, he was just proposing to me," she said, trying to sound airy, but only managing to sound as nervous as she felt.

Crispin's voice was so stern she shivered.

"I see. Well, you've certainly been encouraging him to think you might favour his suit, so that was only to be expected!" A pause, then, "And did you accept him?"

"*Of course I didn't!*"

"Well, that's something, I suppose." But his tone was still cool.

"In fact, I not only told him I wouldn't dream of marrying him, but I s-said I didn't like him, either, and would tell Beatrice not to marry him." She was biting her lip as she added, "Only after I said that – well, I felt a bit afraid of him. He's so very – large."

"It never pays to tamper with someone's affections, Eleanor. Even those of a fellow like him." He eyed her and said firmly, "I've been thinking things over and have decided that as soon as the Dowager has recovered, I shall seek an interview with her – and the earlier, the better. I categorically refuse to continue with this deceit any longer!"

She had never seen him in this mood before. All she could think of to say was, "Yes, Crispin."

"And mind you don't start flirting with anyone else!" He spoiled the masterful effect by smiling at her as he added, "Until we're married, you're only allowed to flirt with me. And after that, I shall expect you to be a dutiful wife."

"Oh, yes, Crispin," she said enthusiastically and they both broke into laughter.

As they got to the south end of the water garden, Eleanor couldn't resist peeping through the hedge at the rose gardens. "He's still pacing up and down," she announced.

Crispin leaned forward to look and they saw Mr Smeathley pick up a piece of fallen branch and swish it viciously at a particularly fine bush, sending a shower of blood-red petals fluttering across the path.

"What a despicable thing to do!" she muttered. "That's Grandmamma's favourite rose bush."

"Shh. We don't want him to see us spying on him."

"I wonder what he's thinking. He still looks angry."

Swish! went the stick and another rose bush lost its blooms, then Mr Smeathley's expression became thoughtful and he tossed away the stick.

"Come away," Crispin said. "I've had enough of looking at that fellow to last me a lifetime."

Ten minutes later, as they were sitting in a leafy arbour, with his arm round her shoulders, they heard footsteps and saw Augustus Smeathley pass by with a grim air.

"What can he be doing?" she asked in astonishment. "That path leads only to the woods."

"Whatever it is, you are not to interfere!" he ordered.

She pulled a face at him and subsided against him again. But they didn't see Mr Smeathley coming back, though they stayed in the arbour for quite a long time. And she couldn't help wondering what he had been doing. And what he had been thinking about to bring that look of grim determination to his face.

–

Dinner that evening was a brief meal, with little conversation. Beatrice took the foot of the table and begged Crispin to sit at its head, opposite her.

Mrs. Smeathley couldn't conceal her annoyance, for she felt that, as the oldest lady present, she should have been awarded this honoured position. What was Miss Dencey, after all, but a poor relative? Consequently, she sat in majestic sulks for the whole meal.

As no one else commented on the seating arrangements and everyone treated Miss Dencey as the hostess, she was even angrier with the young woman by the time the meal ended. Consequently, when her son asked for her help, she was quite prepared to do what he wanted. Not that she approved of his plans, but he was her son and she would be glad to help him to a fortune – and anyway, it served that young woman right.

Beatrice begged the company to excuse her immediately after dinner. "I wish to see how my aunt is feeling and check arrangements for her care during the night."

Eleanor, who was hoping to have a chat with Crispin, went into the drawing-room and began to play softly upon the piano, but Augustus stuck firmly close to the two of them, as if determined to prevent a tête-à-tête. He was insistently affable, as if the incident in the rose garden had never occurred, but he still made Eleanor shiver when he narrowed his eyes and looked down his nose at her in an assessing way.

Justin followed Beatrice from the room and managed to have a word alone with her before she retired by dint of simply pulling her into the library and sweeping her into his arms.

"I'm sure I shouldn't," she sighed, leaning her head against his shoulder.

"I'm sure you should," he countered. "You must be worn to a frazzle with the worry about your aunt on top of the strain of finding something to say to those fools."

"You don't like the Smeathleys either, do you?" She smiled in spite of her worries.

"Can't stand them. Know the type well. The son will get on in the church, though not, perhaps, to as high a position as he expects. He's got an inflated opinion of his own worth, but an imposing appearance and a loud voice isn't all it takes to become a bishop."

She shuddered. "I sometimes wonder if he isn't quite ruthless beneath that affability."

He stared at her in surprise. "I doubt it. He's shown no signs of it, anyway. But what can he do to you, even if he is the most ruthless fellow on earth? You're perfectly safe here in your own home."

"Not what he might do to me, but to Eleanor. She has definitely led him on, but I noticed at dinner she appeared to have completely lost interest in him, didn't you? And he glanced at her angrily when he thought no one was looking."

"I never thought she did have any interest in him." He frowned. "And she told me she'd wagered with you that she could make him believe she was enamoured of him."

"Wagered with me?"

Her amazement was so patent he frowned.

"*Wagered!*" she repeated, in a disgusted tone. "Do you really think I'd encourage her to behave in such a vulgar way?"

"Then what was she up to with him?"

"I don't know, but I intend to find out, I promise you!"

But Eleanor wasn't in her room when Beatrice went to bed, so she was left wondering.

–

The following morning the Dowager was feeling a little better, but the doctor, who had called upon her very early, refused to let her receive any visitors and even Beatrice was only allowed to go in for a minute to ask how she was feeling.

"Tired," sighed the old lady. "I thought I could manage it one last time, but I can't, Beatrice, I can't. What are we going to do about them all?"

"Nothing at the moment," said Beatrice firmly. "You're not well enough to think clearly and as the guests are no trouble to me, we'll just leave things as they are until you're a little better, shall we?"

Lady Marguerite nodded, her eyelids already drooping toward sleep.

Beatrice watched her for a moment, nodded to Lippings and tiptoed out, feeling as if the world were topsy-turvy. She'd never seen her aunt quiescent like this and it terrified her.

During breakfast, Smeathley was so attentive to Beatrice that she couldn't fail to realize he was now courting her again. When he requested that she walk with him in the gardens, she made an excuse of having a lot to attend to in her aunt's place. Something about the way he looked at her made her feel nervous of being alone with him, she couldn't understand why. He put her in mind of a stable cat stalking an unsuspecting bird. Only she wasn't unsuspecting, thank goodness.

Later in the morning Augustus Smeathley took himself off into the woods with a gun, but that was the only period of relief for Beatrice. He was so assiduous in his attentions to her for the rest of the day that she begged Justin to stay near her and not allow Smeathley a chance to be alone with her.

Like Eleanor, she was beginning to find him more than a little frightening. While Justin was with her, she could dismiss her fears, but when she was alone, they returned to torment her.

–

The following day, the Dowager was so much better that she started demanding to get up again. As the weather had turned showery and the whole house felt damp, Beatrice and the doctor both felt she would be better keeping to her well-heated rooms. However, they did allow Crispin and Justin each to visit her briefly, at her request.

Crispin took one look at the pale sunken face and knew this was not the time to press his suit.

It was Justin who left her looking happier, for he chatted quietly of his home and of his closest neighbour, her granddaughter, Jennice. He even made the Dowager splutter with laughter several times.

"How did you do it?" Beatrice asked him afterwards, for she'd been listening outside the door and was awed at his skilful address.

"The secret is to treat old ladies as if they were still young," he told her with a smile. "Did you think that age rendered them impervious to a little attention?"

"*My Aunt Marguerite?*"

"Even your aunt. She's very proud of having outlived most of her generation, you know, and of still being in full possession of her faculties." He smoothed the frown from her brow with a gentle fingertip.

She gasped and clutched him as that feathery touch sent sensations fluttering around her body and made her feel suddenly short of air.

He gave her a quick kiss on the cheek. "Don't worry, my love. Your aunt is on the mend now and will last a while longer, long enough to watch us marry, I hope."

"If we can keep her from shocks and annoyances."

"We'll do that."

She stared into his eyes, still astonished that he should care for her so deeply, and as his arms opened to her, moved into them without hesitation and rested her head against his shoulder, feeling as if she had reached the only safe refuge in the whole world. "I hope so, Justin."

They stayed like that for several moments and neither felt the need to speak.

Somehow the rest of the day crawled past. The weather worsened, with grey skies and more showers, quite in tune, Beatrice thought, with her mood. However was she to bring her aunt round to the idea of Justin as a husband for herself instead of for Eleanor? But she now knew that she would marry him, whatever happened. She couldn't even imagine a life without him, so quickly had he become a part of her.

–

Shortly after Beatrice had retired to her room that evening, there was a knock on the door. She gestured to Tilly to answer it and continued to brush her hair, an activity which always helped her to think clearly.

"It's a note from Mrs. Smeathley, Miss." Tilly held out a screw of paper.

"Oh, bother, what does she want? I've only just left her."

Beatrice opened the note, read it with a frown, then looked at the maid in puzzlement. "She wishes to see me immediately upon a matter of extreme urgency. Well, you can just tell her maid that I've gone to bed and can't see anyone until the morning."

"The maid told me Mrs. Smeathley was already waiting for you in the library, Miss. She didn't wait for an answer."

Beatrice scowled into the mirror, then sighed. "I suppose I'll have to go down to her, then. She *is* a guest, after all, though why she had to wait until now to speak to me, I don't know!" She pulled her hair back and tied it with a ribbon, examining the result in the mirror. "That'll have to do. Don't wait up for me, Tilly. I can easily manage to remove this dress myself afterwards and I know you're tired."

She whisked out of the room without waiting for an answer.

Tilly began to tidy up the rest of the room, then sat down stubbornly to wait for her mistress.

Downstairs, no one was waiting in the library and Beatrice looked round in puzzlement. She heard a sound outside and realized that the French windows were open. It seemed a strange time for an elderly woman to take the air, but then, she found the Smeathleys a strange family. She shook her head irritably and went out to investigate.

Before she had realized what was happening, some thick material was thrown over her head and a heavy hand muffled her mouth. The whole operation was conducted so rapidly and skilfully that she had no time to scream before her mouth was filled with choking layers of cloth and she was dragged forward, away from the house.

Amazement as much as fear prevented her from struggling at first, but then she realized the danger she was in and tried to free her arms from the encumbrance.

When she could not, she bit the hand that held her mouth. A voice cursed and someone cuffed the side of her head, making it spin for a moment or two. Her attacker continued to drag her along the terrace.

With fear mounting, Beatrice struggled desperately, but the man holding her was immensely strong and her efforts were in vain. After a minute or two she was thrown face down upon the ground and he pressed her head against the damp earth with what must be his knee while her hands were tied firmly behind her back.

She suspected there was more than one assailant, but the cloth blanketed out sound as well as sight, so she had no idea of who they were. Something was tied over the material across her mouth, which effectively prevented her from making anything but the most muffled of noises.

This left only her feet free and she tried to use them, kicking out vigorously. At one time, she felt her right foot make contact with something soft and a yelp issued from her mystery kidnapper, which gave her a brief feeling of satisfaction, but apart from that, he was very much in control of the situation and tied up her feet next.

She felt panic surging up. What did this person want of her? Why would anyone want to kidnap her?

She was picked up and slung face down over someone's shoulder, then he began moving. She could hardly breathe for the stifling layers of cloth and terror filled her, as she realised there was nothing she could do to free herself, that she was completely in his power.

After a few minutes of intense discomfort and jolting, she was dumped on the ground again so hard that she could only lie there for a moment, feeling disoriented and helpless. There was the sound of a door opening and she was dragged unceremoniously into what felt like some sort of building. The door slammed shut and she was left alone with her fears. Throughout the attack, her kidnapper hadn't said a word and that seemed to make it all so much more sinister.

She could only lie on the cold floor and wait for something dreadful to happen.

Who was doing this?

When time passed and nothing further happened, she began to recover a little from her fright and grow angry. The darkness seemed suffocating beneath the thick folds of material, but she told herself firmly that she'd managed to breathe so far inside it, so she wasn't likely to choke to death now. She forced herself to take deep, even breaths and gradually her heart stopped fluttering.

For a time, she struggled against the ropes binding her wrists, but in vain, for they were tied tightly enough to bite into her flesh, so she abandoned that.

Her mind kept darting from one thing to another in the most disoriented way. A heroine in a novel wouldn't have been caught out like this, though a heroine would probably have fainted first, then done something ingenious and making her escape against improbable odds.

Only this wasn't make-believe and Beatrice was beginning to realise how helpless one really was when one's hands were firmly tied behind one's back.

–

She heard the door open again and at once froze where she lay, making a quick decision to pretend to be unconscious. But no one touched her. She strained her ears and thought she heard the sound of a scuffle and grunts as if two men were struggling close at hand. A cry, then something fell against her skirts. The door slammed again and she distinctly heard a bolt being shot from the outside.

If she had been able to, she would have shrieked with terror when she felt someone moving on the ground beside her, but the gag prevented this. Hands groped across her body, but she forced herself to lie still. The hands reached her head and to her relief began to unfasten the gag. When the stifling material was removed, a voice asked in the darkness, "Who are you?"

To her astonishment it was Augustus Smeathley's voice. That didn't make sense, so she continued her pretence of being unconscious. The way his hands roved across her body increased her fear and bewilderment, for this wasn't the way a clergyman should behave with an unknown and unconscious female.

When the hands lingered and began to caress her breasts, she decided it was time to wake up. "Uhhh. Where am I?" she asked, annoyed that she could think of nothing more original to say. To her great relief, the hands stopped touching her.

"Miss Dencey! Is that really you?"

"Mr Smeathley!"

"It is indeed I, dear lady."

"Where are we?"

"In a garden shed. We appear to be prisoners here. Are you all right? They haven't hurt you?"

"I'm not hurt, but my hands are tied behind my back, and my feet are tied, too. Can you unfasten them?"

He fumbled with the ropes for a moment and freed her feet, then moved to her hands, but stopped quite quickly and said, "I'm afraid these knots are too tight."

Her intuition told her that his presence here was no coincidence and the feeling persisted that he must have been involved in the kidnapping. It made a sort of sense, if he were now intending to marry her instead of Eleanor, she supposed. He was unsure of her and wished to compromise her. Well, whatever happened, she would *not* marry him! She would as soon marry a toad! Sooner!

"How did you come to be here?" she asked, judging it safer to behave as though she believed what he told her.

"I saw a stranger, an uncouth-looking man, behaving in a suspicious manner near the house, so I followed him. I must have made a noise, because he was waiting for me behind this shed. I fear he overpowered me and cast me inside. I am a man of God, not a pugilist!"

"But why should anyone lock me up here in the first place?" she demanded. "What could he want with me?"

There was a silence, then he suggested dubiously, "Ransom, perhaps?"

"I have no money!"

"But your aunt is an extremely rich woman."

Beatrice sucked in her breath. "And she's a sick one, too. The shock of this could kill her! Mr Smeathley, I've got to escape!"

"We must pray for guidance."

She gave an angry snort. "Well, I'd find it easier to pray if my hands weren't tied behind my back!"

"The knots—" he began.

"Why don't you see whether you can find something to cut the ropes with?" she asked tartly. "Even a man of God should be able to do that!"

"It's very dark in here."

"Your hands aren't tied, so you can surely feel your way around? There must be something sharp that you could use to saw at the ropes."

She dared not let him see that she suspected him of arranging this. She waited impatiently, hearing him fumbling about in the darkness. What if he left her tied up and then assaulted her person? The mere idea of him touching her again in that way made her feel ill.

"I've found something sharp," he said at last. "It's some sort of garden implement, I think."

And you've no doubt realized how suspicious it would look if you didn't release me, she thought to herself. "Thank goodness!" she said aloud. "Oh, Mr Smeathley, my arms are hurting so much."

As he pulled her into a sitting position, his hands again strayed briefly across her body. She said nothing and he began to saw at her bonds. It seemed to take a long time, but at last she felt the bindings slacken. When they fell away and she tried to move, she cried out involuntarily as pain shot up her arms.

"Pray allow me to massage your arms, Miss Dencey," he said in a throaty voice, his breath hot on her cheek.

"*Keep away!* I mean, thank you, Mr Smeathley, but there's no need." She was only too conscious of the size of the body supporting her and was sure he could easily overpower her, whether she was bound or not. "Thank you for your help, but sensation is returning to my limbs and I can move on my own now."

The arm round her shoulders was not removed. "However brave you're trying to be, my dear Miss Dencey, a female in your circumstances must be terrified. Allow me to comfort you until you are yourself again."

"Oh, I always recover quickly when I've been kidnapped," she said as lightly as she could. She pushed away from him and managed to stand up before he'd realized what she was doing, but he did the same and, to her mingled fear and frustration, she found herself trapped in the corner of the hut by his large, well-fleshed body.

"I'm afraid you may faint, Miss Dencey. Too sudden a movement could be dangerous. Or you might trip over something in the darkness."

"Pray move back! Such close contact between us is unseemly, Mr Smeathley," she snapped, losing patience.

"My given name is Augustus."

"I prefer to call you Mr Smeathley. We aren't related."

Still he didn't move away. "Whatever we say or do," he pointed out, "this whole situation is highly unseemly, and I'm glad you've realized that. A young unmarried woman alone at night with a man to whom she is not related is a shocking thing, even when the man happens to be a clergyman with the purest of intentions. However, you need not worry. I shall, of course, marry you afterwards. I can do no less. Your good name is quite safe with me, my dear Beatrice."

She pushed past him. "I need to move around, sir, to restore the circulation in my limbs." She didn't dare tell him what she thought of his offer. As long as she kept up the pretence of believing his tale, she might be safe. She bumped into a shelf and cried out involuntarily. A large hand groped for her and she was firmly seized again.

"Are you all right, my dear Beatrice?" The arm again slid round her shoulders and one of his hands lingered quite openly on her breast. "Ah," breathed a voice in her ear, a voice husky with passion, "you are a very womanly creature." The hand continued to caress her.

She tried to pull away from him, but he was far stronger than she was.

Chapter 14

First half an hour, then an hour passed and Miss Beatrice didn't return to her room. Her maid became more and more worried. Surely Mrs. Smeathley could not be keeping her mistress talking for so long at this hour of the night?

Tilly went cautiously out into the dark corridor from which led the main bedrooms used by the family, and crept along it, listening at doors.

There was a light in the suite occupied by Mr and Mrs. Smeathley and the murmur of voices from inside. The light went out. A short time listening at the door confirmed that husband and wife were both there, settling down to sleep.

There was complete silence at Miss Eleanor's door.

Tilly returned to her mistress's bedroom, fidgeted around for a minute or two more, then lit a candle and went out again. As she made her way downstairs by its flickering light, the suits of armour made her shiver, because the moving shadows made them look as if they were waiting to pounce, but she swallowed hard and pressed on. Let it not be said that she had failed her mistress in time of trouble. She felt quite sure something was wrong.

The house was silent, full of dark shadows and rustling sounds. At the bottom of the stairs, Tilly paused to listen again. Nothing.

She groped her way to the front door, but it was bolted. Where was Miss Beatrice?

She went to listen outside the old lady's rooms on the ground floor. Utter silence.

Even more worried than before, she tiptoed back up the stairs, again checked her mistress's room, but found it as empty as before.

She went to listen outside Miss Eleanor's room again, but that, too, was dark and there was not even a hint of movement from inside.

As she turned to go back to her mistress's room, she saw a man standing in the shadows behind her and jumped in terror, sagging in relief when she recognized him.

"Be quiet!" he whispered. "It's only me!"

"Oh, Mr Serle!" She clutched her breast, for her heart was still pounding, and tried not to sob aloud in shock.

"Shh. What are you doing creeping round the corridors at this hour of the night, Tilly?"

"I was looking for Miss Beatrice, sir. She hasn't come back!"

"*What!* Where did she go?"

"Downstairs to speak to Mrs. Smeathley. A note came, asking for her."

"Who brought this note?"

"Mrs. Smeathley's maid, sir. But that was over an hour ago."

Justin stood motionless for a moment, trying to work out the implications of this. "Where can she have gone?"

"That's what I was trying to find out, Mr Serle. I went to listen outside Mrs. Smeathley's bedroom and I heard her and her husband speaking, so she can't be there. I even went downstairs to check."

"I heard you coming back up the stairs. Look, we can't talk here. Let's go back inside Miss Dencey's room."

Once there, Tilly explained again about the message, ending, "…and I'm ever so worried, sir, for it's all dark and locked up downstairs, even near her ladyship's rooms, so where can Miss Beatrice have got to?"

"I don't know, but I promise you I'll find out. I—"

"What's wrong?" Eleanor was standing in the doorway in her nightgown, with a cloak clutched around her. "And where's Bea?"

Serle turned to frown at her. "Shh! That's what we're trying to work out."

"You mean – she's missing?"

"Yes."

Eleanor stared at him in amazement. "But she came up to bed ages ago!"

Another form appeared in the doorway.

"Oh Crispin, Bea's disappeared!" Eleanor threw herself into his arms and he clasped her to him.

In terse phrases, Justin explained the situation, as far as they knew it.

"We'd better go and look outside, then," said Crispin in a calm, matter-of-fact tone. "She could have got locked out. Come along, Eleanor. You know the house and grounds better than we do."

She refrained from pointing out that if Bea had been locked out, she would only have needed to knock on the door to gain admittance, since Borrill's room was downstairs in this old-fashioned establishment.

They crept down and went out through the library, trying not to make any noise. As they started exploring the terrace, quickly establishing that there was no sign of Beatrice out there, the butler woke up and joined them.

Serle had difficulty hiding his frustration as they were delayed for yet another explanation when Beatrice could be in grave danger.

However, Borrill's presence proved to be an advantage, for he slipped back inside and came out with three storm lanterns, whose light was a great improvement on the flickering candles the two men were carrying.

They all spread out along the terrace and started to search more carefully.

It was Crispin who discovered broken twigs and leaves next to one of the bushes, with an overturned potted plant nearby.

Justin examined the evidence, his expression becoming grimmer and grimmer, then he went further along that side of the house, where he found marks in the soft earth near a flower bed, as if something had been dragged along the ground.

Careful scrutiny of the area, with lanterns held close to the ground, revealed large footprints leading away from the house, with slide marks alongside the first dozen or so, then a jumble of marks, then nothing but the large footprints.

"Someone's been dragged along here, I reckon," said Borrill. "Look at those marks, Mr Herforth. And they stopped here, milling around. I reckon they picked Miss Dencey up and carried her after this."

No one argued with his unspoken assumption that Beatrice had been kidnapped, but Eleanor clutched her beloved's hand and found comfort in the way he gave it a quick squeeze and kept hold of it.

"Yes," he agreed. "I'd say you were right, Borrill."

"Where does this path lead to, Eleanor?" demanded Serle, his voice sharp with anxiety.

"Well, nowhere, really. Just to some sheds."

"Show me!"

Clutching her cloak around her, Eleanor led the way through the shrubbery, holding Crispin's hand quite openly. With his free hand, he held one of the lanterns up to light their way. "That must have been where Mr Smeathley was going yesterday," she whispered.

"I only hope we're in time," he said, then could have kicked himself when he saw her look even more anxious.

"If he's touched Bea, I shall find one of grandfather's dueling pistols and shoot him," she said through gritted teeth.

He squeezed her hand. "No need. I rather fancy we can leave him to Serle."

Her eyes brightened and she looked sideways to see that Serle's lips were a tight, bloodless line and his free hand was clenched into a fist.

The sheds proved a disappointment, for they were empty of anything except garden implements and sacks. Frustrated and afraid for Beatrice, Serle prowled round the bushes behind the huts and then returned, only to stop dead in his tracks, frowning as if in thought.

"Where can she be?" asked Eleanor loudly.

"Shh!" Serle's whisper was so ferocious that everyone fell silent. He stood in a listening posture, then looked at Crispin, who was also listening. "Did you hear some-thing?"

"I'm not sure. Over there, do you think?"

"Yes." They listened again in silence, then Justin said, "I definitely heard something that time. It sounded like a woman's voice." The mere thought that Beatrice might be in some sort of distress made him set off in that direction, without bothering to find out whether the others were following him.

Walking in single file now, they pushed their way along an overgrown path and found that it led them to another hut. This one had its door firmly bolted from outside and had a large key in the lock as well.

"Hello?" Justin called, banging on the door. "Is anyone in there?"

From inside, someone cried, "Oh, thank goodness!"

The voice had a distinct quaver and at the sound of it, Justin thrust his lantern into Eleanor's hand and threw himself at the door, tearing back the bolt and nearly ripping the door off its hinges as he flung it open.

He snatched the lantern back from Eleanor and thrust his way through the narrow doorway, calling almost immediately, "Thank God! She's here!"

When he came out a moment later, he was supporting Beatrice, who was clinging to him openly.

Eleanor threw herself at them, embracing her cousin and Justin indiscriminately. "What happened? Oh, Bea, we were so *worried* about you! Oh, thank goodness you're safe!"

Beatrice shivered and pressed against Justin. "I was abducted."

Eleanor stared at her for a moment, then gasped, "Like in *Cressida's Revenge*?"

"It wasn't at all like those stupid novels!" snapped Beatrice. "I'll have you know, Eleanor, that when one's hands are tied behind one, it's just not possible to wriggle free. Nor can one spirit oneself through a heavy door that's bolted on the other side!"

"Oh!" Eleanor's tone was faintly disappointed.

"And what's more, one can't scream for help with a mouth full of gag. In fact, adventures are not at all pleasant in real life and I hope I never have another one as long as I live!"

"I'll make sure you don't," Justin promised quietly.

Eleanor looked so disappointed that Crispin burst out laughing. "There you are, then, my love. I feel exactly the same way about adventures, so you'll just have to be content with a mundane life from now on."

A groan issued from inside the hut and they all froze.

"What's that?" Crispin demanded, amusement vanishing. "Is there someone else in there?"

"Oh, I forgot to mention that Smeathley is lying on the ground unconscious," drawled Justin, not even turning round toward the hut. "How did that happen, Beatrice?"

His beloved began to fidget with his coat buttons. "I'm afraid I hit him over the head with a flower pot. I – um, I seem to have hit him a bit harder than I intended."

Eleanor gaped at her. "But why?"

"Because he's the one who kidnapped me and," Beatrice blushed, "because he was behaving improperly."

Crispin put one fingertip on Eleanor's lips, and shook his head to warn her not to pursue this point.

"I dare say he has a thick skull," Justin said savagely. "It certainly looks thick. Let's leave him to recover on his own." Though the fellow didn't deserve to come out of this unscathed, and Justin had every intention of coming back once he had seen Beatrice safely to her room to teach him a sharp lesson.

Crispin went to peer into the hut. "His hands appear to be tied behind his back as well."

They all turned to stare at Beatrice. "Well, he kept trying to force his attentions on me and telling me we'd have to get married! As if I'd marry *him*! So I hit him on the head with the first thing that came to hand and then to be sure, I tied him up with a strip of my petticoat."

For all his anger, Justin gave a snort of laughter.

Crispin's chuckle echoed it.

"Well, that sounds just as good as any heroine in a novel to me," said Eleanor approvingly. "How very brave of you, Bea!"

"It wasn't bravery, it was desperation." Beatrice shuddered at the memory of Smeathley's hands on her body.

"As if I'd let you marry anyone else, whatever happened!" Justin drew her closer and kissed her cheek.

"How did you both get in there in the first place?" Crispin stared at the hut. "Since the door was locked from the outside, I gather there must have been some other person involved?"

"I didn't see anyone else, but I did think there were two men involved. Smeathley pretended he'd been following an intruder who'd overpowered him, but Justin, I'm sure *he* was the one responsible for me being kidnapped, even if he didn't do it himself."

Justin's eyes took on a fierce gleam. He set her gently aside and took a step toward the hut.

Beatrice grabbed his coat and dragged him back. "Please don't hit him any more! I think he'll have a very sore head in the morning and that's surely enough."

His voice was harsh with suppressed rage. "A sore head, my love, is not nearly enough punishment for trying to compel you to marry him. Or for forcing himself upon you. You must have been terrified!"

She nodded, swallowing hard. "I was at first. Later I grew too angry to be afraid."

He smiled at that. "Like the time you chased that pickpocket?"

Her answering smile shut out the rest of the group. "A little like that." Then her smile faded. "But Justin, think for a moment! If we do anything to bring him to book, Aunt Marguerite will get to hear of it. She'll be furious and that wouldn't be good for her. Justin, please! Let the matter drop! For her sake!"

Crispin had come out of the hut as she was speaking. "She's right, you know. We don't want the old lady upset, especially now." He grinned round at them, "However, there's no reason why we shouldn't leave Smeathley in there overnight to cool off. I've removed his bonds and we can lock the door again. I dare say one of the gardeners will find him in the morning if he shouts loudly enough."

Eleanor broke their startled silence by gurgling with laughter. "That's not a mundane sort of thing to do, Crispin! That's a *wonderful* idea!" She gazed at him adoringly. "How very clever you are!"

Borrill coughed. "If you would trust me with the key, sir, I can ensure that Mr Smeathley will be found by someone who will not pay much attention to what he says. We have a gardener, Old Henry, who is very deaf and bad-tempered." He gazed blandly at Crispin.

"An excellent idea!" said his future master, passing over the large, rusty key that had been in the door. "We'd be very grateful for your assistance there, Borrill. In fact, you've been of great help to us tonight. I shan't forget that."

"It's been a pleasure, sir. We servants are, if I may say so, very fond of Miss Beatrice." He bowed in her direction. "And you may be sure that no word of this will get out from myself or Miss Hulls."

"I won't say a word." Tilly drew herself proudly upright, then saw her mistress shiver. "But I do think we ought to get Miss Beatrice back to her room now, sir. She's cold."

Justin nodded. "You're perfectly right. And she doesn't even know yet that she owes her rescue to you, Tilly."

As everyone made approving noises, the maid stared down at her feet in pink-cheeked embarrassment.

"Thank you, Tilly," Beatrice said with a warm smile.

Justin turned to the butler. "I'll be down again in a minute, Borrill, if you could wait. I need to discuss a small matter with you."

"Certainly, sir." Borrill shot him a speculative glance.

Crispin looked from one to the other. "Need any help, Serle?"

"No, thank you. I prefer to manage this on my own – with Borrill's assistance." Justin began to draw Beatrice gently toward the house. As they walked, he bent closer to her to ask quietly, "Will you be all right now, my love?"

She smiled at him. "Oh, yes. I'm not the sort of person to succumb to hysterics." She yawned. "In fact, I'm exhausted."

"Be sure to lock your bedroom door."

"Yes. I'll definitely do that." She laid her free hand on his for a moment, marvelling at how strong a man's body could feel.

"I wish—" he began, then closed his mouth.

"So do I," she said softly, not needing to be told what he wished.

For a moment they stopped moving to stare into one another's eyes, then he murmured, "You won't keep me waiting for long, my darling, will you? We can get married very soon, can't we?"

Her voice was slightly breathless. "As soon as you like, Justin."

Eleanor, shamelessly eavesdropping, jabbed her elbow in Crispin's ribs and beamed at him. Behind her she heard Tilly sigh sentimentally and when she glanced sideways, she could see that even the normally impassive Borrill had allowed himself to smile fondly.

–

The next morning, Justin woke just before dawn and made his way down the back stairs very quietly. As he passed the servants' hall, Borrill came out, carrying a lighted lamp, and the two men nodded to one another.

"I thought I'd deal with Smeathley now," Justin said quietly, but with an edge to his voice. "It's light enough to see what I'm doing."

"One of the footmen has spent the night outside the potting shed, with instructions not to speak to Mr

Smeathley or to allow him out until I give permission. I – um, took the liberty of warning Michael, who is a strapping young fellow, that Smeathley's man might try to release his master, and I promised there would be a small gratuity for Michael's trouble."

"Excellent." Justin raised one eyebrow. "Shall we go, then?"

"Yes, sir."

The footman was sitting on a garden chair, with his back against the door of the potting shed and his arms folded, but he jumped to his feet when he saw them.

"No trouble, Michael?" Borrill asked.

"I have heard a few strange sounds from time to time, Mr Borrill. Sounded as if someone was shouting for help from inside the shed." He sniggered. "But I paid 'em no attention, just as you said. Nor I didn't chase after the person who chucked a few stones at me, either." He looked up at the sky and eased his shoulders.

"Thank you for your help. I'd be grateful if you'd not mention this to anyone." Justin slipped a coin into his hand.

Michael betrayed his pleasure at this largesse with a beaming smile, then, as Borrill frowned at him, his expression became impassive again. "Thank you very much, sir. I was glad to be of use."

Not until the footman was out of sight did Justin move towards the shed door. "Do you have the key?"

"Yes, sir."

"I should be grateful if you'd prevent anyone from intervening. Unless there is something wrong with my hearing, we have been followed out here."

"There is nothing at all wrong with your hearing, sir. And you can rely on me to watch your back. I am not, if I may make the claim, a weakling." He presented the key with a distinct flourish.

Justin took it from him, but before he opened the door of the shed, he banged on it several times with one clenched fist.

There was the sound of movement from inside and a rather hoarse voice yelled, "Help! I'm locked in."

As Justin flung the door open, Smeathley staggered out, looking drawn and dishevelled, with a huge purple bruise on his right temple. "Serle! I can't tell you how glad I am to see you! Someone hit me over the head and locked me in the shed last night, and—"

"I know *exactly* what happened last night."

Smeathley grew very still.

"And if you ever mention one word of Miss Dencey's involvement, I shall make it my business to blight your whole future career in the church. I happen to be the godson of your Bishop – and I have certain other connections in high places who would be shocked to hear of your unconscionable actions. It is only to protect my future wife's name that I am refraining from addressing this matter."

"Sir, I deeply regret to tell you that you are mistaken in the lady's character. She led me on. She—"

Not for one second did Justin doubt Beatrice's version of the previous night's events. Such fury sizzled through him at this lie that he drew back his right arm and punched Smeathley on the jaw, putting all his pent-up anger into the blow.

As the man staggered backwards, Justin followed up by another punch to the fellow's soft belly with his left fist. "Only the worst sort of scoundrel would impugn a lady's honour," he declared in ringing tones.

With a soft "Oof," Smeathley folded in the middle, staggering backwards in a crab-like posture and seemed to be experiencing some difficulty in breathing. He was brought short by the wall of the shed and moaned aloud as he huddled against it.

A man rushed out of the bushes, brandishing a big stick, but Borrill moved quickly forward and stuck out one leg, tripping him up and snatching the makeshift weapon from him. "Stay out of this, you, if you know what's good for you." He kept the stick in his hand and so fierce was his expression that the manservant crawled backwards before standing up again.

"Stand up and face me, you scoundrel!" Justin moved forward again, clenched fists raised and ready, but Augustus Smeathley made no attempt to fight back, only cowered against the shed wall.

"I am – a man of – the cloth," he managed to plead in a hoarse voice, seeming to have difficulty breathing properly.

When Justin took another step forward, Augustus shrank away from him, holding one arm in front of his face.

"Coward!"

Smeathley turned his head away and said nothing.

Justin let his fists drop, feeling cheated. "If I ever hear that you've so much as mentioned Miss Dencey's name in public, I shall find you," he said slowly and with savage emphasis, "and make you extremely sorry. Physically sorry. Whether you fight back or not."

"All a dreadful – mistake," Smeathley wheezed. "Assure you – not say another word – complete misunderstanding."

With a snort of disgust, Justin took a step backwards and beckoned Smeathley's manservant forward. "Take yourself and your master away from Satherby Abbey as quickly as you can – and don't ever show your faces here again."

He stood with arms folded, his expression grim, watching the two men move slowly towards the house. His expression lightened into a slightly twisted smile as he noted that Smeathley seemed still to be having difficulty in standing upright and was, indeed, leaning rather heavily on his manservant.

"Nice pair of punches, those, if I may say so, sir," Borrill said mildly.

Justin flexed his left hand, wincing a little.

"Are you hurt, sir?"

"Just a scratch or two. Smeathley's damned fob watch got in the way of the second punch. I doubt it'll ever tell the time again, though."

Borrill exchanged comradely grins with him, then took a deep breath and transformed himself into a butler once again. "I'll send a message to the stables to have their horses saddled and waiting." However, he so far forgot himself as to add, "I wonder how he'll explain the bruises?"

"Just as long as his explanations don't include Miss Dencey." Justin let out his breath slowly. The mere thought of what Smeathley had tried to do to Beatrice the previous night made him want to chase after the fellow and beat him to a pulp.

Thanking Borrill again for his help, he strode off to the house to get ready for what promised to be an interesting day. By the time it was over, he intended to have set a date for his marriage. And no one was going to prevent him, not even an autocratic elderly lady.

–

When Crispin came down to breakfast, Eleanor poked her head out of the door of the small parlour and beckoned imperatively. Before Crispin could join her, however, Borrill moved forward to report in a low voice to his future master that the two unwanted guests had departed post-haste soon after dawn. "Mr Smeathley left a note for her ladyship, but it was delivered to her rooms before I could intercept it, I'm afraid. I hope he didn't say anything untoward."

Justin came down the stairs just then and Crispin turned to wait for him. With a mutter of impatience, Eleanor darted out of the parlour to tug both men inside. She then closed the door and pressed herself dramatically against it. "You're not getting any breakfast until you've told us what happened this morning."

Beatrice came to range herself beside her niece. "I agree."

"This isn't exactly a tale for ladies," Justin objected. "But you can rest assured that Smeathley has departed in haste – and in some discomfort."

"Did you hit him hard?" Eleanor asked.

Beatrice gasped and took hold of Justin's left hand, which displayed some signs of bruising across the knuckles. "You're hurt. What happened?"

"Only a few scratches and a bit of bruising where his fob watch got in the way of my second punch. It was well worth it. He'll be feeling rather sore today, I promise you."

Eleanor clapped her hands together gleefully. "Oh, I wish I'd been there to see it."

"So do I!" said Beatrice.

"Dear me," said Crispin. "I hadn't realized how bloodthirsty you two ladies were."

Justin drew Beatrice to one side, his eyes searching her face. "Did you manage to get some sleep?"

"Not much. But that doesn't matter."

He raised her hand to his lips. "It matters to me. In fact, your welfare is my main concern in life now."

Eleanor nudged Crispin as Beatrice stared up at Serle with what could only be described as a glowing look.

Crispin took the opportunity to put his arm round his own beloved's shoulders and give her a quick hug.

The breakfast gong sounded a few seconds later and both pairs of lovers broke apart. Each gentleman offered his lady an arm and they strolled towards the dining room together.

There was very little conversation during the meal, though the older Smeathleys did wonder what urgent church business had called their son away so suddenly as they ate their way through plates piled high with food.

The four lovers held a conference of war in the library immediately after the meal, the problem being: how could the two gentlemen best approach the Dowager to ask for her permission to marry her niece and granddaughter?

"She must never know what Augustus Smeathley did," Beatrice insisted. "She's taken a dislike to him and will never invite him or his parents here again. That must be enough. And she won't," she blushed slightly as she looked at Justin, "have any reason to try any more match-making of her own after you've spoken to her."

"Definitely not." His smile was a caress in itself.

But they still could not agree on the best approach. Crispin was all for being completely honest with her ladyship about who wished to marry whom.

Justin thought they might approach the matter with some delicacy and delay the final announcement of their intentions for a day or two.

The two ladies were trying to work out how to spare their elderly relative any sudden worry or upset.

Before a decision had been reached, Borrill brought a summons from her ladyship. "Her Ladyship requests Mr Serle and Mr Herforth to present themselves at her private sitting room immediately."

There was a moment's silence, then, "How did she look, Borrill?" Beatrice asked.

"Somewhat better, I believe, miss."

"I'm coming with you, Crispin!" Eleanor declared.

"No. Let's see what she wants first."

"But I'm best at getting round her! In fact, I'm the *only* one who can make her do anything."

He eyed her sternly. "Not this time, my love. *This* time we shall do things my way."

Beatrice intervened. "He's right, Eleanor! You know how she hates it if anyone disobeys her or upsets her arrangements. She must have a reason for wanting to see them. We'll have to leave her to do things her own way, or we'll only make matters worse."

Eleanor scowled at them both, but couldn't maintain her bad humour for long. "Oh, very well! But *do* hurry back as soon as you can, Crispin, for I'm *dying* to know what she wants!"

The two ladies fidgeted around for the next twenty minutes or so, speculating as to what could be happening in the East Wing, then at last the butler came to summon them to join the others.

"Is my grandmother all right, Borrill?" demanded Eleanor, refusing to stand on ceremony with him. "Does she look angry or upset?"

"Her ladyship seems to be in an excellent humour, miss."

Beatrice and Eleanor exchanged bewildered glances. Did that mean she had agreed to their betrothals, or had the matter not yet been broached?

They entered the Dowager's rooms to find Justin standing by the window and Crispin sitting on a couch beside her ladyship. Justin shook his head at them, which they took as a warning to say nothing.

"How are you, Grandmamma?" asked Eleanor, bending to kiss the wrinkled cheek. "You look much better today."

"I'll be better still when the other two Smeathleys have left. That young upstart of theirs wrote me a most impudent letter, not to mention departing without taking his leave of me! Well, he'll not be invited *here* again! None of them will! In fact, I shall cut the connection. They're only related by marriage, anyway. There must be bad blood in their family somewhere. What's the world coming to when a clergyman flirts like that? I've a good mind to write to the Archbishop to tell him not to do anything for that young fellow!"

"What exactly did Mr Smeathley say in his letter?" asked Beatrice when her aunt stopped to draw breath.

"He had the impudence to tell me that he did not wish to offer for either of the two young ladies – as if I'd have let him marry you, once I'd got his measure! – because he didn't feel they would make suitable wives for a clergyman. The impertinence of it!"

When she started rapping the cane on the ground to emphasize her point, Beatrice realized her aunt must be much better, and that, far from damaging her health, Smeathley's letter had quite invigorated her.

"*And* he said he had taken his leave this way in order to spare the young ladies any embarrassment," added her ladyship. "As if *we* could have anything to be embarrassed about!"

"Spare us embarrassment!" exclaimed Eleanor, highly indignant. "Why, that—"

"I must say I didn't care for him myself," Beatrice interrupted, pinching Eleanor's arm, afraid of what her niece might blurt out. "In fact, I found him a great bore."

"Hmm! And what about you, miss?" demanded the Dowager, turning to Eleanor. "It seemed to me at one stage that you were rather taken with him!"

"Oh, that was just a game."

"Game, eh?" She nodded in sudden understanding. "And I suppose you told him so – which is why he took a huff?"

"Well, when he proposed to me, I had to refuse him." Eleanor stared down at her feet, "And – well, I suppose I might have spoken a bit too frankly about my feelings."

The Dowager nodded in satisfaction that her guess had been correct and cast a regretful look at Serle. She would have been pleased to marry him to her grand-daughter. At least she hadn't erred there. He was a gentleman of birth and breeding, unlike the other fellow. "That'll be what upset him, then! Canting hypocrite! And what do you mean by flirting with *anyone*, miss? You are a Graceover, not a kitchen maid!"

"I was just practising, Grandmamma," Eleanor said, all wide-eyed innocence. "It didn't mean anything."

"Practising flirting!" spluttered the Dowager. "Persons of rank and breeding do not even *consider* indulging in such tasteless behaviour! If I ever catch you doing something so ill-bred again, miss, I'll teach you how to flirt, I will indeed!"

Eleanor cast her eyes down, but this didn't prevent her from looking sideways at Crispin. She got no help from that quarter, for he was displeased with her as well about the flirting.

"Anyway, that's all over and done with!" Lady Marguerite said, changing tone and addressing the two young women more temperately. "What I've decided upon for your futures isn't what I'd first planned, but it'll do, yes, it'll do tolerably well, given the circumstances, and I'll thank you two chits to do as you're told about this." She fell silent and stared round the room, studying them all through narrowed eyes.

"What have you arranged, Grandmamma?" Eleanor asked as the silence continued.

"I have decided, miss, that you had better marry your Cousin Crispin. If you must flirt in future, you will kindly do so with your own husband. Though I personally had rather you behaved in a manner more in keeping with your station in life."

Eleanor said nothing, only putting her head on one side, as if she were thinking the proposal over.

The Dowager, never famous for her patience, waited only a minute, then snapped, "Well, what do you have to say to that, hey?"

Crispin cocked an inquiring eyebrow at his beloved, grinning openly.

"Mmm," said Eleanor thoughtfully, "I suppose it might just answer."

"*Might just answer!*" The Dowager glared at her. "It's a perfect solution, given that Serle's affections have settled elsewhere! Your marrying Crispin will keep Graceover blood at Satherby, even if the name has to change. You're to marry him at once and no more arguments, miss. *Might just answer, indeed!*"

Eleanor pouted. "Well, I don't think that's fair at all, Grandmamma!"

"Not fair! What's not fair about it? You just said yourself it might answer. Make up your mind, young lady! Make up your mind! I won't force you into anything you dislike, but he seems fairly presentable to me and you don't seem to object to his company. *He's* willing, that's for sure." She stared at Crispin, and cackled with laughter as he flushed under her open scrutiny.

"It's not the idea of marrying Crispin which is unfair, Grandmamma," Eleanor said, all wide-eyed still. "In fact, I quite like it. But I don't appreciate the way you're both going about it. How do you think it feels when one's grandmother does the proposing? Can't he speak for himself?" She pulled a cheeky face at Crispin. "I don't think it's fair at all if I'm not to have a proper proposal, on bended knee and – and everything!"

Crispin had difficulty keeping his face straight and Justin chuckled aloud.

Even the Dowager's lips twitched. "And is that your only objection, miss?"

Eleanor looked at Crispin, pretending to consider him as her grandmother had. "Well, he's not bad looking, really, and I *should* rather like to stay at Satherby. But I do insist on a proper proposal. I'd feel cheated, otherwise, I really would."

The Dowager let out a rusty spurt of laughter, which she tried unsuccessfully to turn into a cough. "Then you'd better take her away and propose properly, young Herforth! And see that you make a good job of it, too. Bended knee and all."

"Yes, Aunt Marguerite." He held out his hand to Eleanor and with a quick sideways glance at him, she placed hers in it and allowed him to lead her from the room.

The Dowager watched them leave, then turned to Beatrice. "I gather," she said dryly, "that you and Serle have already come to an understanding of sorts."

Beatrice blushed. "I'm afraid so. I – I hope you don't mind too much, Aunt Marguerite. I didn't mean to spoil your plans and become attached to him. It just – happened."

"I should have known you'd do something like this when I sent you to London without me. If Johanna couldn't keep her own daughters in order, why should she manage it with you? Still, you've done quite well for yourself, I must say. It will be a very good match."

Justin made her a flourishing bow in acceptance of her compliment.

The Dowager's eyes were gleaming with suppressed amusement. "You've done better than your father did, that's for sure, Beatrice. Serle is not only a man of breeding, but has enough money, I gather, to make comfortable settlements upon you and your children. I wouldn't agree to the marriage, else! If things are not done properly, the next generation suffers for it. As you did."

Beatrice's face was now bright scarlet. "Aunt Marguerite!" she protested, embarrassed by this businesslike attitude.

"It's true, miss, as you well know. No use denying the facts."

Justin came across to take Beatrice's hand, smiling at her in a way that made her breath catch in her throat. "I think you can rely upon me to keep matters on a proper footing, your ladyship. Beatrice is, alas, incurably romantic, but at least she has had the good taste to settle her affections on me and not on some lowborn fellow."

Beatrice barely smothered a laugh as her joy suddenly began to overflow.

"True, true! I brought her up to know what she owes to the family." The old lady brandished her cane at them. "I suppose she'll complain as well if I say any more. You'd better take her away and make her a proper proposal, Serle. You and I will sort out the business arrangements later."

"An excellent idea, your ladyship."

Neither of them noticed the Dowager's lips twitching or heard the hoarse little chuckle that escaped her control as she watched them leave. "Who do they all think they're fooling?" she asked the air around her as she rang for her maid. "I'm not in my dotage yet, thank you!" Still, although the outcome was not what she had planned, she was well pleased with it.

When Lippings came in, she found Lady Marguerite still chuckling, and this developed into such a hearty bout of laughter that her ladyship fell into a choking fit and had to have her back pounded as if she were a common sort of person and not a member of the nobility.

–

Justin shepherded Beatrice from the room with the greatest celerity and pulled her into the library. The minute the door was closed behind them, he gathered her in his arms.

She held him off for a moment, in mock anger. "How on earth did you persuade her to agree?" she demanded. "Yes, and how dare you speak about me like that! Good taste to settle my affections on you, indeed!"

But before she could take him to task, he had drawn her to him and silenced her with an urgent kiss which left her feeling so breathless that she could only cling to him for a moment and wonder that a man's touch could set her whole body tingling like this. When she had taken a few careful breaths, she demanded weakly, "Well, aren't you going to propose to me properly, Mr Serle?"

"Justin."

She smiled. "Justin, then."

"Dearest Justin, even?"

She blushed, but repeated the words softly, her eyes steady on his, "Dearest Justin."

"I rather thought I had already proposed, my darling. But if you insist on another..." he paused, smiling down at her in a way that made her heart lurch. "Will you," he punctuated each phrase with a gentle kiss on alternate cheeks, "marry me – and next week please – if not sooner?"

"Oh, I think I'd better!" she gasped, clinging to him in a very unladylike manner, "and yes, yes, as soon as possible, if you please, for I'm developing a strong desire to embrace you whenever I'm alone with you, and that sort of behaviour will never do between persons who are not married!"

He brushed a strand of hair from her forehead and looked down at her very seriously, still clasping her lightly around the waist. "Dearest Beatrice, are you sure?"

She didn't try to avoid his glance, but looked him straight in the eyes. "I'm very sure, Justin." Then her smile returned, for she had never felt so gloriously happy in all her life. "Mind, I'll only marry you if you promise not to throw me into any more pools."

He threw back his head and roared with laughter, then pulled her into his arms again to kiss her passionately. "I promise nothing," he said in a husky voice, "except to love you for ever. And I demand the same promise from you."

In fact, considering they were all persons of the highest rank and breeding, there was an extremely vulgar display

286

of feelings and affection that day at Satherby Abbey, and even the Dowager startled her maid several times by giving sudden cackles of laughter for no apparent reasons.